OF DUBIOUS INTENT

A Dark Artifice Novel

by Richard Grantham

 Created with Vellum

Do you think when a man's name reaches my ear, that he doesn't deserve what I bring him?

Cat has grown up as a cutpurse on London's streets — pretending to be a boy to stay clear of the procurers, but that ruse is getting harder to maintain and she needs a new plan. One that will let her keep the gang's next big score for herself, get her free of the streets, and give her the hope of a new life. Then she finds her plan was someone else's all along — and that man's intentions are not at all what they seem.

Ar Hyd y Nos

Holl amrantau'r sêr ddywedant
      Ar hyd y nos
      "Dyma'r ffordd i fro gogoniant,"
      Ar hyd y nos.
      Golau arall yw tywyllwch
      I arddangos gwir brydferthwch
      Teulu'r nefoedd mewn tawelwch
      Ar hyd y nos.
      O mor siriol, gwena seren
      Ar hyd y nos
      I oleuo'i chwaer ddaearen
      Ar hyd y nos.
      Nos yw henaint pan ddaw cystudd
      Ond i harddu dyn a'i hwyrddydd
      Rhown ein golau gwan i'n gilydd
      Ar hyd y nos.

All the stars' twinkles say
      All through the night
      "This is the way to the realm of glory,"
      All through the night.
      Other light is darkness
      To show true beauty

The Heavenly family in peace
All through the night.
O, how cheerful smiles the star,
All through the night
To light its earthly sister
All through the night.
Old age is night when affliction comes
But to beautify man in his late days
We'll put our weak light together
All through the night.

CHAPTER 1

A sudden cramp made Cat's belly clench, but she ground her teeth together and kept walking. The market square was alive with sound and movement, every vendor calling out loudly to the passersby. The smells from a sausage cart made her mouth fill and stomach clench again, but for a different reason. Neither she nor any of the boys in the gang had eaten that morning. Their leader, Brandt, wanted them out in the market and making this score first.

Her prey paused to look at a table of brass lamps and Cat slowed her pace, not wanting to get too close too soon. She'd watched this man before in the market, many times, and he had his habits — one of which would make him the poorer today. And Cat richer, if all went well and as she planned.

Richer and free, she thought.

Another cramp, this one more severe than the last, almost made her double over and she had to stop, breathing deeply until her muscles unclenched.

A hand clasped her upper arm and she turned to find Brandt beside her. The older, larger boy dragged her to the side and leaned down to whisper in her ear.

"What are you about, Runt?" His grip on her arm was painful, but she lowered her eyes and bowed her head. Brandt liked his crew cowed and afraid of him, and didn't hesitate to beat them if they didn't show what he felt was proper deference. "You been following him for ten minutes now!"

"I'm simply waiting for the right time," Cat whispered back.

Brandt cuffed her across the back of the head. "Don't you uppity-talk me!"

Cat grimaced, but kept her eyes down and nodded. She often wondered why Mother Agnes had taught her to speak properly, when all it did was get her into trouble with the likes of Brandt. She kept at it, though, even if it was mostly kept in her head and the words she actually voiced were nothing but the street-cant of the others in the gang. There was more than a bit of Mother Agnes' advice that she didn't understand the reasons for, but the old woman had been proven right often enough to make Cat follow it all regardless.

Another cramp ran through her and she grunted.

Brandt narrowed his eyes. "What's yer gripe? You sick?"

Cat ran a hand over her belly, massaging — that helped a bit.

"Hungry," she said.

That was a plausible enough explanation, for Brandt had dragged them out to the market with no breakfast, but it wasn't the real reason. The real reason was that her monthly courses had arrived and were worse than usual, but she couldn't tell Brandt that. Doing so would let out the secret she'd been hiding for all the years she'd been running with Brandt's crew; the secret Mother Agnes had started when Cat was just four years-old and sat with her at the begging bowl each day. No, it wouldn't do at all for Brandt to learn that Cat was a girl and not the scrawny boy he thought she was.

"We're all hungry," Brandt whispered. "And we'll be hungrier if we don't bring in some coin soon, so cut that fop's purse and let's move on!"

Cat nodded. "I will," she said. "I just want the right time." *And place,* she thought.

Brandt cuffed her again. "It's here and now, you scrawny ginger, so move!"

He shoved her away, letting go of her arm. "We're a full two crowns short of what Marven expects this week and but three days to get them. Hurry up."

Cat nodded again, keeping her eyes downcast. Her reddish hair, even shorn short as she kept it, always did seem to irritate Brandt.

"Yes, sir," she said. Brandt liked to be called "sir," she knew. His shoulders went back and his chest swelled as he nodded back to her, apparently satisfied that she'd do as ordered. He slid off into the crowd to take his place and Cat looked ahead to spot her target again.

Oh, damn! The man was almost to the baker's stall, the one he stopped at every time in the market, and where Cat's plan needed to start. She hurried through the crowd, cursing Brandt under her breath for stopping her.

She'd marked this man as a target weeks ago, long before she'd told the others in the gang, and watched him every time she saw him in the market. He had one habit that was perfectly suited to her plan and now Brandt's petty interruption was about to make her miss it.

Cat's stomach clenched again, this time from anxiety, as she made her way through the crowd. If she missed her chance at the baker's stall, her plan could still work, but it was far more likely to succeed if she could take him there.

She slid her hand into her pocket to ready her purse-knife, the razor-sharp blade mounted to a leather half-glove. Her thumb and first two fingers slid into the glove, leaving her pinkie and ring finger free.

The man was at the stall and Cat walked steadily toward him. Not hurrying, not drawing attention to herself, but closing the distance rapidly.

He started his banter with the baker's wife while he eyed the wares. Always the same, Cat had listened to him many times. How he couldn't decide what he wished today, then a sudden choice and a request to have one of the pastries packaged for him to take with him and one that he'd eat that very moment, for he simply couldn't resist.

The baker's wife simpered and blushed, handing him his selection. Cat reached his side, staying a bit behind him. She cut her eyes to the side, seeing Dome, a boy little bigger than Cat herself, at the next stall, ready to create a distraction if one was needed — then a quick glance behind her. Osraed, nearly as large as Brandt, but not so bright, was about twenty yards away, idling by another shopkeeper's stall, with Brandt behind him — both ready to run interference if her escape was threatened.

She took a deep breath and took her hand from her pocket. The man was busy stuffing his pastry into his mouth, chewing and swallowing noisily. He was making great sounds of appreciation, as he always did, and had the full attention of the baker's wife.

Cat reached forward and slipped her hand inside the slit in his jacket that hid his purse. Her fingers closed around the leather cords that bound it to his belt and she slid the razor over them firmly. The leather parted easily and she pulled the purse up and then to her with a smooth, practiced motion.

In an instant, she turned and was sliding away through the crowd, the man's purse already tucked into the waistband of her trousers and her hand in her pocket to hide the purse-knife. She didn't look back.

Never look back.

Instead she watched Osraed. He kept his eyes on the man at the baker's stall and would signal if there was trouble.

Cat's heart fluttered in her chest. Had it been her imagination or had the purse been heavier than any she'd lifted before? It was certainly larger — bigger than her clenched fist. She'd known the man carried a lot of coin — she'd watched the heft of his purse for weeks and that was part of why she'd decided it was time to run.

That and the fact she couldn't hide that she was a girl any longer. For the months since her courses had first come, she'd lived in fear that she'd be discovered. Blood on her clothes or bedding, or even the physical changes she knew were coming. Her chest was still mostly flat, but it ached sometimes. Mother Agnes had told her what to expect and that she couldn't hope to hide forever. If Brandt, or any of the other boys, ever found out, they'd drag her to one of the buttock-brokers and pocket the coin.

Cat stepped to one side to go around a fat merchant and put him between her and the baker's stall, but her step faltered as she saw the look on Osraed's face change. His face grew puzzled, then his eyes widened and he half raised his hand in the signal that she'd been spotted, but then he paused, as though unsure.

Never look back.

Cat looked back. Her steps faltered again and she paused, standing still. The man had turned from the baker's stall and crossed his arms over his chest. He stared across the market directly at Cat and, as her eyes met his, he smiled.

Then he took a deep breath, pointed at her, and bellowed, *"Thief! Stop her!"*

CAT RAN.

Their gang had a plan for this. As soon as the man yelled, Dome stumbled into the display of wares next to the baker's stall, sending a clatter of pots to the ground and distracting at least some of those nearby. Cat ran toward Osraed, bumping into him and seeming to knock him to the ground, then dashing off. Osraed himself leapt to his feet and started running in the opposite direction — the hope was that anyone watching would think Cat had passed the man's purse to Osraed and some would chase him, leaving Cat free to pass the purse to Brandt as she ran past.

Halfway between Osraed and Brandt, though, Cat dodged to her left and leapt over a table of leather goods. The gang might have a plan, but she'd had her own all along and she saw no reason to alter it now. She needed this purse. Even if it were only filled with copper pennies, it would still be more wealth than she'd ever before held at one time. She needed it to get out of the city, away from Brandt, to escape the fate Mother Agnes had shown her.

The leather merchant grabbed her arm as she ran through his workspace, but Cat pulled her hand with the purse-knife from her pocket and ran the blade over his forearm. The man shrieked in pain, blood flowing freely from the shallow cut, and Cat was free again.

Normally none of the gang would assault the merchants, but Cat intended to be gone and never return.

She slipped between the fabric hangings that backed his stall and into a narrow alleyway barely wide enough for her to pass, feet splashing through the puddles of water, offal, and worse, that lined it. Her shoulders grazed the rough stone of the buildings to either side, but she didn't slow her pace. Any adults chasing her would be hard pressed to make their way through the narrow space, but if Brandt suspected her plan he'd have the gang after her in a shot.

She grunted as her shoulder struck a stone protruding from one wall, but kept on. Ahead of her the alley opened into an inner court-yard filled with refuse from the surrounding buildings. Cat slid the purse-knife off her hand and into her pocket. She'd scouted this route and kept it to herself for months, ever since her courses had started and she'd realized that her time was up and she'd have to run.

She heard a grunt behind her and ran faster, not looking back. It wouldn't help to know who was chasing her.

She ran into the courtyard and cut hard to the right, aiming for a particular drainpipe. She leapt, planting her feet against the building's wall and grasping the pipe, then began climbing rapidly, hand over hand. There was another grunt and a rattle from below her as she climbed and the pipe shook out of time with her own movements.

It had to be Brandt or Osraed chasing her, an adult would never try this climb — probably Brandt, for Osraed wouldn't have made the decision to on his own. He was more trusting than Brandt and he'd see her varying from their plan and think she'd simply meet up with them later. Brandt would see it for the betrayal it was.

She was faster than either of them, though, especially at climbing — they were both bigger and couldn't pull themselves up as fast as she.

And I only need a little more, she thought. *Just a bit higher ...*

She passed the point she'd marked in her earlier scouting and kicked hard at one of the brackets holding the pipe to the wall. Once, twice, and then the third time she felt the bracket give way, pulling out of the old brick of the wall and falling with a clatter. She wrapped her arms and legs around the pipe, her breath coming in panting gasps. She could take her time with the rest of the climb — make it slow and safe to the rooftops and be gone. She looked down.

Brandt, for it was him chasing her, had stopped climbing as well. He was ten or so feet below her — twenty from the hard cobbles and refuse of the courtyard. The pipe, from just below her feet where she'd kicked the bracket free, was swaying side to side, and Brandt clutched it tightly.

He glanced down, then up at her, his eyes wide and his jaw set in anger.

"I'll kill you fer this, Runt," he said.

Cat stretched out her leg, caught the top of the pipe with her toe, and shoved it hard away from the wall.

CHAPTER 2

*C*at settled her back against the bricks of the chimney, the slate tiles of the rooftop sun-warmed under her. She thought she was a mile or more from where she'd left Brandt cursing her from the cobbles of the courtyard. There was nothing else he could use to climb to the rooftops, she'd made sure of that long ago, and the only way out was back through the alleyway to the market square — or through one of the buildings if he could find an unlocked door. She felt safe and well-away from him.

Safe for a time, at least, but with nowhere to go.

Her eyes filled and she pulled her knees to her chest, hugging herself. Bad as it was, Brandt's gang — Osraed, Dome, and the rest — were the only family and only home she'd known since Mother Agnes died and left her alone. She'd found a home with the boys, even if it was built on a lie, and now she was alone.

Cat scrubbed at her eyes angrily with the heel of one hand.

They'd have sold you to a buttock-broker in a heartbeat if they'd suspected, she told herself.

Mother Agnes had shown her what was in store if anyone ever found out she was a girl. The choices on the streets were few for the boys, but fewer for the girls. One look at the women turned out of the houses to make their way on the streets, plying their trade in the alleyways for a few copper pennies, had settled for Cat that she'd never want to be one of them. Even as young as she'd been when Mother Agnes showed that life to her, she'd been able to decide that.

Then Mother Agnes had died, but the lie was already well established. Mother Agnes had a boy begging with her, not a girl — and so Cat had been accepted by the other boys on the street. Odd, perhaps, certainly shy, and small — but they were all smaller than they should be, with so little food to share between them. Only the older boys like Brandt had the strength to command a larger share.

That had been home for ... *Three years*, she thought. *Mother Agnes said I was four when I came to her. Six years begging with her and three winters with Brandt.*

And now she was starting over again, with nothing. What few possessions she'd accumulated were left behind in the abandoned building the gang slept in. There was no retrieving them now. She had nothing.

Not even a proper name.

Cat, though it was how she thought of herself, wasn't a real name at all. It was just the last, and only, memory she had of her real mother. Leaving her with Mother Agnes, Cat not understanding that she was leaving forever, and bending to kiss her forehead, whispering, "I love you, catling, never forget."

She sometimes thought it was odd she couldn't clearly remember anything before that moment, only the words and the warmth of her mother's lips on her skin and the scent of her that always meant she was safe and loved, but perhaps life had been hard. Lord knew there were things that had happened since that she wished she could forget. She raised one hand to her chest and felt the locket beneath her shirt.

Not a proper locket, surely, but that's what she called it. Just a leather thong with two locks of hair tied tightly around it and bound with string. A lock from her mother, that Mother Agnes had given her, and a lock from Mother Agnes herself, that Cat had cut from the old woman's head when she'd found her dead that horrible morning.

Mother Agnes had never called her anything but "boy," a constant reminder of the lie and how important it was to remember it.

When Mother Agnes had died and Cat approached the gang of boys she thought might take her in, Brandt looked her up and down and said simply, "Are you quick, runt?"

Quick, she was, but without a better name to give them, the gang had called her Runt thereafter, never suspecting that she was girl. But the man in the market had, and that was surprising. Her hair was shorter even than most of the boys wore theirs, not only for the disguise, but to hide its reddish tint from Brandt and his bigotry, and her clothes were the same, shapeless rags all the boys wore.

Had he known? Or just guessed at a distance? She supposed it didn't matter. Even if Brandt and the others had heard him and believed it, she could never go back to them anyway. *Would* never go back.

Cat sniffed and pulled the stolen purse from inside her trousers. She squeezed it hard and grinned at the crunch of metal from within. The seams were pulled tight, it was so full, and the shapes of coins were showing through the thin leather.

With this I'll pick any name I want, she thought. *A proper name. And I'll eat proper food.* Her stomach growled and her mouth filled at the thought. She'd walk straight into an inn, slide real coin onto the table, and eat her fill.

"And I'll wear proper clothes when I do it," she said aloud. A dress, like the girls in the market square wore — those who had families and even a bit of respectability that let them take real work. Those who didn't have to hide what they were. They had mothers and fathers and a place to start, not the desperate, gnawing hunger that left you open to doing anything to fill it. Fathers and brothers who'd protect them, not a gang of boys who'd see nothing but what the nearest pimp would pay.

She squeezed the purse again. It was so full. *It's a fortune!*

Cat pushed the thought down, telling herself the purse could be full of no more than pence or farthings, though why would a man of some substance carry so many small coins. Even if it was ... She eyed it, estimating.

Even if it's only pence, there must be hundreds!

She squeezed again, relishing the anticipation. She felt the size of the coins through the leather. Some were the size of pence, but others were certainly shillings. There were larger coins, too, and she tried to think. She eyed the bag. Could there be guineas?

Never, not in all the years they'd worked the market, had the gang seen a guinea coin. Shillings if they were lucky, and the occasional crown, but mostly pence and less. Guineas came out in the wealthier markets. The ones where Brandt and their gang would stick out and be noticed, so they'd never worked them.

Cat bit her lip and stared at the purse. The outline of one coin caught her eye. If it were a guinea ... how much would that be worth? With twenty pence in a shilling and twelve of those in a pound — thirteen in a guinea. Could one coin really be worth that much?

More than two hundred pennies from one coin?

The thought was staggering. Cat stopped breathing for a moment at the implications. Dinner in a pub — *a real dinner* — was but a tuppence. If that one coin was gold it would mean ...

"Months," she breathed, barely daring to hope. She closed her eyes and clutched the purse to her chest. Could there really be a single coin in that purse that would feed her for a month?

She sniffed and scrubbed at her eyes again, then looked up at the sky. It was a beautiful day. The sun was still high and the clouds were white against a brilliant, blue sky. There was just enough of a breeze, here above the streets where the buildings didn't block it, to make the sun's warmth pleasant.

She had a sudden thought and bit her lip again. She'd never prayed. Brandt's gang wasn't the sort to enter a church, even if they'd be allowed. She couldn't even, really, think of the words to a single prayer.

"Please?" she whispered. She couldn't think of any other words, but surely if God were there, if He'd listened, He'd know what she was asking.

Cat swallowed hard and opened the drawstring at the top of the purse. She closed her eyes and reached inside. Her fingertips touched cool metal and she smiled. She chose one of the smaller coins, one she was certain would be a shilling, and pulled it out.

She opened her eyes.

The disk she held was the size and shape of a shilling, but it wasn't silver. Nor was it gold, nor even copper. It was black, mostly, with spots of orange-red.

Cat raised it close to her face and stared at it, then touched it to her tongue.

"Iron?" she whispered in disbelief.

She set the black disk on the rooftop and reached into the purse again, pulling out another. This too was black and flecked with rust. She dropped it and pulled out a handful, crying out at the sight of more orange and black, rather than the copper, silver, and gold she'd been praying for.

"No," she cried. "No!"

She upended the leather purse over her palm, pouring its contents out, staring at the cascade of black disks that fell from her hand to the rooftop and rolled down to the edge before falling to the street below.

Iron, all, and worthless.

CHAPTER 3

*C*at ran.

She seemed to be doing a lot of that since stealing the purse full of iron. In fact, it seemed that was all she'd been doing. She'd moved steadily away from Brandt's territory, trying to find some place for herself. The markets were what she knew, though, and they were all claimed by gangs that had no interest in someone who hadn't grown up with them.

"Get him!" one of the boys chasing her yelled.

And do you think that isn't what the rest of them are trying already?

Her feet pounded the pavement, her arms pumped, she dodged around and between shoppers in the market square, trying to get away. This square was unfamiliar to her. She'd crossed to the far side of the city, as far as she could get from Brandt's territory, trying to find a place, but there were other gangs everywhere. Gangs, or the constables, or private guards.

She hadn't even been trying to make a score today. Her purse-knife was safely hidden away and she'd simply been walking through the market, taking its measure and hoping for a bit of dropped bread or other food no one would miss. But someone from the local gang had spotted her and the chase was on. Her dress marked her as belonging to the streets, and they'd not allow someone new in their territory — any competition had to be driven out.

When she'd first recovered from the shock of finding nothing but iron in the stolen purse, she'd thought to find a new gang. That was foolish, she realized now. She was too old and had no history with any of the other gangs. They'd take in someone who'd grown up in their territory, that was how they got new members, but not someone from outside. None of them knew her, they didn't trust her, and assumed there must be something wrong with her.

Ahead of her, a beggar saw her coming and stretched out his leg into her path, probably hoping for a bit of coin from the boys who worked this market.

Cat leapt over his leg, but missed her footing when she landed — her foot hit the edge of a raised cobble and slipped off it, twisting her ankle. She kept running, but every step sent knife-sharp lances of pain up her leg.

She saw other boys ahead of her, moving to cut her off, and spun to dart between two stalls. Her ankle twisted again, giving way during the turn, and she cried out. That caused her to stumble and she threw her hands out to catch herself on the hard cobbles, grit and pebbles scraping her palms, and pain shooting from her knee as it slammed into the stone.

A body landed on her, driving her to the ground and knocking the breath from her.

"Bastard!" the boy on top of her yelled, forcing her head to the ground with his forearm. "Stay outta our patch!" He drove his fist into her side.

Cat tried to get her hands under her to rise or twist away from him, but his weight held her firmly and he punched her in the side again.

"'Ere now! Off 'im!" a voice yelled and the boy's weight left her back.

Cat scrambled forward, first to her hands and knees, then getting her feet under her before she looked back. A man, perhaps one of the merchants, was holding the boy by the scruff of the neck, but the rest of the gang was closing in fast. She turned away and ran for the nearest alleyway. Her knowledge of this part of town was far less than that of the territory she'd prowled with Brandt's gang. She had no idea if this alley would lead her to freedom or dead-end and leave her trapped.

Her side hurt where the boy had punched her and her knees and palms were scraped and raw. There had been rain earlier in the day and while that always washed the streets clean it only seemed to wash the worst of the refuse into puddles at the center of alleyways. Water splashed up her legs as she ran, smelling of putrid refuse and worse.

Cat's legs burned with the effort of running. Normally she could run forever and never get tired — even scramble up pipes and rough walls to the rooftops, and run across their sloping surfaces for miles, leaping the occasional gap between buildings. The days since she'd run from Brandt's gang had put a stop to that, though. Now her body felt weak and leaden. Her gut ached with hunger. The last thing she'd eaten had been a half-rotted turnip, scrounged from the reeking surface of an alley just like this one.

Something struck her shoulder and a rock flew by her head. The boys behind her were throwing things and there was no way for her to dodge within the narrow alley. She could hear their splashing foot-steps growing closer. Another rock struck the back of her head and she stumbled to one knee, then the boys were on her.

Cat curled herself into a ball as the shouting and kicks started. It wasn't the first time she'd been beaten by a gang — that had happened more than once since Mother Agnes had died. The only question was how far this gang would go and how badly she'd be hurt at the end.

She cradled her head to protect it and she felt something snap in her left hand as a kick connected. At least her hand had cushioned the impact to her head a bit, but she still had to clench her teeth to keep from crying out. Any noise only made it worse by encouraging attack-ers. The kicks eventually trailed off and Cat could hear the boys surrounding her, panting with the exertion.

"Leave off," one of them said. "We don't want a deader around here."

Cat stayed still, not even opening her eyes or peeking at those around her. She heard footsteps and splashes as the gang walked back toward the marketplace. She lay still for a time, until she was certain they were gone, then opened her eyes and sat up.

She used her feet to push herself toward the alley's side until her back pressed against the wall, then slumped gratefully against its support, taking stock. Her back, shins, and forearms were battered and bruised. Some kicks had knocked her protecting arms against her face, battering her nose and jaw. She thought she tasted blood and spat to clear her mouth. That was a mistake, as the motion sent waves of pain through her and her head spun.

Her hand throbbed and she really didn't want to look at it, fearing the damage, but she finally did. Her ring finger was swollen and bent at an unnatural angle. She cradled her hand for a moment, knowing what she had to do.

Cat was no stranger to injuries after years living on the streets, but this was probably the worst she'd suffered herself. She'd seen others in the gang hurt, though. The finger was either broken or dislocated, possibly both, and would have to be straightened or it would heal crooked and useless.

There was a drunken beggar in Brandt's market that the boys went to. Rumor had it he'd been a doctor of some sort, before the drink got to him, and she'd seen him treat a similar injury. It hadn't been a pleasant sight.

She slid her purse-knife from her pocket and used the sharp blade to slice a strip of fabric from the hem of her tunic, then bit down on the palm pad. She gripped the end of her injured finger, took a deep breath, and pulled.

Whimpering behind her teeth clenched on the sweat-stained leather, Cat wrapped the strip of fabric as tightly as she could, binding the last two fingers of her hand together. She spit the purse-knife into her lap and used her teeth to help tie a knot to keep the binding secure.

Her hands were shaking before she was done and she leaned back against the alley's rough wall. The stone under her was cold and her clothes were soaked through with water and worse, but she lacked the strength to move.

Just a little time to rest, she thought, cradling her injured hand in her lap.

She let her head droop and closed her eyes.

It was near dawn when Cat woke. She'd slept straight through the afternoon and night. Her body ached and was covered with bruises and scrapes. Her clothes hadn't dried at all. She was shivering from the chill and her throat hurt. She winced as she swallowed.

There were noises from the mouth of the alley, back in the market. The earliest vendors were arriving for a new day's trading. Her stomach growled at the thought, but she knew she couldn't go back out here. The local gang would be out early too, watching their territory, especially after running her off. They'd want to see she didn't return.

Cat struggled to her feet, cursing as the movement sent spikes of pain through her. She looked around the alley and sighed, wincing and then cursing again at the pain. She limped off down the alley, away from the market. There was only one thing left that she could think to try.

"*Hst! Osraed!*" Cat whispered.

The boy spun around sharply, hands going up in an instinctual gesture of defense, then cursed sharply and lowered them to grasp his exposed crotch. She'd caught him in the act of relieving himself.

I should have waited until he was finished, Cat thought as she watched him dance backward holding up his hands in disgust.

"Who's there, damn you?" Osraed asked. He tucked himself back into his open trousers, then shook his hands and wiped them on his seat. He peered around the still dark alley beside the abandoned building the gang slept in.

"Over here," Cat whispered. She was tucked behind some crates that had been in the alley as long as she could remember.

"Runt?"

Cat grunted. She hated that name.

"I need to talk to you Osraed." Her voice was hoarse even without whispering. The pain in her throat had grown as she'd walked back to her gang's territory and the chills she'd thought were just from the air had gotten worse as well.

"You've got some balls comin' back 'ere," Osraed said, approaching her. "Brandt says yer a dead'un when he finds you."

"I know," she said. "I need to talk to him. To explain."

"What's to explain? You took off with the score."

"It wasn't like that, it was a mistake."

"A mistake, all right." Osraed laughed. "Never seen Brandt so worked up." He shook his head. "I can't believe you did that, Runt. Stealin' from us."

"I didn't," Cat said. "Look, I …" She licked her lips, wondering how she'd be able to get Brandt to believe her story if she couldn't convince Osraed. Osraed was the gullible one of the group, the nice one. That's why she'd picked him to approach. If she could get him to believe it and talk to Brandt first, then she might have a chance of coming home. "I saw the way we planned was blocked, see? So, I had to change up the plan. I never meant to keep it from you."

"So, you've got that big purse, do you?" Osraed asked. "Fattest I ever saw, the glimpse I got when you lifted it."

"No, I —"

"'Course not. Went through it fast and nothing left? Took off to keep it all fer yerself? Selfish instead of sharing with yer mates."

"It wasn't real," Cat said. "It was nothing but some … some iron disks. Not a copper in the lot even."

Osraed snorted. "That's a story. Let's see it, then, all them iron disks."

Cat hesitated. "I threw them away," she said finally.

"Yeah." Osraed looked her up and down in the moonlight. "You look half-dead, Runt."

Cat shivered. "I think I'm sick," she admitted. "And I got beat up.

Look, Osraed, please ... will you tell Brandt I'm sorry? There was nothing in the purse, it was a trick. I ... I just want to come home."

Osraed shook his head. "I'll not tell him I saw you, Runt, but that's all I'll do for you." He spat on the alley's cobbles at her feet. "But you get out of here. I see you on our patch again and I'll raise the cry, right?"

"Osraed, please —"

"No one'd believe that story, Runt. Not me and sure not Brandt." His lip curled up in disgust. "Yer selfish and stole from yer mates, Runt. From me. Now you live with that an' what it gets you. You get on out of here."

CHAPTER 4

*C*at wasn't sure which was worse, the burning in her throat or the burning of the fever. Her head felt light and fragile, like it could come apart at any minute. The bright light from the gas lamps that lined the street sent lances of pain through her head and the constant *clip-clop* pounding of horses' hooves on the cobbles was nigh unbearable.

She'd wandered the city all day since her meeting with Osraed, having no clear idea what to do next and no destination. As night fell, she found herself in a part of town she'd never seen before. A posh, fancy part of town, with wide streets lit by lamps. The buildings were large and well-lit. Not homes, for there hadn't appeared to be many people around until after nightfall, but they'd come then.

Carriage after carriage came down the street, disgorging streams of men and women in fancy dress. Liveried servants held the carriage doors for them and ushered them into the buildings. She heard them talking about shows and dinners and a night of gaming.

The wealth on view was staggering to Cat, she'd never before seen the like. The women wore jewels that were quite beyond her wildest imaginings, the men carried elegant, silver- or gold-topped canes that would have fed the whole gang for a month or more, and the clothes

… well, the least of the ladies' dresses would have sold to a picker for a fortune.

Cat slid into the shadows of one building's corner and watched in awe. She bit her lip and slid her hand into a pocket to finger her purse-knife. One, just one, of the tiny, elegant bags some of the ladies carried would change her life. A picker'd have it apart in a trice, all the fabrics separated and the clasp apart, ready for sale as its parts and unidentifiable if someone came looking. Not that any would bother, she was certain, this lot would hardly notice the loss.

That bag would keep me in style for month, Cat thought, staring at a couple walking by. *And that's without what might be inside.*

She glanced up and down the street. There was no sign of anyone who might be part of a gang, child or adult. The footmen and porters at the doorways were a worry, sure, but she thought she could move quickly enough, even as battered and sick as she was. The ladies' bags didn't even hang from leather, the straps were mostly of flimsy cloth. Her purse-knife would slide through those like air and she'd be off, across the street and into the alley, before the mark even noticed.

A likely couple was approaching. Cat waited until they'd just passed her, then slid out behind them, purse-knife at the ready. She followed for a few steps, then moved close behind the woman and reached out toward the thin straps supporting the bag.

Something struck her injured hand hard and she stumbled as pain flashed up her arm. Then she was struck on the side of the head and was knocked back against the building's wall.

"Damnable urchins!"

Cat blinked back tears from the pain and looked up, too shocked to even run as she should have. There'd been no one for yards beside her or behind her, she was sure of it. Just the couple she was following, so where had this man come from? Her eyes locked on the silver head of the cane he'd struck her with, already raised to bring down another blow.

"Porter!" he yelled. "Why do you allow these creatures near your door? I've a good mind to take my custom elsewhere!" He waved the cane above his head and Cat gasped. Not at the threat, but at the sight of his face and his next words. "Off with you, girl!"

How? How could it be him again?

She recognized the face immediately, the same man from the market. The man with the purse of iron disks.

And twice he's called me "girl"!

The cane started to descend and Cat dashed forward. A sudden flash of anger made her reach out her right hand, the one with the purse-knife, to slash his leg as she went by. The blade wouldn't cut deep, but it would mark him and slice his fine trousers. Cat rarely struck out in anger. She wasn't large enough or strong enough to win most fights, so she'd always relied on stealth and guile, but she suddenly blamed this man for everything that had gone wrong with her life the last week and she wanted to hurt him.

Then she was past and her blade encountered nothing. He'd dodged aside, his leg suddenly not where her blade was striking, but that didn't stop his own blow. The cane's movement changed from a swing to a thrust, and the heavy grip struck the back of her head with a dull *thwonk* that echoed through her skull.

Cat's vision narrowed and she stumbled into the street, staggering her way across and narrowly missing horses and carriage wheels to the accompanying shouts of hack drivers. Somehow, she made it to the other side without being crushed. She tripped over the far curb and sprawled on the cobbled walkway. A porter from the nearest building grasped a cudgel from beside the doorway and started toward her, but she managed to get to her hands and knees, crawling between the buildings before he came near enough to strike her.

CAT SHIVERED, but kept her eyes locked on the doorway across the street. There was a sign above the doorway that read "White's." It had been three hours since she'd seen the man enter White's and certainly he must leave soon. Unless he'd already left by another door, but Cat refused to think about that. This was the main doorway, it was where he'd entered after striking her — surely, he'd leave the same way.

At first, she wasn't entirely sure what she intended to do once he did leave, only that she had to do something to him. She simply blamed him for the mess her life had become — and it still shocked her that her life could be worse than it had been before she'd stolen his purse — and she wanted to make him pay somehow.

What kind of man carried a purse full of iron disks? If only he'd carried proper coins, then none of this would have happened. She'd be safely off somewhere out of the city, well-fed, with enough to carry her through until she found a decent way to support herself. It was not so much to have asked, and he was clearly wealthy enough to not have missed a single purse of coins.

She supposed it was his sick idea of a joke, perhaps. Let someone steal his purse, let her think she'd taken enough to start a new life, then laugh at the thought of her disappointment. Did he have another purse of iron hanging from his belt even now, waiting for a new victim?

And then he'd destroyed her opportunity to clip the lady's bag. The woman wouldn't have missed it and that bag would have gotten Cat off the streets for a time. A decent meal and a warm place to sleep would go a long way to getting her on her feet again. Just a few days, time enough to recover from whatever sickness she'd come down with and fill her belly, was that so much to ask?

He'd ruined things for her twice now. And, worse, how had he recognized that she was a girl? Her hair was short and she was as dirty and poorly dressed as any of the gangs of boys that roamed the streets. No one, not in all the years since Mother Agnes died, had ever suspected she was a girl, so how did he know?

Cat slid her thumb over the hilt of her knife. Her real knife, not the little blade of the purse-knife. It was a short blade, but she kept it sharp. She'd never used it on a person before, usually the sight of a blade made attackers back off. Everyone on the streets knew there was no winner in a knife fight and tried to avoid them, but she didn't plan on fighting the man.

As she waited — shivering from both the cold night and the fever, her broken hand throbbing, every attempt to swallow felt like ground glass passing down her throat, and the back of her head throbbing where he'd struck her — Cat's intent solidified. The blade might be short, but it was sharp, and long enough to reach a kidney from behind.

A part of Cat knew that she wasn't thinking clearly. That she should leave and try to find someplace warm, or at least warmer, to spend the night, and concentrate on getting well and finding food, but the rest of her was focused on making the stranger pay.

The night wore on and Cat began to despair that she really had missed him, but then the door of White's opened and he stepped out. He waved off the porter's offer of a hack and started down the street on foot.

Cat slid out of her hiding place and followed. She darted from shadow to shadow, crossing quickly in front of buildings' entryways so as not to draw the ire of the porters and footmen. She wished her hand wasn't injured and that she wasn't sick, then she could go to the rooftops and follow him from there.

The neighborhood changed within a few blocks. The well-lit, genteel establishments changed to darker, closed storefronts, and eventually to a seedy block where no gentleman should be about. The deep shadows and lack of street lamps made Cat's task easier, and she crossed the street to tail him closer. She kept her blade in her right hand, tucked against her thigh to avoid a betraying glint, and her left hand tight against her middle to protect her injured finger.

The man was oblivious to her. He blithely strolled along, cane tapping absently with each step.

Cat crept closer. *Ten feet*, she thought. *From ten feet I can rush him and have the blade home before he knows I'm coming.*

She increased her pace, closing on the man, but an itch in her chest made her turn aside. She ducked into the shadows beside a building's front steps and took slow, even breaths until the urge to cough subsided, all the while silently cursing her fever and sore throat. She'd almost had him, but now she'd have to make that distance up again.

When she stood and looked down the street, she realized that the tapping of the man's cane had stopped and he was nowhere in sight.

She started moving again, quicker this time, eyes searching for some sign of where he'd gone. They'd been in the middle of a block, with no intersections and little space between buildings, so where had he gotten to? Cat stopped. She strained her ears for any sound, the tapping of his cane or his footsteps.

He banged that bloody cane on the cobbles the whole way, why would he —

She tried to spin toward a sudden movement from the shadows, but wasn't quick enough. A glove-covered hand clamped over her face and pulled her close to her attacker's chest. She reversed the knife in her hand and drove it backward, but he caught her wrist, squeezing hard until the bones of her forearm ground together and she dropped the knife.

Cat struggled to get a breath past the hand covering her nose and mouth and realized that the glove was wet. She caught a sharply sweet scent that went rotten with her next breath and gagged. She reached behind her with her injured left hand, her right helpless in her attacker's grip, to find something to squeeze and twist, but all that accomplished was to trap her hand between their bodies. Blinding pain shot up her arm as she felt the broken ends of her finger grind together.

There was a shout and Cat heard running footsteps. The glove pressed tighter against her face, causing her to gasp and her head spun. There were more shouts and the man jerked her from side to side, as though struggling with someone himself.

Her vision narrowed and the sounds of their struggle grew farther away. She held her breath to avoid inhaling any more of what was on that glove, but her attacker released her hand and drove his fist into her midsection. Air exploded from her lungs and she had to inhale again. Her vision dimmed and her knees buckled. Her attacker lowered her to the ground, hand still clamped to her face.

*C*at came awake slowly. She heard birds singing, but that was puzzling because the gang's hideout wasn't anywhere near a park. She remembered that she'd run from the gang and grew more puzzled. She'd avoided the parks, the gangs that ran there were the most vicious and protective of their turf. None of the places she'd chosen to spend the night had been close to a park or open space at all. She preferred someplace enclosed and small, where her size became an advantage.

She gained enough awareness to realize that there was more than just the birdsong that was odd about her situation and kept carefully still.

None of the places she'd be able to spend the night would be this warm, nor this soft.

She listened for a time, heard nothing but the birds, then slowly cracked her eyes open. They were stiff and sticky as though from a very long sleep.

She was in a room. Not only in a room, but in a bed. Bright morning sunlight streamed through a window covered with white linen curtains. Across the room from the foot of the bed a small fire burned in a fireplace. The bed itself was the softest thing Cat had ever felt, both the mattress beneath her and the thick comforter she lay under.

It was then that Cat realized she was warm. Not chilled or burning with fever, but merely comfortably warm. Her throat was no longer sore, as well, so enough time had passed for her to recover from her illness.

She cast her thoughts back, trying to remember what had happened. She recalled following the man, thinking to kill him, and flushed at that. Whatever had she been thinking to attempt that? There was no profit in it, only risk.

She remembered being attacked and struggling, but nothing after that.

She'd been taken by someone, then, and none of the tales told on the streets had a good ending after that sort of start.

Cat sat up, thinking to find a way out and escape, but her head spun and she fell back against the pillows. Her stomach rebelled too, and she was suddenly aware of being both terribly hungry and sick-feeling at the same time. She clenched her jaw and closed her eyes, waiting for the feelings to subside.

While she waited, she took stock of the rest of her condition. Her broken finger was still bound, but with a clean bandage and wooden splint. So, she'd not lost enough time for it to heal, but someone had tended it. She stretched her arms and legs slowly. An ache or two and the feel of a bruise, so long enough for her to heal somewhat from the beatings.

And to grow quite weak, she realized. Her limbs were leaden and she doubted she could run even if her head and stomach would allow her to stand.

There was a rattle at the room's door, as of a key being turned, and Cat quickly closed her eyes and feigned sleep. She heard the door open and soft footfalls. Someone, a woman, she thought, hummed a tune as she moved about the room. The humming approached the bed and a hand lightly touched Cat's forehead.

"Yer fever's gone and yer awake, I think, girl."

Cat sighed. She opened her eyes and found an older girl, perhaps fifteen or sixteen, by the bedside, hand still on Cat's forehead.

"Am I right yer feeling better?" the girl asked.

Cat swallowed and narrowed her eyes. "Where am I?" she asked.

The girl took her hand away and settled onto the edge of the bed.

"Yer safe, girl, don't you worry," she said. "Yer at me master's house in the country, safe from whoever did you like that."

"How did I get here?"

"Master found ye on the streets, he did. Said ye'd been beaten by some'at had just run off when he found ye. Oy and a sight you were, sure." She rested her hand on Cat's. "Hand all busted an' that great knot on t'back of yer head." The girl frowned. "And ever' inch o'ye covered in filth, girl, whatever were y'about?"

At the girl's words, Cat noticed that her arms and hands, what she could see of them, were cleaner than she remembered. Not *clean*, by any means, it had been years and more since she'd been that, but not nearly as grimy as she remembered. And her clothes were gone, replaced by a white, linen shift and nothing else. She pulled her uninjured hand free and felt at her neck.

"Where's my locket?" she demanded.

"Locket?" the girl asked. "Y'mean that bit o' leather and string?" She frowned again. "Master had me bag up all yer things."

"Where?" Cat struggled to rise. She'd kept those bits of hair safe for years. They were all she had of the only people that'd ever cared for her. It couldn't be gone. Her head spun again as she rose and the girl eased her back to rest.

"Easy, girl," she said. "Sure, it's safe, just there in the wardrobe. Look, y'were dire sick, y'were." She nodded toward a cluster of small bottles on a shelf near the bed. "Cook an' I've tended ye nigh a week an' thought y'd leave us more'n once."

"A week?" Cat was shocked. How could she have no memory at all of a full week's time?

"Easy," the girl repeated. "Aye, been six days today since y'arrived." She smiled. "But yer better now, aye? Fever's gone and some o'yer hurts healed. Could y'eat a bit at all?"

Cat's stomach growled and her mouth filled at the thought. She swallowed and nodded. Whatever her circumstances here, if they were willing to feed her, she'd take the meal first and run later.

The girl rose and made her way to the hearth. She knelt and then rose again with a tray.

"Master said it's warm tea and dry toast to start," she said. "Porridge in a bit, if this lot sits easy."

Cat stared at the tray in wonder. She felt her eyes burn. Real tea and not water scooped from the gutter? Dry toast and not the burned heels of bread scavenged from behind a baker's stall? And the promise of more? She reached out tentatively, unsure if she was dreaming.

"Slowly," the girl warned. "Y'ave not had solid food fer a week, now."

Longer than that, Cat thought. *You have no idea.*

Cat nodded. She was no stranger to long periods without food and knew the danger of eating too quickly after. She picked up a piece of toast and took a small bite, chewing slowly and deliberately. It was a fine bread, really toasted and not burnt, and the tea, when she took a small drink, was plain, with no cream or sugar, but she thought it might be the finest thing she'd ever tasted.

The girl let her eat in silence for a time, then asked, "Have you a name, then?"

Cat swallowed and bit her lip. She couldn't very well introduce herself as Runt, though that was what she'd been called for years. "Cat" wasn't really a proper name either, though. She considered. No, "Cat" was how she'd always thought of herself, and it came from her mother, sort of.

"Cat," she said finally. "Call me Cat."

The girl raised an eyebrow. "Odd name, that," she said. "But all right. I'm Emma."

"Thank you, Emma." Cat slowly chewed another bite of toast and looked around the room. It was very large, with a number of furnishings in addition to the bed. Cat didn't understand what some of them were for, she'd never been in a proper bedroom, or even house, before. Tables and chairs, she knew, and cabinets of a sort, but nothing so rich as this. There were carpets on the floor everywhere except very near the hearth, a padded bench near the window, and a set of padded chairs around a table to the side. "What place did you say this was?"

"It's me master's country house. Mister Edward Roffe, he is."

Cat could see Emma was looking at her expectantly, as if she should know who that was. She wracked her brain, but couldn't recall hearing the name. "I'm sorry, but who is he?"

Emma looked disappointed. "Mister Edward Roffe? Y'never heard of Mister Edward Roffe?"

Cat shook her head, taking the last of tea. The toast was done as well, and had gone nowhere near filling her empty belly.

"Is he some sort of lord?"

"No lord, him. He's a famous artificer, he is," Emma said.

That was a term Cat had heard, though she knew little about it. The Artificers were a new guild or something like that, one that messed about with mechanicals. *And weren't they part of that steam exhibition in the park? The one that exploded and killed all those people?*

"I see," Cat said. "That sounds … impressive."

"Oh, it is!" Emma said. "He's a great man, he is."

"And you say he found me on the street?"

Emma nodded. "Said you were attacked by some bloke what run off when he come by," she said. "And you were all beat and not stirrin' a'tall." She rose and took the empty tray from Cat's lap. "An' that on top o' the sickness." She nodded to the bottles. "Been medicine every day and laudanum to keep you still. Whatever happened to put you in such a state?"

"I … I don't rightly know," Cat said, not wanting to let on what her station and situation had been. *Though my clothes and the purse-knife surely made it clear.* "Is Mister Roffe at home?" she asked. "So that I might thank him?"

"He's in the city, but he left instructions." Emma returned to the bedside. "Do you have people we should send word to?" she asked.

Cat shook her head.

"No more'n the Master expected," Emma said. "He said yer to rest and get yer strength back, and he'll speak to ye when he returns." She smiled. "I expect he'll offer ye a place here, if y've none other."

"A place?" Cat blinked. That would be an unbelievable outcome. A place in a household would mean a bed and roof, regular meals, it was more than she'd ever hoped for. She wasn't put off by the thought of work, even the hard work she knew being a servant would be — nearly anything would be better than the hardness of the streets.

"Nothing grand, mind you," Emma said. She gestured around the room. "And this ain't the servants' quarters, sure. Only put you here so's there'd be room to tend you." She pursed her lips. "I tried t'do as much as I could with the sponge, what with the fever sweat and all, but are you feeling up to a bath?"

Cat glanced at her arms, still streaked with grime but likely cleaner than they'd been in some time. There was little bathing on the streets. The boys would sometimes play in the river on a hot day, but Cat had not for obvious reasons. Being caught out in the rain was about the cleanest she could remember being. She compared what she could see of her skin to Emma's and flushed with embarrassment. Dirt had never been something to be concerned with before, but if she was to have a chance at a place here she must surely look the part, at least.

She nodded.

"Good."

Emma threw back the bedcovers and held out a hand to assist Cat from the bed. Cat took it and rose, having to close her eyes for a moment while her head swam. Emma put an arm around her waist and waited patiently.

"Take yer time," she said. "I were a week abed with the spots once. Takes time to get yerself back again."

Cat nodded and raised a hand to her forehead, then ran it over her head in shock. Her scalp was bare, all her hair gone, with hardly even any stubble remaining.

"My hair!"

"That were the nits," Emma said. She shrugged. "Sorry, but it were easiest. Once those get in a house and bedclothes, there's no stoppin' 'em."

Cat's initial shock faded. She'd always kept her hair short anyway, so it was no great loss, but it was still surprising to wake up and find oneself nearly bald. She opened her eyes and nodded when the dizziness subsided and Emma helped her walk to a doorway and into another room.

"Master's got his ideas, he does," Emma said. "Fitted up three rooms special like this."

This room had a fireplace shared with the bedroom Cat had been in, and in its center was a large, high-sided, copper bathing tub on a raised platform. A white, linen sheet was draped inside it as a cushion.

"Just let me get you settled and I'll see to the water," Emma said.

"I'm sorry to be such a bother," Cat said, worried at the effort it would take to carry enough water to fill that tub. She eased herself into it and leaned back against the linen-covered copper. Her breath was short from just that little walk and her hands were trembling.

"Cor, girl, no bother." Emma went to the fireplace and swung a copper pipe from beside it so that the open end was over the bath. "One thing this house has no lack of is hot water."

She did something near the hinge of the pipe and water began flowing into the bath. Hot water that made Cat yelp as it splashed over her thighs. Emma did something else and the water cooled a bit. It was still hot, but not unbearably so, and began to fill the tub.

"The master's ideas. Copper pipes in all the chimneys," Emma said. "Pipes in the bread ovens, pipes through the foundry next door, bloody pipes everywheres. Can't hardly reach into a cloth-closet without you scald yerself on pipes." She returned to the side of the bath. "Take that shift off, then. I'll get a cloth and some soap and some clean clothes fer after."

Cat hesitated. Wearing only the shift was bad enough, but her weakness had kept her from noticing it before. The necessity of hiding that she was a girl meant that she'd never gone without clothes before, not even when she was with Mother Agnes. It wasn't modesty so much as habit, but she was still uncomfortable.

"Come on, now," Emma said. "I left five little brothers and sisters at home, and I've tended y' these last six days. You've nothing I haven't both seen and wiped clean, so off with it."

Cat flushed but pulled the shift over her head. Even that effort exhausted her again and she collapsed back against the tub with her eyes closed and barely enough strength to cover herself with her hands. The copper of the tub was cold against her skin even through the linen sheet, but it heated rapidly as the water filled it.

The heat of the water stung as it rose up her body, but after that it seemed to sink into her, easing aches she hadn't even realized she had. It also discovered to her the few scrapes and cuts that hadn't yet healed and set them stinging, but that felt good to her in an odd way.

Emma returned with a sponge, several cloths, and two bars of soap.

"I've a stronger soap to get the worst of grime off," she said, "then a softer one to ease yer skin a bit."

Cat saw that the water, midway up her belly, was already dark with grime. She accepted the sponge and a bar of soap, smelling strongly of lye, from Emma, but she soon found that she lacked the strength to work up any sort of lather or to really scrub.

"Lean back," Emma said. "Yer weak as a babe."

Cat did as instructed. She closed her eyes, first with embarrassment, but then with a certain pleasure as Emma scrubbed her. The heat of the water was luxuriant and the scrubbing, while rough to get at the caked in grime and dirt, was almost pleasant.

She opened her eyes once when Emma grunted and there came a gurgle of water. Emma had pulled some sort of plug from the bottom of the bath and the water level was sinking.

"Water's too filthy to do more than move the dirt around," Emma said, nodding toward the window. "Drains out under the window there." She sat back on her heels and crossed her arms on the tub's edge. "You sit back. We'll fill 'er up again when this lot's gone and 'ave another go."

Cat nodded and leaned back. The air was cool on her skin as the water drained, so she wrapped her arms about herself and drew her legs up, partly out of embarrassment, despite Emma's words that she'd seen it all before. While she waited for the fresh water to fill, Cat considered all that Emma had said so far.

"Is a place here very good?" she asked. Any place would be better than the streets, she suspected, but she'd heard dire stories of how servants were treated in some households. Emma, though, seemed quite happy here.

"Oh, aye!" The girl rested her cheek on her crossed arms and smiled. "There's two hot meals a day, and breakfast is more than bread and drippings, mind you, not like some houses. Half a day every Sunday for church and a full Sunday once a month."

"What … what sort of work might I be asked to do?"

"Well, Cook's gettin' on a bit, she is. Might could use a hand in the kitchen." She smiled wider. "Or y'might be put to helping me with the cleanin'. There's only Cook and me, y'see? Well, there's the master's valet and a man-of-all-work, too, but the one only sees to the master and t'other mostly works the grounds."

"I see," Cat said. "So, cooking or cleaning? No … other work?" What Cat really wanted to ask was about the stories she'd heard of how female servants were treated in some households, but couldn't quite think how to phrase it. The question itself must have been enough, however, for Emma's brow furrowed and she frowned.

"Oh," she said, "no. None of that here. The master's a grand, kind man, he is. A real gentleman, for all he's not titled a'tall." She paused. "Has his ways, o'course, as any might. But more than fair, I'll say that."

The tub had mostly drained, save for a thin layer of mud at the bottom, leaving Cat both astounded and embarrassed at the amount of grime that had been on her. Emma rose and swung the pipe from the chimney back into place. Fresh hot water splashed into the tub.

"Three years I been here," Emma continued, "and never a bit o' that. He don' come here much even. Spends most of the time at his city house."

Cat relaxed. Emma was a pretty enough girl, as she understood such things. Surely if this Mister Edward Roffe were the sort to take advantage of his servants he'd have done so with her.

"I think the master pines fer his dead wife," Emma went on. "He's a widower, you see? Wife and little girl died years ago, and he never took another. Very sad, it is."

"Yes, it is," Cat agreed.

The tub filled with water and Emma resumed scrubbing. In all, it took three more fillings of the tub before Emma was satisfied that it was the best they could do in one sitting. Cat's skin stung and felt raw, but a final wash with the milder soap, scented with lavender and chamomile, eased her. The last filling of the tub, almost to the brim, and the subsequent peaceful soaking while Emma saw to fresh bedclothes, eased her even more.

"I've a porridge brought up from the kitchen," Emma called from the other room, "with cream and honey, since the bread's sat easy in you."

This must be very like Heaven, I think.

CHAPTER 6

For Cat it would always be the next day in that house that was the source of some of her fondest memories.

After returning to bed for a rest the day before, she'd gone to sleep warm, clean, comfortable, and with a full belly for, perhaps, the first time in her life. Certainly, the first time she could remember. But to wake up from a restful sleep the same, to be met on waking by Emma, who brought a tray of tea and toast for her to break her fast, this time with butter and jam as well as cream and sugar for the tea, and then to dress in clean, albeit plain, clothes … well, it was quite the most wondrous morning Cat had ever dared dream of. The start of a day that only became more wonderful as it went on.

"It's only plain stuff," Emma said as she helped Cat dress. Cat's experience with clothing being limited to cast-off tunics and trousers, skirts and stays were quite beyond her knowledge. "Cast off bits Cook asked for in the village. The master's a fine one, but just like a man to run off and think nothing that ye'd have naught to wear a'tall."

"I'm grateful for it, Emma," Cat said, "thank you."

"Ye've truly never wore the like?" Emma asked as she tied the stays and handed Cat a loose blouse.

Cat settled the blouse over her shoulders and shook her head.

"Well, when y'ave yer own, don't strait-lace it, or you'll not make it through a day's work." She eyed Cat critically. "You'll do fer now. I've no cap or collar fer you, but yer presentable. Master'll provide a proper kit if yer t'ave a place."

"Thank you," Cat said again. She smoothed her skirts, trying to adjust to the clothing. It wasn't that the clothes were uncomfortable, just that they were so very different than what she was used to. And so many more of them. Skirts and undergarments — the stays, though not tightly-laced, felt very constricting, though Cat could see how the garment might offer some welcome support through a hard day's work. And she wasn't even wearing the whole of it. They'd found no spare shoes or stockings that might fit her, so she was still barefoot.

"'Ave you strength to walk downstairs?" Emma asked.

"I believe so," Cat said. A bit of food and a night's rest without sickness had done wonders for her.

"Cook 'as a proper breakfast in the kitchen."

Cat's stomach growled, even with the morning's toast and tea, and she grinned. "It appears I can find the strength for that, at least."

Emma grinned back. "Sounds it," she said. "Follow me, then."

They left the bedroom and Cat looked around the rest of the house with interest. Whatever this artifice was, there must be a great deal of coin in it, for the house was huge to Cat's eyes. She counted twelve doorways before they reached the staircase and the hallway floor was covered in rugs and runners that she thought would fetch a nice sum from a picker. There were even chairs and pieces of furniture in the hall, which made little sense to Cat.

With all these rooms to choose from, why would they need to sit in the hall?

"Most of t'house is closed," Emma said. "Just the master's room and the one yer in we keep open." She paused and frowned. "The master dint leave word fer what to do with ye when y'woke. Didn't say to move y'to servants' quarters or nothing." She grinned. "I think if he hasn't said, then y'should stay where y'are."

"Should I?" Cat asked. The last thing she wanted to do was anger her benefactor. She was still wary of his intentions — in her experience no one helped another without something in it for them — but Emma seemed to think he was a kind man.

Emma nodded. "He ordered y'put there and said not a thing about movin' ye," she said. She grasped Cat's arm and pulled her toward the stairs. "It'll be a grand lark, now yer better. Y'can play at bein' a lady, an' I'll practice bein' a lady's maid." She nodded. "I've ambitions, I do."

"Is that good?" Cat asked. "To be a lady's maid?"

"It's the grandest thing t'be, I think," Emma said.

"What … what does one do as a lady's maid?" If Mister Roffe truly did offer her a place, then perhaps Cat, too, could aspire to one day being a lady's maid. It was certainly a better thing to be than a cutpurse.

"She helps a lady with her clothes and bath and, well, all manner of things."

"And what does a lady do?" Cat asked, never having seen someone she'd call a lady in the markets.

"Well, I suppose she lazes about and gets dressed and bathed and fed," Emma said.

The lady's role sounds far more what one should aspire to, Cat thought, but aloud, "I'll see if I can play at that for you then, Emma. Just so you can practice, you understand."

"Oh, aye, all fer me, I'm sure," Emma said grinning. She took Cat's arm and the two hurried down the stairs. "You just enjoy it while y'can. A'fore that room's closed up again like the rest of 'em."

Indeed, when they'd descended the stairs most of the rooms on the main floor looked closed up to Cat, with furnishings covered by large sheets. To hear Emma tell it, this Mister Roffe only visited the country house a time or two each year, which made Cat wonder why he kept the home at all. She also wondered if Emma might be mistaken about him offering her a place, since the small staff already there seemed to have the limited work well in hand. Unused or not, though, what she saw of the rooms and furnishings spoke of wealth as much as the upstairs did.

The kitchen and staff areas on the main floor were plainer, but still finer than anything Cat was used to.

She met Mrs. Singley, the cook, who Emma referred to simply as Cook. As did Skiff, the gardener and groundskeeper.

"It's good ter see you up an' about, lass," Cook said, sliding a plate in front of Cat. "It's Cat yer called, is it?"

Cat stared at the plate in shock. She'd thought the toast with jam and the porridge were fine, but before her was a mound of eggs, sausages, and potatoes, not to mention more bread than she thought she could possibly eat. She blinked back tears, remembering what Emma had said about the meals here. *No, it's not just bread and drippings, is it.*

She shook herself.

"Yes, it's Cat, thank you." She looked up from the plate. "This is for me?"

Cook gave her a look tinged with sympathy, and Cat might have taken offense if it hadn't clearly been so kind-hearted.

"Skiff's had a good year with the chickens, he has," she said. "Hardly know what ter do with all the eggs. Between them and the gardens we've plenty." She set similar plates in front of the other two and got one for herself.

CAT ATE her breakfast in silence. The others, perhaps sensing that she was unsure of herself, talked of the coming day's chores and asked her only a few questions. Cat tried to answer as honestly as she could without coming right out and saying that she'd been raised in the gutter, and they didn't pry.

After breakfast, Emma took Cat on a careful walk around the grounds, with frequent stops for Cat to rest, as she was still easily tired.

The house looked immense from outside and the grounds did as well. Emma told her that "only" four acres or so of land made up the grounds inside the estate's high walls and outer fences. Outside those, some distance away, was a fair-sized village and another, larger, estate house.

"They're proper lords of some-such," Emma said. "This were theirs too, at one point, but the master he bought it outright, he did."

Cat nodded. She was a bit in awe already of what Emma had said was inside the estate's walls. Kitchen gardens, a formal garden, a quarter acre or so of wooded land, along with a small carriage house and barn. They'd left by the kitchen door and along a cobbled way for deliveries to the kitchen garden Cook kept.

"I come from a farm, meself," Emma said as they walked through the rows of plants.

"Whyever did you leave?" Cat asked. She couldn't believe that someone would leave a place where food simply came out of the ground for the taking.

"It were a small village," Emma said, looking away. "Not much to choose from fer a husband there. And didn't much want one, come to that."

Cat frowned. She had a sense there was more to it, but didn't want to pry.

They continued walking and chatting. Cat was astounded to learn that nothing from the estate was sold for profit. She'd expected that this Mister Roffe kept it for that purpose. To learn that he kept something so expensive and rarely used it made little sense to Cat.

"Why does he keep the place?" she asked. "If he so seldom comes here?"

Emma shrugged. "No tellin' what them with enough coin'll do."

"Is your work hard here?"

"Easier than most, I 'spect. With none in residence much of the time."

Cat frowned. "Do you really think he'd offer me a place, then? With so little work here?"

"He might need help at the house in the city." Emma shrugged. "Maybe plans to bring you there, or me, and have you take over here. Who's to say?"

Cat thought for a moment. "Perhaps."

They walked in silence for a time and then Cat stumbled and shivered. The day was sunny, but cold, and she shivered again with the chill.

Emma stopped and grasped Cat's hand.

"Yer cold as bone, girl, why'd you never say some'at?"

Cat shivered again and wrapped her arms around her middle. "I didn't notice ..."

"Let's get y'back to the house," Emma said. "A bath to warm y'an bed to rest, I think."

~

"I COULD GROW QUITE USED to this," Cat said, easing herself deeper into the hot water.

"Enjoy it while y'can, yer ladyship," Emma said with a teasing grin. "Afore yer down with us servants. I've never had such as this meself."

"I thought this house had hot water to spare?" Cat asked. "How can you not have?"

"Oh, there's hot water a'plenty," Emma explained, "but no bath like that below stairs. We've a hip bath, but naught like that'un." She held a hand at her midsection. "About t'here's the best, not all soakin' neck-deep like that."

Cat frowned. "With so many of the baths in the house — three, did you say? And this Mister Roffe never at home, why can't you just use the ones upstairs?"

Emma shook her head. "Not done," she said. "Not done a'tall. Even if the master's not in residence. Cook and me, we keep to our place, we do."

Cat frowned. With so much to the house and so many luxuries, why shouldn't the staff make use of them when this "master" wasn't at home? To have such a thing as this tub lying idle and unused seemed a shame.

"Well, if I'm playing at being a lady, then I shall give you permission to use this one," Cat said. "In fact, I order it. So there."

Emma looked shocked, then bit her lip.

"Well," she said and grinned. "If her ladyship orders it …" She began unbuttoning her smock.

"I …" Cat started to protest. She'd meant for Emma to use the bath another time, not right this minute — certainly not for Emma to join her. But her voice trailed off as she watched the other girl.

Emma slid into the bath at the other end and Cat jumped, startled, as their legs touched beneath the water. Cat froze, uncertain of what to do and equally uncertain about what she was feeling.

"Oh, this is nice," Emma said, leaning back and closing her eyes. "It's like being right inside a fire, it's so warm."

"Yes. Yes, it is."

CHAPTER 7

$\mathcal{C}$at spent the next fortnight living in luxury she'd never dreamed possible.

As her strength returned, she spent her days walking the grounds of the estate and even took the short walk to the nearby village, though there were more than a few stares and whispers. Her close-shorn hair made her quite the oddity, she knew. She stopped going to the village and limited herself to the Roffe estate when three of the village boys taunted her over her lack of hair and threw clods of dung at her. Cat resisted the urge to chase them down and make them pay for that, not wanting to jeopardize her chances for a place in the Roffe household by brawling in the village.

Emma took her opportunity to play at being a lady's maid quite seriously, waking Cat with toast and tea every morning and helping her dress, and Cat spent her days learning the ways of a housemaid from Emma. She thought that knowing the work might help her chances of Roffe truly offering her a place in the household.

Neither set of tasks took all of their time, especially with Cat helping at the cleaning tasks, and the two girls spent hours each day simply talking or walking the paths of the estate. For Cat it was, indeed, heaven itself. She was safe, warm, fed, and, for the first time in her life, she felt she had a friend she didn't have to lie to every day.

Still, though, she could not shake the man with the iron-filled purse from her thoughts. Without him, she would certainly never have been rescued by Mister Roffe and would never have the hope of a place in this household, but still he'd cheated her, struck her, and even tried to ... what had he been trying to do with her when she'd been rescued? Kidnap her? Murder her?

No, there was a score to settle there, still, and even if she were offered a place here, Cat knew she'd be on the lookout for that man all the rest of her days. And when she next met him, she'd be surer of her strike.

Then the word came that Mister Edward Roffe, artificer and master of the house, would be arriving the next day.

At noon, Cat was sitting beside a small brook that ran under the estate's wall and through the patch of woods. She looked up as she heard Emma calling her name from nearer the house and saw the other girl waving to her. She rose and made her way back.

"There's word come," Emma said. "Mister Roffe'll be here fer supper, but he's sent a package fer you."

"A package?"

Emma grinned as they walked toward the house. "Boxes an' such, Cook said. Look t'be the master's finally thought of you having no clothes o' yer own an' sent some'at fer you."

"That will be a relief."

They returned to the house and upstairs to Cat's room. Cat stopped in shock at the sight of the packages on the bed. Boxes and paper-wrapped parcels covered it, far more, and of finer quality, than could be accounted for by a maid's uniform.

Cat went to the bed, hand at her mouth. She opened the largest box first. The packaging itself was a work of art. Bound not with twine as she'd expected, but with ribbon, and of a heavy, expensive stock. She untied the bow and carefully pulled the ribbon aside, then lifted the top. There was something dark beneath the white tissue paper in the box and she pulled that aside as well, then gasped at the sight.

The dress was exquisite. A deep, emerald velvet that seemed to sparkle as it caught the light, trimmed with black that only made the greens more vivid. Cat reached out a tentative hand to touch it, then pulled it back.

"This can't be for me," she whispered. "It's a mistake. Emma, this can't be for me, can it?"

When Emma didn't answer, Cat turned and found the other girl frozen in the doorway, eyes wide and one hand to her mouth. She was staring at the open box as well.

"Emma?"

Emma stared at the boxes, then at Cat. "I'm sorry, miss." She ducked her head and stared at the floor.

"What?"

"I'm sorry, miss," Emma repeated. "I should'a known."

"Should have known what?" Cat asked. She stepped toward the girl. "Emma, whatever's gotten into you?"

"Should'a known," Emma repeated, not looking up. "But y'said y' had no people, miss, that y'were no one in particular." She pointed at the boxes. "But I should'a known. Y'talk all proper-like and —"

"Emma, what are you saying, what do you mean?"

"Them's no servant's clothes, them. Yer some kind'a lady, miss," Emma said. "I should'a seen it. I'm sorry I was so familiar, miss." She looked up and Cat saw real fear in her eyes. "Please don't see me put out, miss?" She ducked her head again. "I'll behave as I should, I will. I swear it!"

Fear shot through Cat as well, but for a different reason. She realized suddenly just how much she cared for the other girl, how much she relied on her friendship. Something she'd not had before.

"Emma!" she cried. She grasped the other girl's hands, holding them tightly. "I swear to you, I have no people. I grew up on the

streets, for goodness sake! I'm certainly no one in particular. This —"
She jerked her head at the boxes. "This has to be some mistake."

Emma raised her eyes and Cat saw that they shone with tears. Just as her own did, she felt.

"Emma, please," she said. "You're my only friend here. Anywhere. You're ... the only friend I've ever had. I could not bear to lose that, please."

"Do y'mean that, miss?"

Cat released Emma's hands and cupped the other girl's cheeks. "Don't you dare!" she said. "Don't you dare call me 'miss' like that. I am Cat and you are Emma and nothing in those boxes, mistake or no, will ever change that, do you hear?" Emma still looked uncertain, so Cat took her hands again and squeezed them forcefully. "I swear it, Emma."

The older girl's face cleared and she smiled. "All right, then, Cat," she said and bent forward to kiss Cat on the cheek.

The knot of fear in Cat's middle dissolved and as Emma straightened Cat darted her own face forward and gave her a quick kiss on the lips with a playful grin. That caused Emma to smile again, and Cat marveled for a moment at how important the other girl had become to her. Not since Mother Agnes died had Cat truly cared about another person. The feeling was odd, and a bit frightening.

"Y'should see what's in the rest o'them boxes," Emma said, pulling her hands from Cat's and moving to the bedside.

Cat stared at her empty hands for a moment, then raised one to touch her lips.

CAT WAITED with equal parts eagerness and trepidation for Roffe to arrive. He was due before supper, but as the day grew later, she began to wonder if he'd appear at all. She was waiting in her room with Emma, dressed far more elegantly than she ever had before.

Over the past days she'd settled in her mind that this Roffe was as Emma described him. A kind sort of man, who'd chased off her attacker and brought her here to be cared for when he discovered she was ill. Someone likely to offer her a servant's position as a further kindness. But the sort of clothes he'd sent …

"Emma, what do you suppose these clothes mean? They're certainly not the sort one gives a servant, are they?"

"No, miss, they're not."

"Emma …"

"Sorry," Emma said with a shy grin. "Cat, then."

"I'll not be his doxie," Cat said firmly. She was young for that, and hardly filled out, but some men had those appetites, she knew. "Not for anything."

Emma shook her head. "None of that here. Never since I've been here. The master's never even had a lady to supper here."

"But you say he's seldom here at all. There's no telling what he does in the city."

"Mister Roffe's a good, kind gentleman, he is. He gave me a place here when … well, he's a good, kind gentleman is all I can say. You'll see."

Cat was unconvinced. She was a girl straight from the streets with no talents beyond the cutting of purses and being light of foot on rooftops — neither of those was anything a gentleman might have an interest in. "If not that, then what explanation could there be?"

Emma frowned. "Maybe yer some sort'er lost heir? Like in the tales."

"Tales aren't real, Emma."

"Well, they're gilded some, sure, but has t'be some truth to a tale, don't there?"

"And how would your Mister Roffe know if I were?" Cat asked. "I've no great birthmark like the lads in a tale."

Emma frowned again. "No, that's for certain. Maybe, the master, he knows that fellow what attacked you? Knows him fer a villain and all, somehow? Followed him on that street and when he saw you attacked like that he just knew it?"

"I think we've gone far afield now," Cat said. She shook her head and sighed. "I know you think this man's kind and generous, Emma, but where I grew up there's no such thing. No one does a thing without there's something to be gained."

Emma gave her an odd look. "Not even fer love, then?"

Cat thought of her gang and others on the street. The closest thing she'd seen to what the tales called love was what she'd had with Mother Agnes, and even that she doubted.

"Especially not for that."

They heard horses in the drive and Emma rushed to the window.

"He's here!" she called.

Cat went to the window as well, but all she could see was the roof of a carriage and a hat-covered head hurrying to the house's door. Cat smoothed the front of her dress and skirts, then checked herself in the cloudy mirror. The dress was fine, she had to admit, but her newly short-cropped hair did nothing for her appearance.

"What should I do?" she asked. "Do I go down and greet him? Or do I wait here?"

"It's so close to time fer supper, you should be going down," Emma said after a moment's hesitation.

Cat nodded. "Very well, then."

The two girls left Cat's room and had no sooner made their way to the top of the stairs than a man appeared at the bottom.

"'At's Clanton," Emma whispered. "The master's valet."

Clanton was a thin, dark man with greasy hair. He reminded Cat instantly of any one of the pimps or fences she'd seen on the streets and she paused, wary and uncertain.

"Mister Roffe's in the dining room," Clanton said, gesturing impatiently for them to come down. "Hurry up now, it's been a long ride from the city and he's no desire to wait on supper for your sake."

Cat hurried down the stairs, Emma behind her. Though she'd taken an immediate dislike to the valet and distrusted him instinctively, she didn't want to keep her benefactor waiting.

She followed Clanton to the dining room where he nodded to her and opened the door.

Cat paused outside the dining room and ran her palms down her skirts. She looked to Emma, who gave her a grin and a nod of encouragement, then steeled herself and stepped through the door to meet this Mister Edward Roffe, artificer.

He stood at the room's far side, near the sideboard, back to her, pouring himself a glass of wine.

"Well, girl," he said, and Cat froze at the voice. He turned and she could see his face. "You look better than last I saw you, at least."

It was him.

The man with the iron-filled purse. The man who'd struck her.

The man she meant to kill.

CHAPTER 8

"*W*ine?"

Cat was unable to move, frozen in place like her namesake caught in a lamp's beam with no shadows in reach.

Stupid, she thought to herself. She'd never considered that the man she'd been following and the owner of this house, her benefactor, might be the same person. She'd accepted without question Emma's repetition that her "master" had come across Cat being attacked by someone else, not that he was the attacker himself. She'd allowed herself to be lulled by Emma's friendliness and forgotten the first rule of the street: No one, *no one*, could be trusted and now she was trapped with this stranger and no telling what he wanted of her. All those days here when she might have looted the house of portable valuables and been safely on her way — all wasted because she'd believed the fairy story of a man, anyone, being kind.

Stupid, foolish girl!

The man raised a different decanter. "Brandy, then?"

Cat stared at him. He hadn't moved from the sideboard except to turn. Perhaps she could escape. She edged backward, but the door had been shut behind her. She reached back, never taking her eyes from the man, and grasped the knob. When she found it locked, her worst fears were realized.

"To drink, girl," the man said. "What will you have?"

Cat's eyes darted about the room, sliding over anything that might be used as a weapon. There were bottles on the sideboard, but the man stood before it. She dashed forward to the table and grasped a knife from the nearest place setting, then put her back to the wall. She started to sink into a crouch, knife held loosely in her hand, but straightened. Better to have him think she didn't know a thing about how to fight. She held the knife with both hands, close to her chest.

The man took a drink of his wine and shook his head.

"I suspect you know more of knives than that, girl," he said. "Enough to see that one's useless for all but butter." He snorted derision. "Better to have grabbed a fork. Now this —"

Cat jumped as a knife *thunked* into the wall beside her head. She'd barely even seen him move. The knife had appeared in his hand, been thrown, and he'd resumed his casual stance before she was even aware of it.

He poured a second glass of wine and stepped toward her to place it on the table near where she'd grabbed the knife. Then he turned his back to her and went to the far end of the table to sit.

"I assure you, girl, you'll go hungry if you kill me before supper. I trust my staff has that much loyalty, at least."

"Who are you?" Cat whispered.

He frowned as though disappointed in her. "Wrong question."

"What do you want of me?"

"Better. Let us say, perhaps, that I saw some bit of potential in you that day in the market." He smiled. "Not the day you took my purse, mind you, but the first day, when you decided to."

He'd noticed her then? That early? She'd watched him for days on his visits to the market, waiting for the right set of circumstances that would allow her to take his purse and get away from Brandt and the others.

He nodded as though to confirm her thoughts. "Yes, you're

nowhere near as good as you think you are, girl. Not so bumble-footed as most, mind you, but far from your opinion of yourself."

Cat frowned. If he'd noticed her that soon and yet kept coming to the market, kept to all his habits. "You planned this."

He took a sip of wine, smiling.

"You carried that purse full of iron knowing I'd take it. Why?"

He shook his head. "You don't know enough of the whole to ask that question yet. Think it through, girl."

"The toffs," she said. "The lady's purse. It's no coincidence you were there."

"And now too far, yet, in our story. Find the other dots you must connect to get from one to the other."

She puzzled and he gave her a disappointed look.

"The markets, girl, the markets." He sighed. "Did you not wonder how the gangs always seemed to stumble to you so quickly?"

She should have, she realized. It seemed every time she stepped into a market square the gangs were on her in a heartbeat. It shouldn't have been so quick. Should've taken them time to realize she wasn't just some shopkeeper's errand boy there on fair business.

"You set them on me," she whispered. "You were following me all that time? Why?"

"Perhaps to keep you from falling in with bad company again." He pointed at the chair. "Sit. Take the knife, if you like, but sit."

Cat pulled the knife from the wall and sat. She grasped the glass of wine and started to drink, then set it back on the table. She'd been drugged once by this Roffe, or whatever his name truly was.

"If I wanted to drug you, I could have done it without revealing myself first," he said. "Drink or not, it's your choice." He rang a small bell set next to his plate. "Eat or not, as well."

The door was opened by Clanton. Cat had a moment's thought to dash through it and try to escape, but she wasn't sure she could get by the valet in the confines of the doorway and corridor. Better, perhaps, to wait for a surer opportunity.

Cook carried in a tureen of soup and ladled out two bowls to set before her and Roffe. She gave Cat an odd look, probably wondering what her place at the table meant, and left. Clanton closed the door and Cat heard the lock turn again. She wondered if not running had been a dire mistake. She looked at Roffe, but he was concentrating on eating his soup.

Well, if I'm in it up to my neck, I suppose I must wait and find out what it is.

The only explanation, if Emma was to be believed that he wouldn't expect her to be his doxie, seemed to be if he wanted her thieving skills for some reason — perhaps to steal something he wanted? But that made no sense either, for there were far more accomplished burglars to be had with just a word spoken in the right ear and the right tavern. The thought that this Roffe must be a thief himself became more what Cat thought. That was where the boys all moved up to, after all, either to thieving gangs or hired muscle if they were dull and strong.

This elaborate charade, though, was far different from what those who'd been tapped to join such gangs described.

Roffe's home was more than they'd described of a master thief's patch, too. So perhaps he was more than that.

If he truly was a proper burglar, one who dealt in more than the few coins a cutpurse would bring, there might be an opportunity here. He might lead a gang of thieves and need recruits. Brandt, after all, recruited from the beggars. And Brandt paid Marven a fee to work the market, and some of the boys went into Marven's gang when they grew older, though what it was Marven did Cat had never learned.

She looked down at her own bowl of soup and her stomach growled. Cook had served them both from the same tureen, and there were easier ways to poison or drug her. Cat spooned up a mouthful of the rich broth and in what seemed like moments she'd emptied the bowl.

The ringing of the bell startled her into looking at Roffe again as the door opened and Cook entered with the next course.

"Do you have a name?" Roffe asked, "or should I keep calling you 'girl'?"

Cat glanced at Cook as a fresh plate was set in front of her. She didn't want to give Roffe her name, but if she gave a false one now, Cook would hear it and wonder at her purpose.

"I've not the staff for a full supper," Roffe said as his own plate was set before him. "And little reason with just the two of us, so you'll have to settle for a full plate from the kitchen. A name?"

"Cat," she said finally, not wanting Cook to think ill of her and confused by his comment. She looked at the full plate before her, with slices of beef, roasted potatoes, and some sort of squash, and wondered how this could be thought settling.

"'Cat'? Roffe asked. "An odd name. How did you come by it?"

She looked up and found Roffe staring at her, eyes intent. Before he'd seemed to barely regard her, but now she had his full attention and it was disconcerting. His stare bored into her.

"I … it was something my mother called me," Cat found herself saying without thought.

"Your mother?" Roffe said quickly. "Is your mother alive? I'd assumed you were an orphan, running with that lot."

"She died," Cat said, looking down at the table to avoid his gaze. "When I was very young."

"But you remember her?"

Cat shook her head, she wished Roffe would apply himself to the beef as he had to the soup and leave her be. "No, I … only a bit."

"Enough to remember she called you Cat, though? A very odd name, as I said."

"It was just something she called me. Not really Cat, I think."

"What then?"

Why was he so insistent? What difference did it make? "A pet name only," she said. "I remember her calling me 'catling,' and I —"

She broke off as Roffe laughed and she looked up in shock.

"'Catling?'" He laughed again and then said, almost to himself, "You remember your mother calling you 'catling.'"

Cat flushed and looked down at the table again. It was bad enough to have told him something so private, something she'd never told another soul, but for him to laugh at it?

"How very, very droll," Roffe said. "No memory at all of a father, I'm sure."

Cat's temper flared. One thing Mother Agnes had assured her was that her mother had not worked the streets. She'd been properly married, though what had happened to her father she didn't know.

"What is it you want of me, Mister Roffe?" she asked.

"You're well-spoken for a gutter magpie," Roffe said, ignoring her question. "Where did you learn that?"

"I had a very good teacher," Cat said, remembering the nights with Mother Agnes, both of them hungry and cold in whatever alley seemed to offer shelter, but Agnes still insisting that Cat take the time to learn a bit of her numbers and letters before drifting off to sleep.

"Who?" Roffe demanded. "Not your mother, for you say you remember nothing of her but this silly name."

Again, Cat bristled, but the intensity of Roffe's gaze and questions had her answering. "A woman on the streets," she said. "I stayed with her for a time."

"Her name?"

"Agnes."

"Agnes," Roffe said and grunted. "What became of her?"

"She died."

"Some time ago, I assume?"

Cat nodded.

Her stomach growled again and Roffe gestured at her plate.

"Eat," Roffe said, turning his attention to his own plate.

Cat did, glancing up periodically to watch Roffe, who now seemed completely focused on his food and ignoring her.

Midway through the meal Roffe filled his wine glass and gestured questioningly to Cat's. She shook her head, but took the opportunity to ask again, "What is it you want of me, Mister Roffe?"

Roffe took a deep breath and sat back. He placed his knife and fork on the table, resting them against his plate with a soft *clink*. The sound in the quiet room reminded Cat of just how alone she was with the man.

"As you surmised," Roffe said, "my work is not entirely of a public and legitimate nature."

"Emma told me you were a famous artificer."

"Emma? Oh, yes, the maid." Roffe shrugged. "That is my public persona. It explains my wealth and provides a certain access within society." He frowned. "Do not, please, take this to mean that I have no actual skill in artifice. This is not the case. It is simply that the public examples of my skill are the least of my talents."

"I see," Cat said.

"No, you do not, but I hope you will. When I saw you in that market the first time, I expected you to try for my purse then and there. I found it curious that you didn't, and more curious when I returned and you still did not. That act, or lack of act, exhibited a certain patience and willingness to risk losing an opportunity that is unusual in a common cutpurse. Why did you wait?"

Cat hesitated. She wasn't used to talking openly about such things with someone who wasn't part of the gang, certainly not with someone who'd been a target.

"I needed a way out of the gang," she said. "Enough to make my own way, but those first times I wouldn't have been able to get clean away."

Roffe nodded. "So, you passed up taking a sizable score for your gang in order to have the chance to keep it all for yourself."

Cat flushed again and looked down. Put that way it sounded as selfish as Osraed had accused her of being.

"My business is not one of teamwork," Roffe went on. "Nor of kindness, nor generosity. One must have a certain ruthlessness, which I saw in you that day."

"I would not say that is so," Cat objected.

"Of course you wouldn't. You'd prefer to think of yourself as kind and generous, no matter how you've made your living these many years. Think about it … *Cat*. You've lived by stealing bread from the mouths of others."

"From men like you who can afford to lose it!"

Roffe snorted. "Never lifted a purse from a servant in the market and given no thought to what he'd tell his master at the loss? Never taken from a cart without care to how the merchant would feed his own children?"

"All of them —"

"Never held back a bit from the rest of your pack of gutter snipes?" Roffe interrupted. He waited while Cat said nothing. "Before that day you stole from me, yes? Are they rich toffs who can afford it, then?"

Cat remained silent.

"That was no wealthy man's market I found you in. You stole from working men who'd labored hard to feed their families. You're a thief. Don't speak to me of scruples." He paused. "Or if you do, then do it from the street, for I've no use for you."

Cat struggled with what he was saying, but couldn't argue. She was a thief, after all. It was what she was good at, and though she could honestly say she'd mostly stolen from those who had more than she, that was only because she'd had so very little.

"You seem hesitant," Roffe said.

"I think I have little reason to trust you, Mister Roffe."

He raised an eyebrow. "Indeed?"

"You struck me."

"I kept you from getting nicked," he said. "You'd have been five steps closer to White's door when you took that purse. The porters would have caught you."

"I'm quicker than that."

"You were sicker than you think. It slowed you."

She considered that. No doubt she hadn't been in her right mind that night. The fever had clouded her judgment in more than one instance, not least of which was following this Mister Edward Roffe from White's.

"You knew I'd follow you."

"I suspected," he said. "If not then, certainly at some point."

He'd been driving her. Driving her to try to kill him? No, that seemed wrong. He'd taken her from her gang, kept her from others, he'd been driving her to solitude and despair. Perhaps even driving her to the anger necessary to attack him.

"Why?"

"If I had approached you on the street and suggested there was an opportunity for you with me, what would you have thought, girl?"

She knew what she'd have thought and done, especially if he'd indicated he knew she was a girl. *Thought he was a buttock-broker and run like blazes.*

"You see, then?" He spread his hands to take in the dining room and house. "Now you are in a position to consider my proposal without false concerns."

It made a certain sense, she supposed, though she thought there must be more to it. More he wasn't telling her. Still, what could he want of her? If he wasn't after her for a doxie, then what skills did she have that he could possibly want? There weren't that many things she was very good at.

"You're a thief," she said and narrowed her eyes when he said nothing. "Not some bauble-nicker, but a proper thief."

"I have been known to acquire the occasional item which was not, strictly speaking, mine to take."

"And what?" she asked. "This is your recruiting? I should trust you after all you've done to me?"

"What I've done to you? Indeed."

His calm demeanor infuriated her after all he'd put her through.

"That iron purse!"

"I may, I think, walk the streets with a purse filled with horse dung, if I wish," he said. "It harms no one, after all, save those who would steal from me."

"You struck me!"

"A moment before a stranger's purse was cut. I plead defense of others."

"You drugged me!"

He raised an eyebrow. "Indeed? Shall we then discuss your own intent at that moment?"

Cat flushed. To hear him tell it, it was all, all her misfortune, her own fault, yet he'd just as good as admitted that he'd driven her there deliberately.

Roffe tossed something toward her and Cat flung an arm up to protect her face and dodged to the side. Her heart beat rapidly in her chest, but she calmed as what he'd thrown came to a rest near her plate. The glint of gold from the table made her heart race again, though. A golden guinea lay before her, the very coin she'd hoped to find in Roffe's purse.

"Take it and go, if you like," Roffe said. "I have no need of you if you're reluctant and I won't hinder your leaving."

Cat reached out and touched the coin, staring at it intently.

"Or more, if you wish."

A small leather purse landed beside Cat's plate with a dull *clunk* and Cat jumped. She'd been so intent on the gold coin that she'd missed him throw the purse. She took it up and slowly pulled the drawstring open. It was small, much smaller than the purse she'd stolen from him, but this one didn't contain iron. More gold glinted up at her from its depths, a full dozen mates to the coin that lay on the table.

Would he really let me leave with it? She looked up and met Roffe's eyes.

"You won't know unless you try," Roffe said as though reading her mind. "But if you leave, my offer is withdrawn and you may never return." He shrugged. "I can afford to throw away a dozen guineas, will you throw away the chance at wealth enough to do the same?"

Cat looked back at the purse in her hand. Roffe's offer to be his apprentice, to learn his trade and work the jobs he couldn't be bothered with, would surely earn her more than this. If he could be trusted. Her mind spun with the possibilities and risks.

In the end, though, it was neither her distrust of Roffe nor the thought of more wealth that made the decision. It was Roffe's words that she could never return … and the certainly that Emma would not go with her if she left. Cat might be willing to make her own way, but Emma would not. She sought nothing more than the stable place she had and perhaps the hope of some small advancement in the future.

Friends are a weakness, she thought. *They make you vulnerable ... and daft.*

She picked up the lone guinea from the table, dropped it into the purse, and pulled the drawstring tight. With a flick of her wrist she sent it toward Roffe.

"What do you require of your apprentice, Mister Roffe?"

CHAPTER 9

"*B*reakfast, Miss Catherine?"

Cat smiled and opened her eyes. She'd been awake for some time — since dawn had first started brightening the room through the closed curtains — but chosen to stay in bed and drowse until Emma came to wake her. That the other girl had called her Miss Catherine instead of simply Cat told her that Mrs. Hinds, the new tutor, was close by outside the bedroom door.

Cat sat up and patted the bed beside her.

"Yes, a bit of toast first thing would be lovely," she said, winking.

Emma set the tray of tea and toast she carried across Cat's lap and sat down. She chose a piece of toast herself and began nibbling on it.

"She's just outside," Emma whispered with a grin. "Like to boil over that it's not at all proper fer her t'come in and wake you herself an' she 'as to wait on me to do it."

"I've enough dealings with her as it is," Cat whispered back, spreading jam. "My bedroom is your domain and I'll not have her intruding."

Since the bloody tutor, Mrs. Hinds, had arrived shortly after Cat's acceptance of Roffe's offer to become his apprentice, Cat had, for the months since, engaged in a delicate balancing act to keep Emma as her lady's maid. Mrs. Hinds did not approve, which was not so very surprising, as Mrs. Hinds approved of very little to do with the Roffe household.

And yet the tutor had accepted a place here. That spoke to the woman's desperation and gave Cat another hint that there were further secrets in this household. Hints and hesitations from Singley, the cook, and even Emma made her think that the servants here had as many things to hide as Roffe did with his thieving.

Hinds was not as happy an addition to the household as those already there, though. She found Cat's insistence on keeping Emma as a lady's maid distasteful to say the least. She felt the small staff — augmented only by a new maid-of-all-work, a timid creature named Lexie who rarely left the servant's quarters except to work, and even then, bolting from any room as soon as someone else entered it — was a sign of the household's common origins. That Cat herself could not be referred to as Lady nor Roffe as Lord caused her to sniff with disdain.

That the titled family she'd last worked for had sent her packing when they could no longer pay her wages, or so the whispers Emma passed along said, made little difference to her opinion. The Roffe household was built on commerce and commerce was beneath one so grand as Mrs. Hinds. She felt, she'd told Cat often enough, that this was merely an unpleasant interlude before she once again found a place in a Great House. In the meantime, she deigned to teach Cat the ways of a proper lady, never failing to remind her charge that Roffe's money could never properly buy him, nor Cat, acceptance in those circles.

For Cat's part, she merely ignored the woman's rants on proper breeding and birth. It was not, after all, as though she was truly seeking a place in Society. No, Roffe had made it clear to her that these lessons were simply to give her the facade she'd need at times as his apprentice.

"Aping my betters," as she says. I do wonder what Hinds would do if I told her I planned to use her teachings to steal those betters blind.

"I wonder what she has in store for me today?"

For the most part, Cat didn't mind the lessons themselves. She could see the use of being able to move in all kinds of circles, especially the upper circles of society. She might think much of what Hinds had to teach was silly, but that didn't mean it was useless. Some of it was even quite enjoyable.

The reading, for instance, once Cat became proficient at it. The house had an extensive library and Cat had found that reading books was quite a bit different from reading the random words Mother Agnes scratched in the dirt of an alleyway.

"That's the thing what's got her riled," Emma said, still keeping her voice low. "A message come at first light an' that Mister Clanton's comin' by mid-morning."

Cat's spirits lifted at that. She still thought the valet, Clanton, was a vile fellow. More so since she'd had to spend so much time with him, but she did enjoy his lessons far more than those of Hinds.

Clanton, she'd found, was quite a bit more than a mere valet. More of an assistant to Roffe in his real work, with myriad skills that fascinated Cat.

The first inkling of those skills had come shortly after Cat had accepted Roffe's offer, when Clanton had come into the dining room and presented her with a bundle of papers. All worn and aged, but with a warning to be gentle as much of the ink might not be dry.

Papers that clearly named her one Catherine Somersby, daughter of James and Anne Somersby. Anne being the sister of one Edward Roffe, master artificer, and both James and Anne being deceased. Birth, marriage, and death certificates all bundled together, along with the deceased couple's express wish that their daughter Catherine be cared for by her uncle. And with the stroke of a valet's pen, Cat had become Catherine, and Roffe's legal ward.

"Well, that will certainly make for a more pleasant day," Cat said with a grin.

She'd actually come to look forward to Clanton's visits, which occurred about once a fortnight. In addition to being a forger, he was also quite accomplished in mimicry and could ape any number of dialects, a skill which he drilled Cat on relentlessly.

He never spent more than a day at the house, but would arrive in the morning and leave to return to the city before sunset. Cat would spend the day closeted with him in a locked room practicing — the scandalous nature of Cat being closeted away unchaperoned with a male servant nearly sending Hinds into apoplectic fits.

Clanton would simply start talking to her in one dialect, which Cat would have to answer in the same. Then he'd change, expecting Cat to follow and alter her speech to his. She sometimes felt like she was taking a verbal tour of the country, from the West to the very steps of the Bow Bells.

"'At's the other thing," Emma said, her face turning serious. "Message says 'e's not stayin', but that yer to go with him back to the city. You alone."

"This is quite improper, Mister Clanton."

Cat stood by the coach and four Clanton had arrived in, attempting to repress her amusement. Mistress Hinds had been put out to find that Clanton was returning so soon after his last visit — when she'd discovered that he intended to take Cat away, unchaperoned, she'd been beside herself.

"*Most* improper, and not at all what I expected when I agreed to take this position."

I do believe she's in a tizzy, Cat thought, biting her lip to keep from grinning. *I've never seen a tizzy before.*

Clanton said nothing, simply slung the single valise he'd allowed Emma to pack for Cat onto the coach.

"Mister Clanton!" Hinds stalked toward him. "Have you nothing at all to say for yourself? I simply cannot *believe* that a fine gentleman such as Mister Roffe would allow his ward to travel in such a ... a *scandalous* way. With no accompaniment *whatsoever.*"

Clanton secured the valise to the rear of the coach and opened the door. He jerked his head at Cat to enter, but before she could do so Hinds grasped her arm and held her back.

"No. No. Not at all. I shan't allow it. I *may not*, in good conscience, allow such a thing. Simply, no." She ended with an emphatic nod of her head.

Cat thought she might actually be sniffing with disdain while she spoke.

Clanton stared at Hinds for a moment. Cat could see a small muscle in his neck twitching. She'd noticed early on in her lessons with the valet that this was a sign of his displeasure.

He stepped toward Hinds, stopping more than arms' length away, but Hinds took a step back regardless, pulling Cat with her.

Clanton reached into his jacket and pulled out a folded sheet of paper, then held it out to Hinds.

"And what is that?"

Clanton grunted, as though speaking to the woman was a great effort.

"Reference."

Hinds' eyes widened and she took a further step back, as though the paper held some contagion.

Clanton waved the paper at her, then dropped it to the cobbles. When he spoke, he dropped his voice into the lowest accent of the city's gutters.

"Stay 'er go as y'like, but bugger off, either. If yer stays, then y'don't question the master, see?"

Hinds fled back into the house and it was all Cat could do not to burst out laughing.

"Should you feel the need to slit that woman's throat some dark night," Clanton said, "I've a fine spot for the body."

He turned his head to meet Cat's gaze for a moment before returning to the coach. A shiver ran up Cat's spine. Clanton had always spoken quite roughly during their lessons, but she'd found it more amusing than anything. Despite his ability to mimic accents, he was still a gentleman's servant, after all. Cat had grown up in the streets amongst those who'd slit a man's throat for the scent of a pence, what could a gentleman's valet know of such violence?

In the moment their eyes met, however, she'd thought he was quite serious.

She took a deep breath and started for the coach, but Emma rushed forward from where she'd been waiting. She wrapped her arms around Cat in a hard hug.

"Be careful," Emma whispered into Cat's ear, then released her and stepped back.

"I'll be all right," Cat assured her. "Whatever Mister Roffe wants of me, I'm sure I'll be all right." She smiled to reassure the other girl, wondering at the sudden warning. Neither Emma nor the other servants had ever said a thing against Roffe. "Do you know how long we'll be in the city, Mister Clanton?"

Clanton grunted. "Long as is required, I expect."

Emma glanced at Clanton, then hugged Cat again, hard.

"Don't trust him," she whispered. "Neither of them." Then she dashed off for the house.

Cat watched her go for a moment, but Clanton grunted again and she hurried for the coach. Clanton climbed in behind her and pulled the door shut. He rapped on the coach's ceiling and the driver put the coach in motion with a jerk.

Clanton glanced out the window toward where Emma had gone, then settled back in his seat and closed his eyes.

"Pretty girl."

THE COACH RIDE to the city fascinated Cat. She'd been unconscious when Roffe had taken her to his house, after all, and she'd never been out of the city before that, so all she knew was Roffe's manor, the small village, and the city itself. She'd had no real idea how far from the city Roffe's manor was, and it surprised her how far they had to travel. She counted seven villages, each growing progressively larger and busier, before they reached the outskirts of the city — and those outskirts seemed to go on forever.

Several times she thought she recognized the area they traveled through, but then the coach moved on to somewhere unfamiliar.

Finally, the coach came to a stop.

Cat followed Clanton out of the coach and into the house. The house was as finely furnished as the manor, but much smaller. Cat was a bit surprised that no servants at all greeted them, but she had no time to question it as Clanton started up the stairs and gestured impatiently for her to follow. He opened a door at the end of the upstairs hallway and gestured her through into a bedroom. This, too, was finely appointed, but smaller than her rooms at the manor.

"Will you tell me now what this journey's purpose may be, Mister Clanton?"

Clanton said nothing, he simply dropped Cat's valise on the floor and returned to the door.

"Are there servants at all? Shall I unpack my own things or would that be improper here?" Cat frowned. It had been quite a long journey and they'd not stopped for anything to eat. Breakfast had been a long time away and she was hungry, which gave her little patience with Clanton's obstinacy.

"It's growing late, Mister Clanton, will there be a meal? Should I prepare a meal?" Would the man not speak at all?

"Food's in the kitchen," Clanton said. He tossed a small roll of leather at Cat's feet. "Just come down when you wish to eat."

He closed the door.

Cat's brow furrowed. Clanton had been acting quite strangely the entire time and it disturbed her. It was as though he was deliberately distancing himself from her. They'd not grown close at all while he tutored her in dialects at the manor, but he had at least talked some. Now it was as though he wanted nothing to do with her.

She thought she might change clothes before going down to eat, but she had little in her valise. When Clanton had limited her to the one bag, she'd assumed there would be clothing here in the city somehow, but a quick check of the room found none.

Curious, she picked up the roll of leather Clanton had tossed to the floor. She untied the thongs holding it closed and unrolled it to find a collection of long, thin, metal picks. Cat knew what they were, she'd seen them on the streets a time or two in the possession of one of the boys who'd been taken up by a proper band of thieves.

Why would he ...

With a sudden realization that filled her with anger and horror, she rushed to the door and turned the knob, only to find it locked.

CHAPTER 10

Cat quickly dismissed the idea that trapping her in a locked room might be some sort of odd joke on Clanton's part. Neither Clanton nor Roffe had ever struck her as prone to any levity. No, this was a test.

She sat down on the edge of the bed and examined the lock picks. They were all of different shapes and angles, finely made, and seemed to be of good steel. She had the beginnings of an idea of how locks worked and were picked from those in the gang who'd been pulled up out of the gutters to become proper burglars. Some of them had come back a time or two to brag about their new status to old mates. So, she knew it had something to do with moving pins inside the lock in some way until the lock would open — the details of how one went about it, however, were a mystery.

Still ... most of those taken up were certainly not the brightest. If they could learn the way of it, how hard could it be?

An hour later she was willing to admit that, though not the brightest, those boys must have been attentive in their training.

"Damn it all! You buggering, *cack-handed twat!*"

Cat flung the latest lock pick she'd tried across the room and sat back on her heels.

She thought she had the way of it, at least in theory, but the practice evaded her. She scrubbed at her face with one hand and ran the other through her hair. The hair had finally grown out a bit, so she no longer looked like a new-shorn sheep. Not so long as it had been before she'd been taken up by Mister Roffe, though, and she was looking forward to it growing longer than that, now that she didn't have to hide being a girl any longer.

Cat noted that it was growing dark. She'd been trapped in the room for some time and she was growing both colder and hungrier. There was no food in the room, nor any wood or coal to start a fire, but she found she could do something about the darkness at least. A few moments with the fire striker had the gas lamps lit and she took the opportunity to warm her hands over the flame.

She shivered and her stomach growled, bringing her attention to the gnawing ache in her middle.

Sheltered, a lit room, and breakfast this morning, yet I'm thinking myself cold and hungry?

She thought of all the nights she'd spent huddled in an alleyway, soaked to the skin, and with her last meal a fond memory of days gone by.

Soft. I've grown soft.

She considered that for a moment, then shook her head.

No. There's no virtue in starving on the streets. I've known hardship and now I've known comfort and plenty. Of the two, by God, I'll keep the second.

The test, the challenge Clanton had set her, was not, at least to her mind, so much to pick the door's lock, but to get out of the room at all.

"Food's in the kitchen," he'd said, "just come down and get it."

His expectation might be that she'd pick the lock, but there was more than one way to achieve a goal.

She looked around the room, searching for some other way out.

Unfortunately, determining that there was none did not take long. Her rooms were on the back side of the house, overlooking the courtyard and carriage house. It was only the second floor, so she was confident she could find some way down the house's walls, but the windows were barred and it took but a moment to determine that the space between the bars was too small to allow her to pass.

The window in her dressing room was similarly barred, and the door that led from there to the water closet was locked as well.

The fireplaces, one in the bedroom and one in the dressing room, were both unlit, but she didn't relish the thought of trying to make her way out through one of them. She doubted she was small enough any more to do such a thing.

Cat began searching the room again with new determination. She would not allow her situation to make her soft, it would make her harder. Hard and determined to never return to that life on the streets, no matter the cost, she vowed.

She hefted the fireplace poker and returned to the window.

The space between the bars might be too small for her to fit through, but only just. She tried using the poker to lever the bars farther apart, but there was nothing to push or pull against. Then she tried prying at the edges of the bars, to see if the entire casement might be dislodged, but stopped as the poker began to bend.

She stepped back and tried to think, eyes darting from the door to the lock picks to the window bars and back to the poker in her hands.

The bars were not so close together that she needed much more space, she thought. Only an inch, perhaps two, and she'd be able to slip between them. She had only to bend them a very little bit.

Cat stripped the beddings from the bed and used one of the sharper lock picks to start a tear in one of the sheets, tearing off a strip. Then she wrapped it around the window bars, from one of the center pair to outermost, and tied it off.

The night had clouded over and a drizzle started, wetting her clothes as she stood at the window and making her feel even colder.

She slipped the poker through the loop of cloth and began twisting it tighter and tighter. Her knuckles were barked painfully more than once trying to force the poker to turn past the bars, but she thought the bars were starting to bend just a bit.

Then the loop of cloth tore and she muttered oaths as her hand slammed into one of the bars with the released force.

But the bar had bent a bit, she saw. Just a bit, but noticeable when she looked for it.

Cat tore another, wider strip of cloth from the bedclothes and carefully folded it along its length, then returned to the window.

It seemed harder to turn the poker with the thicker cloth, but she kept at it, forcing the rod round and round. With each turn she thought she could hear the iron bars groan a bit, or perhaps that was just herself. Finally, she felt she could force the poker no farther.

She examined the bars. They had bent. Both bowed in the middle and she measured the distance with her hand. The gap between the two center bars was perhaps an inch greater at its largest, but still not quite enough to get her entire body through, she thought.

The knot on her loop of cloth had been pulled so tight that she had no hope of undoing it, so she ripped yet another strip from her bedclothes tried again.

More struggling with the poker, more barked knuckles, more screaming muscles, and she'd forced the other center bar to bow as much as she thought possible. She was shivering with the chill when she was done, clothes and hair wet from her exertions and the falling rain, but she had a space that was enough.

She managed to get her head through, by turning it and not being too particular about the state her ears were in when she was done, and was able to examine the outside wall. There was a ledge and stonework near the window that led right to a drainpipe where this house met the next. She'd not even need to sacrifice more bedding to make a rope.

I do love a convenient drainpipe. Good as a road laid out before me.

The courtyard and side of the building were dark, as well, lit only by a pair of gas lamps on the carriage house next door. The lamps in Roffe's courtyard were unlit, leaving deep shadows, so she'd have no worries about being seen either.

She looked down at herself and eyed the gap between the bars.

No, clambering down the side of the building in a dress was right out. Nor would her stays provide any benefit in this exercise.

Cat stripped to only her chemise and drawers, both already damp, but quickly wet through from the increasingly heavy rains blowing through the window. Her slippers would offer no help either, so off they went. She knew there was nothing more suitable in her valise, only a few other dresses and underthings.

I'll have to speak to Clanton about a proper thieving wardrobe if there'll be more tests like this.

She forced her head through the bars again, ignoring the complaints from her ears. Then her shoulders — the cloth of her chemise caught and tore, but she slipped farther out. Another moment of discomfort.

Those'll be a worse burden soon, she thought wryly as she forced her way on.

She twisted so as to be able to grasp the bars and pulled her hips and legs through the gap, finally hanging from the bars for a moment before her feet found purchase on the wall's stones. That and her hands' grip on the window ledge that ran to the corner allowed her to make it to the drainpipe.

The journey to the ground was one of hands and feet slipping on the rain-slick metal of the pipe from one bracket to the next, but she was finally able to set her feet on the cobbles of the courtyard.

With a grin, she hurried over to the house's courtyard door, grasped the handle, and found it locked.

Cat's grin fell as she continued to stare at the locked door.

"I'm a bloody fool," she whispered.

She'd grown so used to the way things were at Roffe's country home that she'd not considered they'd be different here.

Soft. Not thinking.

The outer doors at the country house were never locked, so far as she'd ever found. On clear nights when she couldn't sleep she'd gone out to walk in the garden or look at the stars, a novelty after growing up under the city's frequent pall of fog and coal smoke. Of course, though, a city house would be locked up at night — in the day even.

As if to further mock her, the rain intensified.

Cat raised her hand to pound on the door and summon Clanton to let her in, but hesitated. *Come to the kitchen*, he'd said and damned if she'd let him see her do less.

She backed away from the house, scanning it for any way in. Five stories, all with their windows barred. She might be able to bend those as she had her bedroom's, but the thought of trying to do so while keeping a hold on the outside wall in this rain made her dismiss that idea. The windows on the front of the house were likely barred as well, and no doubt the front door was locked. She could try it, and the kitchen door at the front, as well, but the house was midway down a block of others, all similar and all touching side-by-side. She'd have to get through the carriage house to the alleyway and then around the block to the front.

All barefoot in a soaking wet chemise and drawers — no, there'll be no attention drawn by that at all, will there?

She wrapped her arms around herself, rubbing her shoulders as she shivered in the cold rain. Possibly try the front later in the night, when it was less likely she'd be seen. For now, though, a bit of shelter wouldn't go amiss.

She turned to the carriage house at the other end of the courtyard and went to check its door. Just to the right of it, were the steps leading down to the house's basement. That was locked as well, though, and she had a moment's thought that she should have brought her lock picks with her. Perhaps Roffe had put a particularly difficult lock on her bedroom door in preparation for this test, but others might be easier?

Regardless, it was a moot point now. Not unless she fancied climbing up that rain slick drainpipe and forcing herself back through the window bars.

I may have to resort to summoning Clanton to the door. At least I'll have made it part way to the kitchen.

The carriage house door, she found, had no lock. It was latched from the inside, but there was a pull-string hanging just above the door, and that unlatched it. Cat pulled the door open and slid inside, grateful for the shelter and the warmth generated by the coach's four horses housed there.

It was dark inside, with only very narrow windows high up on the walls. She could make out the vague shapes of the horses, shuffling as their sleep was disturbed by her entrance. Clanton had told her the coachman was hired on when necessary and did not sleep at the townhouse, so she knew the structure was empty of people, at least.

The carriage house had two bays for carriages at the alley side with a walkway for the horses between them and stalls for the horses at the courtyard side where she'd entered. The smell of horse and fresh dung came to her. She shuffled forward, hands outstretched. The cobbles were cold on her feet, but still a relief from the colder, wetter stone of the courtyard, even with the occasional prick of straw.

Feet are getting soft — need to remember to toughen them, not go about in slippers all my days.

If she remembered right, there were stairs just between the carriage bays and the stalls which would lead up to the rooms above where the grooms and coachman would stay if Roffe kept those on.

Odd, that. I do wonder why he has servants to care for his country home when it's never used, yet only Clanton here in the city. Does he entertain no one?

There were so many things that were odd about her benefactor that these were just more to add to the pile. Even knowing he was a thief didn't explain all the oddities.

Past the horses she turned and stumbled into the stairs, then made her way up. There were more windows on the upper floor to light the servants' rooms and she found a candle and flint in one of them. More importantly, once she had the candle lit, she found blankets and a thick coachman's cloak.

Cat stripped her wet things off in the candlelight and rubbed herself vigorously with one of the blankets, then wrapped herself in the heavy wool cloak. It dragged the ground and smelled of horse, as the blanket did, but it was admirably warm.

She went back down the stairs for a moment to look about. The big doors to the alleyway were chained and locked from the inside. Not surprisingly, really. That was where thieves would come from and they'd have to get over the carriage house, a two-story climb, to reach the courtyard and the unlocked inner door. Not many would be able to accomplish that, and if they did, there'd still be the matter of not having a key to the heavy padlock on the outer door before they could think of stealing a horse.

Back upstairs, she settled onto a cot in one of the groom's rooms and watched the main house through the window. She blew out the candle so its light wouldn't be seen by Clanton if he happened to look outside. There was little risk of that, she thought, but best to be careful — the main house was well-lit. Not just her upstairs window, but most of the ground floor windows shone with the steady glow of gas lamps.

Somewhere church bells sounded. Cat didn't know what church — she still had little idea what part of the city they were in — but they sounded nine o'clock. Still early and far too soon to attempt checking the front of the house for a way in.

Cat let herself drowse, still watching the main house from time to time, but not closely, until the bells sounded three o'clock, then she stirred.

She'd spent her time pondering how to get into the house. First, really, now to get to the front of the house, as the carriage house access to the alleyway was locked. She didn't relish the thought of trying to climb over it in the rain.

The key to the lock, though, should be nearby. The coachman, had there been one, would have had it, and she didn't think Clanton would carry a carriage house key with him, nor keep it in the house. He'd want it nearby and likely on the ground floor of the carriage house, not upstairs. A brief search once her candle was relit turned it up, tucked into a hollow in one of the stalls.

Cloak wrapped about her and some tools and bits from the horse's tack rolled up in her chemise and drawers to keep them from clinking, she slid the carriage house door open and made her way down the alleyway, over to the main street, and back to the house's front.

The front door was tried first, but locked as she suspected. As was the kitchen door down the steps from the street. She grimaced as she saw all the windows on this side were barred as well. No more than she'd suspected, but it left only one possibility for getting into the house, and not one she relished the thought of. Had hoped to avoid so much, in fact, that she'd made the useless trek around the block to the house's front on the chance it could be avoided.

She paused and glanced at the door. A bit of pounding, perhaps a shout or two, and Clanton would swing it open for her. Or not. He might find it amusing to leave her standing about on the street in a freezing rain with nothing but a cloak and her underthings.

And it would be a failure of sorts.

Cat pulled the cloak tighter about her and made the walk back up the street and around to the alley and the carriage house. She bent over the round metal cover of the coal hole — the metal disk that covered access to the basement room each house's coal was stored in. The coal man would pry that up and dump his bags of coal down it for delivery, rather than carting them in through the kitchen doors.

It had been nearly a year since Cat had been sent down one by the gang to pilfer a bit of coal to heat their squat, but she remembered the experience all too well. Lowered head first into the dark with a rope tied to her ankles and held by Brandt and Osraed, she'd barely fit then. Now she wondered if she still could or if this would be her worst decision of the night.

She shook her head and fished through a hole in the cover with a length of leather and a bit of metal tied to the end for the cover's internal latch. There'd be a cord strung down the basement where a servant could unlatch the cover for a delivery.

After a moment, she'd caught it and freed the cover so that she could lift it a bit and slide it aside.

Staring into the dark maw of the hole led her to second thoughts again, but she determined to move forward.

She bundled up her things and dropped them down the hole, careful to be sure her flint would strike no sparks, then slid feet first into the hole and pulled the metal cover shut atop her.

The coal hole was drier than the street, with only a few trickles of water seeping around the edges of the cover, but no warmer. It was pitch dark — only a tiny dot or two of light from the streetlamps shone through the small holes in the cover. The rough brick of the interior scraped at her everywhere she touched, which was most of her in the tight space, and every movement dislodged more and more coal dust, that seemed to fill her nose and irritate her eyes.

Arms outstretched above her, she inched her way down. Grasping the seam between bricks, then letting her feet lower to find some purchase farther down, and repeating the process. Inch by inch, brick by brick, not able to bend her arms enough to lower herself more than a brick or two at a time in the tight space.

Eventually, her foot scrabbled against empty air to find purchase and she knew she'd found the bottom of the hole where it emptied into the coal room. That was a relief. There'd been the possibility that the bags of coal would have been left blocking the hole, blocking her way and forcing her to climb back to top and try to push the cover aside from within.

It also meant she'd reached the most difficult portion of the climb, though, as she'd have to keep herself in place with only her finger tips and as much of herself as she could leverage against the rough walls. The bricks scraped more until there wasn't enough of her left inside the coal hole to hold her up and she had to let herself fall the rest of the way. It was only a short distance, but came with more and worse scrapes from the bricks and a jarring impact as she struck her cloak and the cobbles of the coal room's floor.

Cat eased herself to a sitting position and rested for a moment. She ran her hands over herself, assessing the damage. A few spots were scraped raw and more than one had a trickle of blood running from it. She'd have to wash thoroughly if she wanted to keep coal dust from healing up inside her, marking her for weeks or months — even permanently if it were embedded deep enough. She'd seen more than one boy who'd gone to work for a chimney sweep man and wound up with markings like a sailor's tattoos.

Finally, Cat eased her way to her feet and began feeling about the coal room. The sides and back were stacked waist high with rough bags of coal, which made finding the door easy, and her shoulders slumped with relief as the door eased open at her touch. In a proper household, with many servants, the coal room would have been locked to keep the lesser servants from pilfering a bit more for their rooms or for sale. She'd counted on Clanton not bothering, as there were no other servants in the house.

Once the coal room was shut behind her, she groped along the wall until she found the first gas lamp and sparked it to life. She had to grin at that, as it marked her success. More lamps lit her way to the kitchen and scullery where she did her best to wash, though the water was cold — as were the ovens, which would explain the lack of hot water if this house was set up as Roffe's country home was.

She'd remedy that quickly enough after she'd eaten, though she didn't know how long it would take the ovens to heat water for a proper bath.

That thought led her to the pantry, where she discovered that Roffe's town home lacked not only servants, but any real provisions. It was empty, save for a bag and a pair of half-wrapped parcels next to a barrel on the shelves.

Cat pondered that for a moment as she assembled a meal from what was available. Half a loaf of bread, not stale, yet neither was it entirely fresh, an indifferent cheese, and a sausage whose origins Cat preferred not to speculate on. The barrel was half full of small beer.

She settled in at the kitchen table and began to eat. She'd eaten poorer for longer in her life, but this was nothing like what she'd grown used to at the country house and certainly not like what was served when Roffe was there. It was more like what she'd expect a man like Clanton to have when left to his own devices. So that meant that not only servants were absent from this house, but Roffe himself. What did that mean?

Footsteps in the hallway outside the kitchen interrupted her thoughts.

In a moment, Clanton appeared in the doorway, stared at her for a time, then left.

Cat continued to eat until Clanton returned.

He went to the pantry and gathered up food and a mug of beer for himself, then sat across from her. After a long drink of beer, he slid the leather roll of lock picks across to her.

"Left these behind. Take better care of your tools," he said. "Goin' out a window — best to wipe up any rain spill and pull the curtains and window shut behind you. Bars y'can't do nothing about, but leave 'em hid and there might be no notice took for a time."

Cat nodded.

They ate in silence, then Clanton drained his mug and stretched. He eyed the cloak she had wrapped around her, then the bundle of her underthings on the table.

"I'll stoke the ovens," he said. "Best wash in the scullery ... Roffe's particular about his carpets."

CHAPTER 12

The next day dawned with Cat aching in muscles she'd never heard from before and with the sting of scrapes in places she'd prefer not to think about.

She jerked awake as Clanton flung the door to her rooms open with a loud, "Up, girl, and be about it!"

He tossed a bundle of cloth onto the bed at her feet.

"Dress and meet me in the courtyard. Bring yer picks."

Cat rose, wincing with every move. She supposed he meant to dress in what he'd brought her, for she could see that the dark bundle was clothing of a sort. They were close, in pattern and style, to what a common woman in the city would wear — utilitarian stays, a loose blouse, a similarly loose skirt — but with significant differences. Firstly, each item was dark in color — not black, but still dark. There were a sort of trousers for under the skirt, and the skirt itself was sewn oddly, with a loose seam up the front and back. It was not at all what she'd grown used to wearing — and it surprised her somewhat that she could grow so used to so very different dress in such a short time — in Mister Roffe's household. Her naked journey through the coal hole the night before notwithstanding.

Once dressed, she splashed a bit of water on her face, and took up her leather roll of lock picks to make her way downstairs.

The sky was grey with overcast and somewhat cool as she stepped into the courtyard — still a bit damp with morning dew. Clanton stood in the courtyard's center, waiting for her.

He looked her over and nodded with some satisfaction.

"Fits you well enough, I suppose." He approached her and jerked her shirt up roughly.

"What!"

Cat tried to step back, but Clanton held her in place.

"The stays are metal an' hollow, see?" he asked, grasping the bottom of one of the ribs in her stays.

His fingers worked at it, pressing against her belly with only a thin chemise between them and her skin. The bottom of these stays weren't fully sewn, exposing the lower end of each rib. Clanton pulled a plug of thick sealing wax from one. Sealing wax, unlike candle wax, was very firm when cool.

"See?" Clanton asked, holding it up. "Heat it a bit if it gets loose and reseat it."

He released her and Cat stepped back from him now, flushed and wary. She'd never had a man handle her so — not when she wasn't disguised as a boy, at least, and she found that it felt different somehow. Clanton seemed oblivious to both her discomfort and wariness. He nodded to the roll of lock picks she still held.

"Slide them picks in and they're hid, see? Or aught else you wish."

Cat nodded.

"Good, then." He tossed his head toward a stone bench near the courtyard's wall. The yard itself was mostly clear, with only a bench to each side. "Put the picks there for now."

Cat did so and when she turned back Clanton was rolling his head on his shoulders and stretching his arms.

"Right, now I'm t'teach you to fight," he said.

"What do you mea —"

Before she could finish her question, Clanton sprang forward, unbelievably fast for a man of his size, and his open palm *cracked* into the side of her face. The force of the blow knocked her to the side. She staggered and then fell to the courtyard's cobbles. Her cheek stung and her ear rung.

Clanton remained where he was, gesturing for her to rise.

"Should'a blocked that," he said.

THE REMAINDER of the morning went much like that, with Clanton striking her, kicking her, sometimes grabbing her and holding her while she struggled, all the while carrying on a running commentary of what she should have done to avoid it. Most of which Cat would have been more than happy to do, if the man hadn't been so bloody fast.

"Duck that'un ... all that space behind you? ... grab the arm an' strike back, there ..."

No amount of her protests seemed to dissuade him, and she eventually gave up speaking, concentrating on either avoiding his blows or minimizing them as best she could.

After some time, he stopped and frowned at her.

"You're not very good at this."

Cat picked herself up from the cobbles for an uncountable time and watched him warily. He didn't seem as though he were going to rush forward and strike her again — but then he never did. The man could go from standing still, seemingly enthralled by a passing bird, to crossing any amount of space between them and striking her in the blink of an eye.

Which was quite fast enough, given that she seemed to have only one eye left to blink with, the other being swollen and tender to the touch.

She crouched and backed slowly away from him, thinking that this time, as soon as Clanton moved, she'd simply throw herself to the cobbles and be done with it.

His frown deepened and he shook his head.

"Not good at all." He shrugged. "Right, then, breakfast."

BREAKFAST WAS BREAD, a bit stale, cheese, a bit moldy, sausage, fatty and salty, and small beer, which Cat cared for not at all. It was a far cry from what she'd grown used to at the manor house, but still better than she remembered from her time on the streets.

Clanton ate with his head down, forearms making fortress walls around his plate, except when he tilted back to take great gulps of the beer.

Cat ate, but drank sparingly, and kept a wary eye on the man.

"I'll not strike you in here," he said, catching her look. "Done with that for the day."

Cat winced. "For the day" seemed to imply that they weren't done with it at all.

"There'll be more then?" she asked.

Clanton nodded. "Mister Roffe said to teach you to fight." He pointed to her. "In them clothes, first, then in propers."

"And you suppose this knocking me about will teach me something?"

"Taught you to duck a bit. And watch a man closer." Clanton shrugged. "How m'Da taught me an' I'm still alive. Fancy stuff I learned with Roffe'll come later."

"And this?" Cat pointed to her eye, which she still couldn't see out of. "Mistress Hinds will certainly have questions when I return to the manor — what am I to do about that?"

Clanton regarded her for a moment.

"Duck better, I suppose."

WHEN DARKNESS FELL, Clanton set her to running roofs.

He showed her how the skirts of the outfit she wore could be bundled up to free her legs — or even split along those seams front and back, if she were rushed.

The splotchy green and grey blended marvelously with the shadows, making Cat nearly impossible to see.

Impossible except for Clanton, that was, for he set her to following him from the rooftops as he made his way through the city, and if he spotted her, which was often, he cuffed her harshly and boxed her ears when they returned to the townhouse.

He relented, some, in the morning beatings — beginning to teach, instead of just insist she learn to avoid his blows. Though his idea of teaching was rough, as well.

"Hips forward, chest back, arm thus," he said, grabbing and shoving her into position until her form met his satisfaction, with no regard for what parts he grabbed and shoved along the way. "Now, move as I showed you."

Cat did so. To hesitate would get her sent to the courtyard's cobbles by a heavy blow.

"Why," she asked, "must I do this over and over?"

"Yer body'll remember," Clanton said. "Learned this with Roffe in the East — the Chinee'll send a man to the floor with their bloody fingertip. Now again."

Clanton's foot swept her legs from under her and she slammed to the cobbles, driving her breath from her.

"*Not* like that, girl — *balance!*"

There was work with weapons as well. Cat thought she was a fair hand with a knife, but Clanton showed her different, easily disarming her with a blow to hand or forearm, even twisting her up so that her own blade became his weapon against her.

He brought out staves, as well, and a length of rope, knotted at both ends that he told her to tie about the waist of her green-and-gray outfits as a sort of belt.

"It's t'be armed and not look it," he told her. "Y'can't carry sword nor pistol, so learn what y'can have t'hand."

"If I'm to be a thief, as Mister Roffe is," she wondered aloud, "then why so much of weapons and fighting? I'd think escaping would be better. And I assume you assist him in his endeavors? Would you not be better able to fight than I am?"

Clanton gave her a long look, then shook his head. "It's a hard world, girl, have y'not learned that already? Y've got yourself and no one else — worse than that, y've yourself and everyone else is out to gut you. Least that's what my Da taught me."

"But —" Cat still didn't see the point of the weapons and fighting. Perhaps if she were still on the streets — well, definitely if she were still on the streets — but at the sort of places Roffe was taking her? Robbing the Quality couldn't carry the same risks as a market bully-boy, could it? "In the circles Roffe intends me to work, will this really be necessary? These are gentlemen, after all."

Clanton laughed. "Oh, aye, all gentlemen," he said, laughing more. "And this gentleman'll be taught proper fisticuffs, and that gentle-man'll be taught his dueling, and all the gentlemen'll be taught not to strike a girl, sure — and some of those *gentlemen* behind closed doors, won't be, will they? Bother if you're caught at Roffe's … thieving, as you say, girl; it's being alone with some bloke at those dances I'd have you ready for."

As time went on, though, Cat's worries about how to explain the bruises to Mistress Hinds were allayed, either by Clanton being more careful not to strike her where it was visible or her getting better at the ducking.

It was then that Roffe began appearing and taking a hand in training her for other things — not frequently, but often enough, he would escort her out. To garden parties, to teas, to the park or exhibition of this and that, where the protocols and manners drilled into her by Mistress Hinds were all on display.

All on his arm, never let alone for very long, and always — at least after the first time she'd proudly opened her bag in the carriage home and shown him the bit of silver she'd nicked — with the admonition that there was nothing she could fit in her bag, nor under her skirt, for that matter, that would be a bigger score than those to come.

Roffe's reaction to that first bit of pilfering had chilled Cat to the core, though. He'd not yelled, not struck her, not said a word.

He simply thumped his cane on the carriage's roof and called to the driver, "The other destination!" then sat in silence, ignoring Cat's queries until she eventually sat back and stared out the window as Roffe did.

Her heart began to pound as she recognized the area they were in, none of the posh townhomes and city manors they'd passed on their way to the affair — instead it was the dirty, crowded streets of the market she'd grown up in.

The carriage pulled to a stop in the middle of the street, ignoring the shouts of outrage from the drayman blocked behind them, and Roffe reached across her to fling the carriage door open.

"Get out," he said.

Cat stared at him, wondering if this was some sort of test of his.

"Out," Roffe repeated, "and back to this if you like."

"Mister Roffe, what have I done?"

"I've no time for you if you wish to be a petty thief taking up the common cutlery," Roffe said. "Get out, or follow my rules, you understand?"

Cat glanced from him to the growing crowd of market folk gathered around to see who might get out of the posh carriage. The drayman shouted again.

No more urging or explanation than that was necessary for Cat — she understood. While she'd thought to please him with a little nick — only a bit of a game, really — clearly, he had larger game in his sights and she should work toward that. She sat back on the carriage bench and smoothed her skirts as Hinds taught her.

"I understand, Uncle."

Roffe thumped his cane on the roof again and the driver swung the carriage door shut and put the horses into motion.

"Oh, Catherine," Roffe murmured. "I've so much more in store for you than a bit of silver traced with gold."

❧

CAT CAME to enjoy the outings with Roffe, though he was always distant and would never speak of future plans, even in the privacy of the carriage to and from some place. She never stole again at these times, though it was a lark to stroll amongst the Quality, even enter their homes, and plan how she *might* rob them blind — always, after that first bit of silver, she set her sights much higher indeed.

Not just the jewels the lady wears now, but how would she discover where the jewelry was kept? How to best get into the house in the night and take not just the diamond bracelet — which a brush of thumb and forefinger against the clasp, Clanton had taught her, would send it falling into the cuff of Cat's dress — but the whole lot.

Those were the things that occupied Cat's mind as she sipped tea and chatted with other girls her age, whom she found interminably boring.

All they ever talk about is clothes, Cat thought through a set smile of polite interest as one of them droned on.

And, oh, the clothes.

Cat almost broke her role to scowl and sigh at the thought.

The outings with Roffe made necessary outings with Clanton, and not of the sort Cat would prefer. No, the one gown Roffe had given her, fine as it was, was not nearly enough.

There must be gowns for tea and for the garden and for the theatre and for the ...

Whatever this is.

And all of them, every one, required a different sort of gown — and more than one, for she must not be seen wearing the same one twice in a row.

That meant trips to the dressmakers and what seemed like hours of poking and prodding while the things were fit properly.

Then, to make it worse, none of the things were such that Cat could reasonably get them settled properly on herself alone. Roffe had still not staffed the townhouse and allowed none of the staff from the manor to travel, which meant leaving Emma behind and left Cat with Clanton to act the lady's maid.

That the man was both uncommonly deft with the intricacies of a lady's garments and seemingly utterly indifferent to what lay under them did little to lessen Cat's discomfort.

Moreover, there was more than the one wardrobe to fill — Cat had two.

There was the wardrobe of Catherine Roffe, niece and ward of Mister Edward Roffe, master artificer — and then there was the wardrobe of Cat, apprentice, she supposed, to Clanton, born, to all appearances with no given name as it was never spoken, and master of every sort of villainy Cat could imagine.

Of the two, she preferred the latter, even though it did require more trips to the dressmaker.

Or several *dressmakers* … and a ragshop or two.

Clanton's idea of a wardrobe was an outfit for all occasions, but while the occasions of Mister Roffe were teas and suppers, Clanton's occasions were people in and of themselves. All of which meant sets of clothes acquired at very different places for very different purposes.

There was Cat the *Parson's Niece*, Cat the *Flowergirl*, Cat the *Sea Captain's Daughter*, Cat the *Merchant's Sister*, Cat the *Fishmonger*, and myriad others, even Cat the *Lady's Maid* sent to market by her mistress — all of which required a different mode of dress and trips to a shop of some sort.

"Do you not fear we'll be recognized?" Cat asked as they made their way home one day. "Going about in different clothes as we do?"

"Recognize what, my dear?" Clanton asked, his voice perfectly suited to the dark suit, round hat, and ecclesiastical collar he wore.

Cat glanced over at him and resisted the urge to walk a bit more distant from him, certain the clear sky above could still produce a proper lightning strike for such blasphemy as this.

"Well, we were not very far away from here just yesterday, with me as the *Sea Captain's Daughter*," Cat said. "Suppose someone from then should see us now."

"Nonsense — today you are the *Parson's Niece*," Clanton said. "There's a vast difference between the two."

"What do you mean? For all these fine shops, the docks are but two blocks that way." She nodded.

"Again, nonsense," Clanton said. "The *Parson's Niece* is a proper girl. She walks with her back straight —" He glanced at her, cleared his throat, and Cat straightened her posture. "— her hands thus, yes, and with a delicate stride."

"Hobbled, you mean," Cat said.

"As may be," Clanton said. "The *Sea Captain's Daughter*, on the other hand —" He jerked his head toward the docks they'd walked the day before. "— has a rolling gait, a tarry mouth, and when she seeks to rouse her father from his drunken stupor in a wharf side pub, she resembles not at all the proper *Parson's Niece*. They are two different people, all entirely."

Cat pondered that for a moment, then struck on something else that bothered her.

"Why, in all these roles, must I be this one's daughter or that one's niece?" she asked. "May it never be for myself alone?"

Clanton paused a moment, as though pondering it.

"No."

"That's —"

"The way it is," Clanton said. "Unless you have both wealth and power — and by power, I mean a title of some sort. Even then, best to be such's widow." He looked her over and narrowed his eyes. "You're young, but we can paint your face a bit — get you widow's weeds tomorrow."

Much to Cat's chagrin, there was also Cat the *Market Beggar*, in which role, she took a bit of umbrage at Clanton's correcting her behavior. She thought she should come to that naturally, but Clanton would always have his way.

THINGS CHANGED at the manor house as well, though not to Mistress Hinds' liking.

Roffe decreed that Cat should have a lady's maid, but one who could be trusted, and, at Cat's suggestion, gave the nod to Emma for the job. Thus Hinds, in addition to the task of teaching Cat to be a lady, was placed of teaching Emma while Cat was at the townhouse.

Emma rose to most tasks that had to do with caring for Cat, but balked at Hinds' insistence that she work on her speech.

Cat insisted as well, though, and Emma eventually, grudgingly, began to practice. She still spoke as she always had when alone with Cat, but took the effort, usually, to follow Hinds' lessons when others were about.

None of this, though — none of what she learned — gave her any more insight in to Edward Roffe and what he was about.

That lack gnawed at her, and she determined to learn more. Curiously, there was little of Roffe at the country manor, despite Cat's searching. She determined to search the townhouse as well, when next she was there.

CHAPTER 13

*H*er chance came soon enough, as Clanton arrived to take her off for another stint in town. His sudden announcement that he would spend the evening at a nearby pub instead of the townhouse that evening proved to be Cat's chance. Roffe himself was seldom at the townhouse, coming by only to pick Cat up for those events he took her to. She wiled away her time at Clanton's lessons in ever more complex locks until the man took his leave.

No sooner had Clanton shut the door than Cat was in motion.

There were things she wanted to know about this house and its master. Things she'd have no opportunity to find with Clanton in the house and aware of her every move.

She rushed upstairs to her room to retrieve a candle and her lock picks, then went across the hall to the locked door.

Roffe's rooms. That was where anything of interest to her would be.

She set the candle and its reflector to shine on the door's lock. The gas lamps would provide better light, but she didn't want to light up the room's windows once she was inside. If Clanton returned unexpectedly, she'd have to dash out and lock the door behind her, but he'd know regardless if he saw the room's windows lit.

The lock was stubborn, more complex than others in the house. More complex, even, than the locks set to her as tests.

Roffe has something he wants kept hidden.

It gave way to her picks eventually, though.

Cat sat back on her heels with a satisfied smile and rolled up her picks. She tucked them into the small of her back, then wiped her face and neck. She'd actually started perspiring while picking the lock, despite the cold in the unheated hallway. She eased the door open and entered, pulling it closed behind her.

The room, shadowed as it was in just the light of her single candle, was still much as she'd expected. A large canopied bed took up most of it, with chests and bureaus against the walls. Rich carpets on the floor and hangings on the wall, all dark colored and adding to the shadows.

Cat made her way to the bedside to see what was on the table there.

Nothing but a candle in a holder, and nothing in the drawers at all.

She began going around the room methodically, checking each surface and drawer, careful to return things to their place if she moved them. The surfaces had a slight layer of dust, so she avoided moving anything there.

Nothing out of the ordinary, though, simply clothing and the sorts of every day devices a man might make use of.

She worked her way around the room, but paused as the light from her candle revealed a wide space between two cabinets. Instead of wall hangings, this space held a painting.

Cat moved closer and held her candle up.

It was a large painting. A portrait of three people — Roffe, only much younger, with a woman and infant. Roffe stood while the woman sat, his left hand on her right shoulder. Cat moved closer, there was something about the woman's face —

"My brother's family."

Cat jumped, almost shrieking in startlement, and dropped the candle. It went out as it struck the floor, droplets of hot wax stinging her feet.

She spun to face the now darkened room, eyes darting about for some sign of who'd spoken.

There was the rasp of metal on flint and a gas lamp came on, illuminating Roffe in the room's far corner. He moved to the next lamp and lit it as well, then around the room, all the while saying nothing.

Cat alternated between watching him and examining the room as it grew brighter. How had he known to be here? How had he even got here, with her in residence all day? She'd not seen him arrive.

Once the lamps were lit, Roffe moved to her side and looked at the portrait.

"Long gone, all of them," he said.

Cat looked at the portrait as well, then narrowed her eyes. In the better light, the man pictured looked even more like a younger Roffe, but it was the woman who drew her attention. She hadn't noticed before, but the woman sat slightly turned away from the man. She cradled the child with its head toward the edge of the canvas, as though she were sheltering it from the man who stood beside her. None of those pictured were smiling, but the woman's face, especially, seemed unhappy.

This was not a happy family, Cat thought to herself.

Still, there was something about that face that she couldn't quite place — the face and the woman's copper hair, falling in waves around it.

"Long gone?" she asked.

"Quite," Roffe said, without elaborating. He turned and walked away.

Cat turned as well to keep her eyes on him. She supposed she should offer some explanation for being in his rooms — especially for having picked the lock as she had.

"I'm sorry, Mister Roffe, I —"

"Do you think I am unaware of everything you do, Catherine? Or that you are not predictable?"

"What do you mean?"

Roffe raised his eyebrows. "You don't ask why I'm here."

"It makes little sense to ask a man why he happens to be in his own bedroom."

"True, but if he's there unexpectedly, your impertinence in asking might buy you a bit of time to think of a reason for your own presence."

"What on earth are you doing here?"

Roffe smiled. "Better." He gestured toward her. "I was waiting for you."

Cat frowned. "I don't understand."

"Do you suppose it was some accident that Clanton decides to spend an evening away just after you've managed to master those lock picks tucked into your skirt?"

"So, this is some kind of test?"

"Everything is a test … or if not a test, then an opportunity for me to learn more about you. Do not think for one moment that I am not still judging your every action."

"Then, what? You expected me to break in here?"

"After so long without your curiosity about me being satisfied and then being given this opportunity? I should be quite disappointed in you if you hadn't." He started for the door. "Come along — you'll find no answers about me in there. Only the odd bit of clothing."

Cat followed him to the stairs and then up to the third floor.

"I've converted this floor to servant's rooms, as I've no family to take them and another use for the top floor," Roffe said. "They're empty, so explore them as you wish."

He continued upward to the top floor, which would be where the maids would sleep in other households.

As her head crested the floor she saw that he had, indeed, made other use of it. The entire floor was one open space, with all the walls knocked out and only necessary support columns still standing. Well, open space in the sense that there were no walls, as the space was filled with benches, tables, cabinets, and chests.

"My workshop," Roffe said, spreading his hands wide.

Cat looked around, trying to take in as much as she could. The workbenches were covered in metallic bits that meant little to her and the walls were covered with large sheets of paper covered in drawings that made no more sense. One entire wall appeared to be nothing but huge slabs of slate covered in chalked writing and drawings. The skylight which let light into the stairwell had been expanded over the street-facing end of the house and a large metal tube stuck up through it. Cat found that odd, because its ends went nowhere, unlike the myriad copper pipes that ran from lower floors to this one and around the room to various devices.

Cat wandered about the room, very aware of Roffe watching her every move.

I wonder if my reaction is to be some sort of test, as well.

She came to one bench covered with a cloth. She glanced at Roffe, but he didn't appear concerned, so she lifted the cloth. Underneath, covering the work surface, were coils and lengths of copper wire, all wrapped in different substances. Some leather, others cloth, and some that seemed to be wrapped multiple times, with other metals as well.

"Electricals," Roffe said. "Useless, really, when they're entirely inoperable six or seven days of every month and utterly unreliable the rest." He walked over to the tube stuck through the skylight. "But I had this thought that perhaps … here, come and look at this."

Cat went to him and Roffe pointed at a smaller, glass-ended tube sticking out of the larger.

"Put your eye just here," he said.

Cat did so, then jumped back quickly as an image of the moon filled her vision. She looked from the tube to the skylight, where the moon itself was visible, full and near, but not nearly so large as she'd just seen.

"Like a spyglass, then? Only writ large?"

"Indeed." Roffe gestured for her look again.

She leaned over and placed her eye to the glass again, this time prepared for what she saw.

The moon, larger and clearer than she'd ever seen. Each of the many craters finely outlined and the deep gash of Halley's Crevasse facing her fully, like a mouth cut across its face. She could tell just how deep it went and the odd coloring of it, so unlike the grey rest of the orb, was even more striking than with the naked eye.

Cat straightened and looked up through the skylight again.

"Was it truly whole once?" she asked.

"Oh, yes," Roffe said. "Round as an orange. Before my time, of course." Roffe shook his head slowly. "Halley. Poor man, really. To be so lauded as a great scientific mind for predicting the comet's return, and then to be vilified and blamed when it came right in earlier than predicted and struck like that. I know they say he hung himself, but he was quite old when he finally saw his prediction realized. I rather think he had some help along the way. The Mob is … unforgiving in its reactions."

Roffe stepped quickly from the giant spyglass toward the bench of electricals.

"Now, my theory," he said, whipping back the covering.

Cat thought that he was quite a different person up here. He seemed genuinely enthusiastic about his workshop's contents.

"So," Roffe continued. "We know that the material either left behind or exposed in Halley's Crevasse has some effect. We see them on those days the Crevasse most faces us and the moon looms larger."

"The pigeons dance," Cat said. It was a sight to see, with all a market's pigeons lining up and shuffling about, unable or unwilling to fly and all moving together as though marionettes on the same strings.

"Exactly," Roffe said. "And as the pigeons dance on those days, so do compasses. Which makes navigating a ship somewhat more complicated, you see?"

Cat nodded. She did know that compasses had something to do with ships, but wasn't entirely clear on what. For her part she didn't see why they didn't just pick a spot on shore and steer for that. She knew the oceans were large, but how much larger could something be than the Thames at its widest?

"Electricals," Roffe said, waving at the items on the bench, "are much more sensitive to these effects for some reason. They'll spark and spit and do their best to kill a man for six or seven days of the month." Roffe grinned. "Much like a wife." He barked laughter. "I had the thought that if distance and the angle of the moon in relation to the Crevasse mitigate the effects, then there might be some material that would shield my electricals from it and allow the electricity to work as it should." He sighed. "If that were possible, then it might work on compasses, as well. Ships that could sail true when all others are amiss would turn a much greater profit."

Roffe flung the cover back over the bench.

"Sadly, I found nothing which would work for that."

Cat stared at the bench for a moment. She had questions — many questions about the room in general and all of its contents. There was something about the workroom she found oddly appealing, with its benches covered with half-assembled bits that must have some purpose she longed to know. She wondered how much of this Roffe might be willing to teach her, in addition to the thievery.

Her brow furrowed. "What's this electricity, then?"

CHAPTER 14

*C*at returned to the upper room, which she dubbed the Mechanicals Room, as often as she could in the weeks that followed — on those days when she was resident in the townhouse, that was. Clanton, with little rhyme or reason she could determine, would drive her back to the manor for days on end, then retrieve her back to the city.

The days at the manor were both wonderful, in that she was able to spend time with Emma, and horrid, in that she must endure the lessons of Mistress Hinds — the townhouse was equally dichotomous, with the fascinating mechanicals and those lessons Clanton taught. Most of those latter were interesting to an extent, and more useful, Cat thought, than the endless etiquettes of Hinds, but his attempts to teach her to fight continued to leave her battered, despite Clanton's infrequent grunts of what she thought might be approval.

The mechanicals, though — well, they might make all the bruises worth it. Cat rushed through whatever tasks Clanton set her, not laxly, for that would prompt a beating, but the promise of free time prompted her to great efforts.

Alone in the Mechanicals Room, she studied both the devices and their associated drawings. Questions to Roffe, in those infrequent times she saw him, about their purposes were rebuffed, but she did learn, to her surprise, that few of the devices there actually worked. The townhouse, it seemed, was not Roffe's primary workspace, but rather a dumping ground for failed projects.

Nevertheless, Cat studied them.

The drawings were an odd lot, each seemed to have been done originally in different hands and styles. The lettering itself, she took for other languages, and could make no sense of it. On all, though, a second, or rather the same hand, had made notations — not so neatly as the original, frequently scrawled, almost illegible, and often scratched out and blotted in what Cat took for frustration on the writer's part.

These writings looked like Roffe's hand to her, and he seemed to be expressing his thoughts, and then frustrations, at attempting to make the devices work as they ought.

Does he take in failed projects from other artificers? Cat wondered.

One device in particular caught Cat's attention. A bit over two feet across, and circular, it stood several inches tall, but on a low set of swiveling wheels. The drawings indicated a tightly coiled spring inside a well-sealed box, wound, she saw, via a steam powered drive on the wall.

This house, like the manor, lacked nothing in the way of piping, either for hot water or steam.

Clanton looked on in amusement as she stoked the kitchen fires for the boiler and then rushed upstairs again.

The winding mechanism appeared to be functional and, when she threw the switch on the wound device, the spring did release its energy into its workings, but the device itself merely sat there while some few of its inner gears spun round.

Cat sat back and stared at the drawings again, understanding the frustration in Roffe's notations and quite wishing she could scribble a few choice words herself.

The more she stared at the drawings, though, the more she thought there was something just a bit off with them.

With no little trepidation at what Roffe might think, she took up tools and began disassembling the device to see its workings for herself, carefully setting each piece and screw she removed aside and making notations as to how it should go back to its place.

The more she peered into the device and compared its workings to the drawings, the more she concluded that something was quite off indeed. It was assembled as it should be, as the drawings said, but … well, she became convinced that would never work at all.

No, the drawings must be wrong — curiously, and almost deliberately, she thought, for there were several key mistakes which certainly bolloxed up the whole.

This gear should mesh with *that* and not the other. The hose from the little pressure tank of steam should lead *here*. This bit? Well, that appears to have no purpose at all, other than to block these others, and if we remove it … and move this just here, well then …

Cat stood and watched in sheer delight as the flipped switch now sent the little device skittering across the floor, propelled by the tightly wound spring, which also drove long, round brushes in its underside. Steam billowed around it and hissed straight up into the air from a linen-covered screen on its top.

She laughed out loud as it reached a wall and the ingenious bumper on its front *clicked* loudly. That triggered it to reverse, change the angle of its wheels just a bit, and move forward again, just as she'd thought it might. In a moment, the little scamp had bumped the wall several times, each at a different angle, then scurried off again having found a clear path.

The path behind it, though, was its true purpose, for the grimy, scuffed floorboards of the Mechanicals Room were left clean where the device passed. Well … *cleaner*, for this room was truly filthy, but the device did make a difference. The steam out its bottom loosened the grime while the brushes scrubbed, and then the steam venting out its top sucked much of it up to be caught in linen-covered screens.

In minutes, the thing ran to a stop, steam sputtering and hissing as the last of it ran out. Cat's mood went from delight to disappointment that it hadn't cleaned nearly the whole of the room's floor, but then she dashed to the workbench in sudden excitement.

Of course, the first wouldn't do a whole room, it was just a toy, really — a sort of way of proving that the thing could work, she thought. Now that she'd seen it, though, the way was clear. A larger spring, a larger steam tank — that was all that was needed. Her mind spun like the brushes on the cleaner's underside.

What if it encounters a stairway? Wouldn't want it damaged. We could block the stairs off, but that's a chore — what if …

Yes, exactly, she thought, scribbling furiously.

Just a bit of a piece, much like the wall bumper, to detect the floor falling away — then reverse away to safety!

She was still working at it, trying to figure the way of getting proportions right in the drawing, when she heard a voice behind her.

"What are you about?"

Roffe stood at the head of the stairs, staring at her with narrowed eyes.

"Mister Roffe … I'm sorry, perhaps I shouldn't have …" Cat's eyes darted around the room. Her eyes and neck ached, and her fingers were cramped from drawing — she had no real idea how long she'd been at it, and worried that Roffe would be angry, thinking she might break his devices.

"But look —" she hurried on, wanting to show him what she'd done.

Cat quickly charged the device with steam, its spring wound, and she placed it on the floor. She set the switch and it began moving.

"You see?" she asked, grinning. "It was only a bit of —"

Crack!

The sound stunned her nearly as much as the blow, Roffe's hand against the side of her face. Even with Clanton's training, it was so unexpected that she didn't even raise a hand in defense before she was flung to the floor.

Roffe's booted foot struck her midsection with a dull *thud*, and she cried out in pain.

"*Little fool!*" Roffe yelled, face mottled in rage. "Do you think I need your meddling? Do you think the way of making that thing work wasn't already in my head, merely waiting for the time to make it so?"

He kicked her again, and Cat curled up into a ball to protect herself. "Do you think I need your help, you bloody, scheming, *gutter cat?*"

Roffe left her and grasped the little cleaner, lifting it off the floor. Its wheels and brushes spun wildly, and steam gushed from its bottom in a hissing plume.

"*I'd have had it!*" he screamed, heaving the device across the room.

A screech of metal from inside sounded as the device struck a workbench and then the floor. It wound up on its back, side dented in near the springbox. Cat could hear the scraping sound of the spring against that dent as it continued to unwind. Steam continued to hiss — slower and slower until it gave out with a last, sputtering gasp.

"I'd have had it in time," Roffe said again, panting from his exertion.

He glared down at her, jaw clenched, and Cat covered her head with her arms as he drew is foot back again. The thought to attack him entered her mind, but where would that leave her? She'd be out on the street sure, then — perhaps would be now, angry as Roffe was.

His kick landed low on her back this time, beneath her ribs, and she was thankful for the sturdiness of her stays there even as she felt the pain.

Footsteps sounded, but she kept her head covered, not trusting that it was over and not understanding why it had begun.

"These are *mine! Mine!*" Roffe yelled as he descended the stairs. "*I am the artificer, damn you!*"

ROFFE'S FOOTSTEPS descended the stairs and there was the sound of more shouting from below.

Cat stayed where she was for a time, afraid to move, then just as she thought she might try to stand, there came the sound of more footsteps.

She curled into a tighter ball, then, torn between anger and the desire to stand and slip a knife under Roffe's ribs, and the urge to stay down, take what punishment he deemed necessary, as the lesser members of her childhood gang would do when Brandt was on a tear.

Cover your head, take it, and hope there's a place for you in the morning — hope you're not to be turned out to fend for yourself.

Memories of being alone on the streets, hungry and cold, kept her in place.

A hand touched her shoulder and she flinched.

"Easy," Clanton said.

His hands ran over her back, probing, and she winced as he pressed where Roffe had kicked her. Clanton's blows in training were hard, they bruised and battered her, but Cat realized he must be pulling them — they hurt, but did no real damage. Roffe's were different — unrestrained and aimed to harm.

"Where else he get you?" Clanton asked. "Any to the head?"

"No," Cat whispered. It came out ragged, sounding on the verge of tears and she vowed that wouldn't happen. She'd not give Roffe the satisfaction. "Gut."

"Roll here," Clanton ordered, easing her to the side. His hands probed at her midsection as well, eliciting another gasp.

"I'll want these off," he said, tugging at her clothes. "Need to see the bruising. Roffe knows how to kill a man, much less you, and he was off his head."

Cat didn't have the energy to argue, nor the strength to help. Her cheek stung and her thoughts felt addled. Had she told Clanton she'd not been struck in the head? But she had, hadn't she? That first blow — yes.

She opened her mouth to tell him so, but instead cried out as he tugged at her clothing and it moved something deep inside her in quite the worst way.

"Nothing for it," he muttered.

The sound of steel on leather came to her and a moment later another tug, this time as Clanton slid a sharp blade into her clothing and cut it away, stays, chemise, and all.

Mistress Hinds would find that quite improper, Cat thought, but it didn't bother her. Clanton's touch had nothing of impropriety in it, as though she were merely a piece of meat he was examining — or some sort of animal.

"Not so bad. Try to sit up," he said, and assisted her in leaning back against a workbench. He examined her face. "Thought you said he'd not struck your head."

Fingers probed her midsection again and she was saved from answering by the need to cry out.

"Tell me if you piss blood," Clanton said. "But I think you'll not die of it."

"That is not encouraging, Mister Clanton," Cat managed.

Clanton ignored her and sat back on his heels. He looked around the room.

"Messing with Roffe's devices, eh?"

Cat tugged the halves of her clothes closer about her now that the man's examination appeared to be over. She glanced over at the cleaning device, upside down on the floor, case dented, a bit of a *ticking* coming from it occasionally. She thought that might be the last of its spring slowly unwinding.

"Why did he do this?" she asked.

"Worked on that near a year," Clanton said, nodding to the device, then to another on a bench at the back of the room. "That one two, I think."

"I don't understand it," Cat said. "Why are all these drawings in different hands? Why couldn't Roffe just ask the drawers if he had trouble making them work?"

"Man who drew those is dead," Clanton said. "Man who drew *those* is dead." He looked back at Cat. "Wager on the others, will you?"

CHAPTER 15

Cat followed Clanton downstairs slowly, wincing every few steps.

As they passed Roffe's rooms, Cat glanced guiltily at the door. She'd entered those more than once, in addition to the Mechanicals Room above, and shuddered at the thought of how Roffe might react to catching her there again.

The painting there drew her, though, in an odd way — she found it both disturbing and, somehow, comforting. She'd determined in her own mind that the woman was clearly afraid of the man, but loved the babe — and she became more convinced with every viewing that the man was a younger Roffe, and no brother. Not unless they were twins, as the resemblance was too close — and hadn't Emma said that Roffe's wife and child were dead, not some brother's? Why would Roffe claim a brother instead of saying the portrait was of his own family, as Cat now suspected it must be?

Clanton seated her at the table and laid out a simple supper.

"Nothing to do for you but wait to heal," he said. "No bones broke, at least."

Cat took a bite of the coarse brown bread and chewed. Proper meals were another advantage of the manor house and she found herself longing to return.

"Why didn't you warn me?" she asked. Clanton must have known she was going up to that room.

"Not my place," he muttered around a mouthful of cheese, then took a large gulp of beer. "My place is teach you to fight and those other things." He drained the rest of the beer, then looked at her critically. "Best you didn't fight back today, but did you even block a blow at all?"

"I wasn't expecting him to strike me."

Clanton laughed. "Weren't expecting it? You suppose a fellow sends bloody invitations?"

Cat flushed. "I suppose I felt safe here — at least when you aren't training me."

Clanton stared at her for a moment. "Have to fix that," he said, which Cat felt bode ill for her future stays in the townhouse.

"*Why* was Mister Roffe so angry, though?" Cat still couldn't understand it — even if Roffe had been working at the thing for a year, as Clanton said, shouldn't he be happy that she'd got it working?

"Not my place to say," Clanton said, starting in on a sausage. "But if you suspect a thing is his, best not to touch it without his leave. He's particular about what's his, our Mister Roffe."

Cat pushed her plate of sausage across the table to him and concentrated on her bread and cheese. She'd seen enough sausages of the sort Clanton chose on the streets to last a lifetime, and would rather wait for something of more certain provenance.

"You said the men who made those drawings were dead — all of them?"

Clanton nodded.

"Is that what Mister Roffe does? Buy the ... what, estates? Of other artificers? Try to get working what they hadn't time to in their lives?"

Clanton stabbed her sausage with his blade and moved it to his plate.

"Not my place to say."

"But the original drawings were all wrong," Cat pressed. "The thing would never work like that, so why write it down in the first place?"

Clanton sighed. "A man writes something down, any can read it."

Cat frowned.

"What do you mean?"

"Any can *read* it; any can *build* it," Clanton said. He rose and refilled his mug from a barrel on the counter, drained half, then filled it again before returning to the table. "Where's the profit in that?"

Cat frowned further, puzzling it out.

"Do you mean an artificer might make his design ... wrong? In putting it to paper, I mean. But wrong in a way he knows it's wrong, but others don't?"

Clanton laid a forefinger alongside his nose and tapped it there.

"So, Mister Roffe knows the designs will be wrong, unworkable, yet buys them from the estates in any case — then tries to figure out what the original designer's done to bollox things up? That makes no sense. Who would buy a design they know won't work? Who would buy such a thing without the key to fixing it?"

"Mister Roffe's business is Mister Roffe's business," Clanton said, "and it's —"

"Not your place to say. Yes, I gathered that."

Clanton grunted.

Cat pondered all this while they ate.

Was Roffe even an artificer? What did it mean that Cat had seen how to make the cleaning device work when he hadn't for, what was it Clanton had said, a year?

And the man's anger — Roffe was normally so calm and controlled, yet he'd come suddenly unhinged merely that she'd touched something of his?

She thought of leaving — if Roffe was so mad as to beat her for so slight a crime, then what might he do for some real transgression?

In the end, though, she couldn't leave. There was nowhere to go — she might be able to make her way as a thief with what she'd learned so far, but she'd never be able to achieve the sort of success Roffe had. Both the manor house and the townhouse were too comfortable, the food too plentiful, for her to leave now — not when there was more to learn, and all that for the taking and nothing asked of her yet.

As though her latest sojourn to the townhouse had been some sort of turning point, perhaps triggered by Roffe's anger at her working with his mechanicals, her return to the country manor was marked with changes as well. Where before her days had been much her own, save for the rather light schedule of classes with Mistress Hinds, they were now so full that Cat had barely a moment's breath from one thing to the next.

Mistress Hinds increased her own workload, demanding more and more of Cat, and presenting everything from mathematics to literature to the ways of proper society at a speed Cat found dizzying.

More, she was expected to find time each day to spend with Mistress Singley in the kitchen. Not cooking or learning to cook, but decocting odd notions in the manor's stillroom. Notions that were decidedly unsavory, for, it turned out, Mistress Singley was an able maker of all things less nourishing than bread or pies.

"Now, this one," Singley muttered, "you'll want to be careful with."

She carefully poured the liquid from one container to another, her hands encased in thick leather gloves.

"Be sure of your stopper," she said. "Cork's no good, lessen you seal the outside with lead or wax — lead's better, but wax'll do if you must. I'll show you the wax now, so you can see, but remember lead's best."

She grasped the newly filled and corked vial with a pair of tongs and poured red sealing wax all around its top until the vial was covered halfway down its length. Then she dipped the vial, tongs and all, deep into a half-filled barrel of water, even though, as Cat had seen, not a bit of the clear liquid had gotten on its outside.

Singley set the vial on a rack to dry, then moved all of the items used to make the substance into the barrel as well, including the thick leather mat that lined the work surface. She ended by dumping in the tongs, then her leather gloves, and seating the barrel's top firmly in place.

"Skiff will dispose of that," she said. "He knows how."

"And that will kill a man?" Cat asked, nodding at the innocent looking vial.

"In minutes," Singley said. "One or two, if you can get it in his mouth — less than ten, still, if by touch."

"Touch?"

"A few drops on the skin, don't take much."

"Why … why would you teach me this?" Cat asked, not wanting to ask the other question of how the pleasant cook would even know it in the first place.

"Master Roffe's instructions."

Master Roffe's instructions applied to Skiff, as well, who began taking Cat on runs about the manor grounds and then out into the surrounding woods.

Those were hours spent in some odd, draped gown Skiff had her wear, with ragged strips of cloth attached, all the time trying to keep him from spotting her.

She was to move from one place to another amongst the trees, and every time she made a mistake, Skiff would toss a pebble at her —

which was annoying, but far less so than the heavy clout she got when Clanton caught her in an error, so Cat didn't complain.

To this Skiff added more mundane tasks, such as harnessing the horses and driving the cart or carriage, even riding, which Cat found she quite enjoyed. These, at least, seemed useful skills to her — as any cart, carriage, or horse could now become her transport clear of a heist gone wrong.

The woodcraft, though, seemed out of place. She thought most of her thieving would certainly be done in a city, not the country — still, she could see its use if she were to need to make her way to some lord's country home and out again with the goods.

It would be handy to be able to hide from any he sent after her and handier to flee.

Singley's concoctions, though, still confused her. Those that put a man to sleep or took his memory of the last few hours' time, those would be useful, but the poisons? Perhaps Roffe hadn't been specific about what the cook was to teach her, yet she still wondered at how Singley knew these things — and how Skiff came to be such an expert at moving about forests.

It seemed like everyone in Roffe's employ had some secret.

It was not so very long before the new schedule began to wear on Cat.

She'd spend a week with Clanton, being battered about the town-house's courtyard in the mornings, set to picking locks, now sometimes paired with the cleverest of traps, in the afternoon, then sent onto the city's rooftops for half the night, before starting it all up again the next dawn — after which, she'd get to doze in the carriage from townhouse to manor where the schedule was almost as grueling.

Lessons with Hinds, distilling with Singley, traipsing through the trees with Skiff — or set to first harnessing the horses, then to driving carriages and riding, as he began adding more for her to master — more lessons with Hinds, who seemed to take great pleasure in loading Cat down with further things for her to study before the next day's lessons and the cycle began over again.

The only person not demanding more and more of Cat's time and effort was Emma, who Cat saw less and less of every day.

Her fatigue and anger at the never-ending demands grew until one morning she simply laid down in bed and crossed her arms when Emma held out her dress.

"No," she said.

"What?" Emma asked.

"I shan't get up today." Cat crossed her arms and sank back into the pillows.

"Are you sick?" Emma set the dress aside and came to feel Cat's head.

"I'm exhausted," Cat said. "I've just got back from the townhouse, where Clanton had me up half the night, and now Hinds has loaded me down with texts I'm to read — but not during the day, as she requires I attend her in the drawing room to learn the proper steps of some dance and Mistress Singley must teach me to create some vile concoction and Skiff has yet another sort of harness he must, without delay, make me familiar with ... I cannot think, I cannot learn — there is not a bit of space left in my head for one more thing — and I must *sleep!*"

With that, and feeling near tears, Cat rolled over and burrowed into her pillows.

CHAPTER 17

Cat spent three glorious days refusing to do anything at all.

She slept late, then made her way to the solarium to simply sit.

Some might have found it boring, but for Cat it was a welcome respite. The peace and view of the gardens helped her to think, and she was still thinking of what to do about Roffe. The man frightened her, but she wanted what he offered, too. The thoughts, the dilemma, clouded the days and made her a bit melancholy.

In all, she would agree she was not good company these last few days, but Emma, bless her, stayed by. Even now, she guarded the solarium door from the fearsome Mistress Hinds who sought to drag Cat off to some horrid lesson in greater maths.

"She's not well," Emma said.

"I heard you the first time," Hinds snapped. "Mind your place, girl!"

"Mistress Hinds," Cat said, not wanting the woman to have any more excuse to harangue Emma than she already did. Though all of the servants found themselves on the bad side of the tutor's tongue, the woman had an especial dislike for Emma.

"I find myself too out of sorts for lessons today — perhaps tomorrow?"

Hinds sniffed again, started to say something, then spun and left the room. Cat knew it was frustrating for the woman. She was used to teaching younger children in a home with the parents in residence. Here, not only was Cat older, but she was, to all intents and purposes, the lady of the house, despite being too young for that. Neither would any of the other servants here support Hinds in insisting Cat study, as the tutor's attitude had alienated them all.

I've allies in that, at least.

"She's gone," Emma said.

Cat heard the sound of the solarium door shutting.

Emma sat next to her on the settee, hands folded in her lap. The girl was still for a time, looking through the glass as Cat was, then she took a deep breath and let it out slowly.

"Is there something you'd like to say?" Cat asked.

"Oh, no, miss."

They'd agreed that Emma should address her so whenever they were out of Cat's rooms, so that she would never worry about slipping in front of another. She was also to practice the accents for proper speech Hinds taught her, so that her role of lady's maid would be more believable.

More minutes passed and Emma sighed again.

Cat found herself torn between amusement and irritation at the girl for being able to amuse her when she was trying to be morose.

"Are you certain there's nothing you'd like to say?"

Emma shrugged.

"Well, miss, only that it's the same clouds out there as yesterday ... well, not the same, I'm sure, but much the same, if you take my meaning?"

"I do."

"And, well ..." She turned to look at Cat, jerking her head toward the window. "Don't you find it a bit tedious, miss?"

"You're free to be elsewhere, Emma. No need for you to spend all day sitting with me." She regretted it almost as quickly as the words left her mouth, for she didn't want to be alone. Or she did. Or didn't, but resented not being so.

"Oh, no, miss, I couldn't. What if you should need something?"

"I'd call for you, I suspect, or get it for myself — but I don't suppose there's anything I'll need."

"Nothing?" Emma slid a hand into her skirt pocket. "Not even a book?"

"A book?"

The one lesson Hinds offered that Cat enjoyed, was on reading. She'd learned the basics from Mother Agnes, though had little cause to practice it until she'd been taken up by Roffe.

Emma slid a volume out of her pocket. "While you was ... *were* away, that woman went through the library pulling out books to have you read."

Cat nodded. She recalled Hinds saying something to that effect when she'd returned.

Emma grinned wickedly. "But what that woman dint ... *didn't* know, was I was watching her."

Cat frowned, not understanding what this was about.

"Watching her?" she asked.

Emma nodded. "Watching what books she left, see? An' what she turned her nose up at, like she does."

Cat could well imagine Hinds turning her nose up and sniffing at any book she felt inappropriate for her charge.

Emma held the volume out.

Cat opened it and read the title.

"*The Life and Most Surprising Adventures of Robinson Crusoe, of York, Mariner, who lived Eight and Twenty Years in an Uninhabited Island on the Coast of America near the Mouth of the great River Oroonoque. With an Account of his Deliverance thence, and his other Surprising Adventures.*"

"I looked in it — there's pictures of ships and islands and this man with his guns ..." She hesitated, then a lower, scandalized whisper which lost her proper accent all entire, "An' some near *naked* savage man."

Cat raised an eyebrow. She could well imagine Hinds' disapproval of such things.

"And you suspected I might need this book?"

Emma lowered her head, but kept her eyes on Cat.

"I thought you might, if you were to find the clouds too tedious-like, care to read it to me."

Cat's lips twitched and she felt an odd, sudden warmth run through her. It was as though Emma's hopeful gaze made any number of things far more bearable. She opened the book and began reading.

After a time, Emma slid her slippers off and raised her feet to the settee, curling up and wrapping her arms around her knees. It wasn't a proper way to sit at all, in fact Hinds would be scandalized to see the maid sitting at all in the presence of the ostensible lady of the house, but Hinds wasn't there and Cat considered Emma a friend more than anything. More than a friend. And the look in the girl's eyes as she listened to the story quite drove away Cat's melancholy over Roffe. Of no less effect was the sight of Emma's pink toes peeking out from the edge of her skirt so near to Cat. She couldn't explain it, but nearness made her warm and somehow feel right with the world.

Cat read on, losing track of time, until the solarium door was thrust open and Lexie, the new maid, stuck her head in.

"A carriage come up the lane!" she burst out with. "I'm sent to tell you the master's come!"

She was gone in a shot, likely back to assist Singley with preparing to greet Roffe.

Cat frowned at the news, Roffe had not visited the manor since that first time, preferring his home in the city. That he'd come now, with no notice or reason, couldn't bode well. Her good mood suddenly evaporated at the prospect of confronting him again — she hadn't settled in her own mind how she felt about him at all after his explosion in the Mechanicals Room.

Emma stood quickly, sliding her feet into her slippers. She gave Cat a quick glance and frowned.

"I'll pull a nicer dress for you, shall I?"

Cat looked down at herself. The dress she was wearing seemed quite good enough to her, it had even met with Hinds' approval — at least the tutor hadn't seen fit to sniff disapproval and comment on it.

"No," she said, "if Mister Roffe will arrive unannounced, then he'll take me as I am. I'll not scurry off to better myself for him."

"Will you go out to meet him, then?" Emma asked, looking at the doorway.

Cat shook her head. The servants, few though they were in this household, would be hastily assembling at the front door to welcome Roffe home.

"No," she said, "I'll greet him here. So far as any know, he's my uncle, after all."

"Aye, miss, but I should go."

Cat nodded and Emma hurried out. She returned to staring out at the leaden skies and trickles of water on the glass, waiting for Roffe to come.

Which he did, shortly. The solarium door clicked open behind her.

"Catherine."

"Uncle," she responded without turning, voice as leaden as the sky outside.

Roffe made his way to the windows without looking directly at her. He joined her in staring out at the gardens for a time, then sighed.

"You know," he said finally, "I had hoped to introduce you to my work more gradually. There'll be time for you to learn the mechanicals, if you wish, but it's best you learn other things first."

"I'm sorry to have spoiled your plan, Uncle, though I'm sure I've been suitably chastised for it."

Roffe grunted.

"Don't touch what's mine, should be the lesson you take from it, and that I'm not to be trifled with. Your little bout of sullenness is disturbing not only my plan, but your education as well." He glanced back at her, eyes narrowed, then returned to looking through the windows. "I'd have sent Clanton to retrieve you to the city for more education there, but I hear you've accomplished nothing with your studies *here* these last few days. They're both important, Catherine. Clanton can't teach you to move in society, nor keep you from giving away your origins with some lack of simple knowledge. Your tutor can."

"Is that so important?"

Roffe turned and glared at her.

"It is if you want this," he said, gesturing at the room. "If you don't want to return to the streets and whatever life you can make for yourself there."

"It's too much, too fast," Cat said. "I only wished a brief rest."

"Well, you've had it," Roffe said. "Get back to work — there's much for you to learn."

Cat bristled at that but said nothing.

Roffe's jaw tightened and his eyes narrowed. "I'd hoped the carrot would be enough for you, *niece*. Perhaps it's time you learned I've more than one stick to bend you to my will, as well."

Cat chilled at the look. She'd never fully trusted Roffe, but her time since waking here in the manor house had softened her view of him a bit. This look, though, brought back the Roffe she'd first encountered. The one on the streets who'd knocked her to the ground so casually. Still, if he thought the threat of a beating would cow her, he was mistaken.

"I've felt your stick, Uncle. You were quite thorough with it in your Mechanicals Room."

Roffe snorted. "You angered me, girl, that's not a punishment. Come here."

Cat shook her head, if he thought she'd come to him for his beating, he was mistaken in that too.

Roffe moved, faster than she expected and faster even than Clanton. He was beside her in a moment. His hand gripped her arm like a vise and dragged her to her feet, then to the solarium's windowed wall. He shoved her against it, the waist high, wrought-iron rail pressing hard against her stomach.

"Look out there," Roffe commanded.

Cat could hardly do anything else, as she was pressed so closely to the glass. The manor's terrace was immediately before her, a flat, well-manicured half circle of grass. A low wall retained the earth of the terrace from falling into the lower garden. The terrace itself was where she imagined lawn games would occur, if such things ever happened at this house.

"Are you familiar with the tradition of a whipping boy, Catherine?" Roffe asked, pressed close behind her and keeping her at the window.

"No, I'm not, and you're making me —"

"Watch," Roffe said again. "The term comes from the children of the king — when the king was thought to rule by divine right, that is. Who would dare correct the future king? Who was worthy? What does one do when a prince misbehaves? From a purely practical point of view, correction might be remembered when the boy becomes a man and wears the crown, after all, and what revenge might he take? Do you see?"

Cat didn't, but said nothing. Clanton was on the terrace now. He strode to its center and turned to look at Cat and Roffe. His shoulders rose and fell as though he'd taken a deep breath or sighed, then he strode to the edge of the terrace where a tree from the garden over-hung it. He drew his belt knife and clipped a branch, stripping away leaves and twigs.

"Do you mean to beat me again?" Cat asked. "Or have him do it?"

Roffe went on as though she hadn't spoken.

"The other use of the whipping boy, Catherine, is that he was the prince's companion and playmate. In theory, if the prince was a decent lad, he'd regret seeing his playmate punished in his stead and correct his behavior."

Clanton motioned toward the house — not to Cat and Roffe, but to their right where the great hall opened to the terrace. Emma stepped forward, head cocked as she listened to Clanton still speaking. Cat couldn't hear the words, but a chill ran through her.

"No —"

"Be still and watch!" Roffe grasped her arms, holding her in place, pressing her more roughly to the iron railing.

Clanton met Emma at the terrace's center and with no warning cuffed the girl to the ground.

"Stop it!"

Cat struggled, but Roffe's grip was solid. She tried to strike at him with an elbow or kick him, but she couldn't connect.

Emma looked up at Clanton, hand to her cheek, surprise and hurt writ on her face. Clanton looked toward the solarium, then raised the switch he'd cut and brought it down.

"*Stop it!*"

Cat threw her head back, hoping to catch Roffe in the face, but he merely laughed.

"I took you off the street," he hissed at her. "Brought you into this home. Offered you more —"

"*Emma!* Damn you, Roffe, she's done nothing!"

"— luxury than you could dream of. The opportunity to learn —"

The switch in Clanton's hand rose and fell over and over again. Emma hunched on the ground, not trying to escape — likely thinking this was her lot in life and that it was better than being on the streets. Much as Roffe was saying himself.

"Which will it be, Catherine, from this point on? The carrot or the stick? If you won't bend for your own sake, will you do it for hers?"

"*Damn you!*"

Roffe shook her roughly. "Do I have Clanton strip her and beat her bloody? Do you doubt I will?"

"*No!*"

Clanton's arm fell again.

"What do you want?" Cat asked. "Tell me what you want and I'll do it!"

"Learn what I set you, Catherine. Whether by Clanton or your tutor or any else I say. Learn your lessons, girl, and become of use to me."

"*All right!*" Cat wanted to look away from the scene on the terrace, but couldn't — she simply wanted it to stop. "All right, I will! *Make him stop!*"

"Very well." Roffe rapped his knuckles on the glass loud enough for Clanton to hear. The valet glanced over, nodded, then tossed the switch to the ground. "Do not forget the consequences of defying me, Catherine. They will only grow more severe."

With that, Roffe released her and left. Clanton walked away from Emma, leaving her in a sobbing heap. Cat spun around and rushed from the solarium. She might have caught sight of Roffe in the great hall, but was oblivious to it. Even Clanton, who passed her on his way through, though she wished nothing more than to strike him, was nothing to her in that moment.

She dashed out onto the terrace, and dropped to her knees beside Emma.

CHAPTER 18

"She'll be herself in no time," Singley assured Cat with a pat on the shoulder.

Cat nodded her thanks, but her attention was all on Emma. The girl was settled in Cat's own bed, carried there at Cat's insistence by Skiff, the groundskeeper.

Roffe and Clanton left immediately, not even waiting for the servants to assemble, and leaving the household stunned at their quick arrival and departure, as well as the violence of it. All of the small staff rushed to the terrace — they'd been watching from whatever discrete position they could find, in any case.

"Skiff, you be off with you, now." Singley gave her own nod to the groundskeeper. "And you as well, Mistress Hinds — I think the girl needs rest."

Hinds sniffed, as she had more than once since Emma'd been brought inside — sniffing and objecting to everything from the girl being carried to her placement in Cat's room.

"It is not your place as the cook to dismiss —"

Cat rounded on her, furious and at an end of her patience. She was certain it was Hinds who'd reported to Roffe that Cat was missing her studies, which made the tutor complicit in what had been done to Emma, so far as Cat was concerned.

"But it is mine in my own chambers, Hinds," Cat said, deliberately leaving off the honorific. "You may set me lessons, but *I* am the lady of this house in Mister Roffe's absence."

"Of course, Miss Catherine, but —"

"*Out!*" Cat yelled.

Hinds jumped, startled, and made her way to the door.

"I do trust you'll be resuming those studies," Hinds said from the doorway, and Cat became certain that the woman knew this was a result of her handiwork — knew and took pleasure in it.

She clenched her jaw and fists, wanting to fling herself at the woman.

"I will see you at the appointed times, Hinds."

"Of course, Miss Catherine."

"And Hinds," Cat couldn't resist calling out before the woman had completely left. "Do remember your place. As we've all seen today, the discipline in this household is strict indeed."

Skiff left after Hinds and shut the door after them.

Cat collapsed to the bedside, clutching Emma's hand.

"Let her sleep," Singley said again. "She's not badly hurt."

"How can you say that?" Cat felt the tears come and welcomed their release.

Emma was still battered and muddied from the beating and the bedding was the worse for it, but Cat didn't care. The girl lay on her side, the back and skirt of her clothes bloody in spots. But Singley was correct that she was resting — asleep at least.

Singley snorted. "Not the first nor the worst beating that girl's taken."

"He's done his before?"

"Not here," Singley said. "But she's told me —" She pursed her lips. "Not my place to tell, and there's other worries now. Let her rest for now, then a bath with salts will set her right. Her stays will have protected her back — they're good for that. Mostly bruises, I imagine, and she'll ache all over, but she's not hurt."

"Are you certain?"

Singley nodded, then gave Cat a hard look. "It's good of you to think of her, but better she were in her own room."

Cat shook her head, returning her gaze to Emma's face, which was peaceful in sleep despite the streaks of mud and wet hair escaping her cap.

"No, I want to look after her. And the bath's just there — you said a bath when she wakes."

"Aye, I'll send up salts." Singley sighed. "And tea with a bit to eat."

Cat nodded. "Thank you."

Singley pursed her lips, started to speak, stopped, then, "This was a message to you, then?"

"What?"

"From Mister Roffe? That Hinds woman's unhappy you've not studied as he wants —" She nodded at Emma. "This was his message?"

"I —" Cat faltered for what to say. There was no denying the truth, but she didn't want Singley and the others to know that this was her fault. Didn't want Emma to know, if she didn't already, for that would surely make the girl hate her.

"I don't know what his business with you is, girl, but be careful." She took a deep breath. "His hooks run deep and he knows how to set them."

Cat frowned. She'd thought the servants here were happy with their lot. A small household with the master gone much of the time meant little work. But Emma had said something odd when Clanton had first taken Cat to the city — not to trust them, she'd said. Did the servants know what Roffe was? Surly Clanton did, but she wouldn't think Roffe would trust that to the others.

"What do you mean?"

"There're hooks set in all of us — just ..." She sighed and nodded to Emma. "She'd do better in her own room. He does this when you're friendly with the girl, what'll he do if he knows it's more? If he suspects that, if he can use it —"

"More?"

"Keep your secrets close, girl, as we all do. Don't let that man own more of you." Singley turned and left. "I'll send up the salts and tea."

~

EMMA SLEPT FOR SEVERAL HOURS, and all the while Cat stayed at the bedside. At first, she simply held Emma's hand and waited, then, as it grew toward evening, she rested her head on that hand, keeping her eyes on Emma's face.

After some time, Emma woke. Her eyelids flickered, opened, and her eyes rolled, at first unseeing. Then they opened fully and focused on Cat. She smiled for a moment, then her eyes widened in alarm and she tried to sit up.

"No," Cat said, "rest easy. You're hurt."

"No, miss." Emma tried to rise again. "I shouldn't be here. Not in your bed like this."

"I had you brought here so you could rest."

"Should be in my own room."

"No." Cat pressed her firmly back down to the bed. "I want to see you're taken care of."

Emma flushed, but settled back.

"Mistress Singley said a bath with salts would do you well once you woke. Do you think you could manage that? There's tea and toast, as well, though the tea's likely cold and bitter by now."

Emma nodded and started to rise again, wincing. "A bath would ease these aches, I think. I'll go down and ask her —"

"Nonsense," Cat said. "She brought the salts up here and my bath is just in the next room. You've shared it often enough with me."

"That were just playin', miss," Emma said, "and weren't proper." She flushed. "It's not my place."

Cat frowned in confusion. Emma'd been a steadfast friend to her here and had, indeed, shared her bath more than once since that first time. Why the girl was suddenly so insistent on it being improper, which it likely was, she couldn't understand. Nor did she care.

"You stay there," she said firmly. "I've seen the hip bath you have below stairs and it's nowhere near big enough for the proper soaking you need."

Cat went to the bathing room and started the bath filling. She poured salts from the box Cook had delivered, but wasn't sure how much to use, so she simply added more and more as the bathing tub filled and what she'd already added dissolved. When the tub was filled, water steaming and somewhat opaque with the dissolved salts, she returned to the bedside.

Reluctantly, it seemed, Emma took her outstretched hand and accepted her assistance in walking to the bath. She limped and her right leg seemed to pain her more than the left.

Once in the bathing room, Cat helped her undress and the extent of the injuries became clear. They weren't as bad as Cat feared — Singley had been correct that the solid ribs of Emma's stays had protected her back from the cut of Clanton's switch. There were bruises there, though, where the impact of the blows had made it through.

Emma's shoulders fared worse, and there were livid, red welts there, some of them bleeding. As well, on the backs of her thighs and buttocks. Some of the blood had dried to her shift and underthings and they were painful to remove.

With every new injury revealed and every hiss of pain from Emma, Cat cursed Clanton and Roffe anew.

Once undressed, Emma eased herself into the bath, needing support from Cat to do so. Her right thigh had taken the worst of it, somehow, and was a mass of bruises and welts that made Cat want to look away.

The heat and salt seemed to ease her, though, at least after the initial sting, and Emma leaned back, eyes closed, her face softening in relief.

"I could lie here forever, I could."

"As long as you like," Cat promised.

She took up a cloth, wetted it, and began washing the now dried mud from Emma's face.

Emma's eyes flashed open and she protested again.

"I can do that, miss, not you."

Cat frowned again. She had a sudden fear that Emma knew — that Clanton had said something to the girl as he beat her, told her that Cat was the cause, and that was the reason for Emma's new formality.

"Emma," Cat asked, steeling herself for the answer, "what's the matter?"

Emma looked down at the water.

"It's — Mister Clanton, miss, he didn't say why. He didn't say what I'd done wrong —" Her eyes clenched shut and filled with tears. "I've been too forward, I think — and Mister Roffe, he's displeased I didn't keep my place."

"No, that's not it."

"Well what else could it be?" Emma asked. "I know I've done my housemaid chores well — Cook would cuff me herself if I haven't." She looked up, eyes wide and fearful. "I've not displeased you, have I, miss?"

"No — no, absolutely not."

Emma nodded. "I left my place. Thought I could be a lady's maid and put on airs. I —" She looked away. "I'm sorry, miss."

"That's not it. And I'm Cat to you when we're alone, remember?"

Emma shook her head. "What is it then? Why would Mister Roffe have me beaten like that?"

Cat opened her mouth to answer. She wanted to tell Emma the truth — about Roffe and his story of the whipping boy — but what would Emma think of her then, if she knew it was Cat's fault she'd taken this beating.

"It's —" She paused. "I don't know, Emma. I've no idea why Clanton did this, but Mister Roffe isn't displeased you've been my maid." That much was true, at least — Roffe was almost certainly quite pleased with it, as it gave him Emma to use as a control over Cat.

"He's not?"

"No."

"Then why?"

"I don't know. Perhaps Clanton was … I don't know."

"Do you suppose he just wanted to, that Clanton?" Emma asked. "He's a frightening man."

"He is … perhaps that might be it."

Cat wrung out the cloth and dabbed at Emma's face, hating herself for the lie, but her limbs were chill with the fear of what Emma might say if she knew the truth. Would she forgive Cat for being the cause of Roffe's wrath? She couldn't bear the thought of losing her only friend, so stayed silent. As the mud came off, she spotted a dark red welt on the girl's cheek where one of Clanton's blows had landed, as well as a bruise where he'd cuffed her to the ground and vowed she'd give Roffe no further cause to do such a thing again. Surely that would make up for the lie, wouldn't it?

"Let's drain this and fill it again to have the water clean," Cat said, wanting to change the subject.

She drained the tub and Emma huddled in place, going all over goosebumps in the chill air. Then she started the tub filling again with fresh hot water and added more salts. The girl continued to shiver even as the hot water rose.

"What's wrong?" Cat asked.

"I'm all over cold," Emma said. "I ain't been beat like that since I come here — not since I left …" She clenched her eyes shut. "Is this how it's t'be? Ever' time a carriage comes up the drive, will it be old Clanton comin' for me?" Her voice dropped to a whisper. "I can't find another place — I can't —"

Cat knelt beside the tub and wrapped her arms around Emma's shoulders.

"It will be all right," she whispered.

"It won't, it — Cat, your dress! It's in the waters!"

"Well, I'll not leave you shivering with fear like that."

"But —"

Cat grinned, it was just like Emma to worry about the clothes before herself.

"Very well, then, there's nothing for it."

Cat stood and began to undress to join Emma in the bath. It was more awkward to get at the complicated stays and ties of a lady's, not a servant's, garments without Emma to help her, and somehow, oddly, more intimate to do it herself with Emma watching than when the girl helped her.

She slid into the tub, grateful for the water's warmth after the chill air. Beneath the cloudy water, her legs and feet touched Emma's softly, and she felt the tremble in her insides she so often did when they shared a bath or lay together on her bed before Emma went to her own.

Her gaze caught the bruise and welt on Emma's face and she slid around the tub to draw Emma into her arms. She held her for a time, until the shaking subsided, then took a deep breath and sighed heavily. Her own thoughts and fears seeming to come as the other girl's withdrew.

"What's wrong, miss?"

"Cat."

"What's wrong, then, Cat?"

She could hear the start of a smile in Emma's voice, and that cheered her for a moment. For a moment, until she realized that this closeness was exactly what Roffe wanted and that it put Emma at risk. But Cat had never had this before and didn't want to lose it. The desire to both keep her friend and protect her warred within. An idea occurred to her.

"Are you happy here, Emma?"

"Oh, aye, I could stay in the bath like this forever, I think."

Cat smiled. "Not the bath, goose, I mean here, in this house."

Cat saw Emma looking confused.

"Where else would I go?"

Cat saw that wasn't an answer to her question and it gave her hope. Emma would never be safe from Roffe here, but what if they simply left? What if they both took service in some other house? The life of a servant wouldn't be so grand as what Cat had now, but neither would it be as dire as life on the street. Was there more she truly needed than a warm bed and a full stomach?

"Some other house, perhaps? One with a more conventional family?"

Emma was silent for a moment. Cat glanced up and found the girl was now looking down at the water herself.

"When I first arrived here," Cat went on, "You said Mister Roffe was a kind master, but today ..." She shook her head. "Whether by Roffe or his man, this doesn't seem kindness. And you warned me not to trust them, when Clanton first took me to the city. Singley, just today, said something about them, how Roffe set his hooks deep." She took a deep breath. "Perhaps another place would be best — for the both of us."

"It don't work like that, miss — Cat," she corrected herself. "With no reference? What do you think a girl just shows up at the kitchen door and she's hired?" Emma shook her head. "No, there's who you know and who knows you — the footman's sister's husband's cousin is who gets to fill a place." She paused, longer, and Cat remained silent, somehow sensing there was more she'd say.

Emma started to pull away from Cat's embrace, but Cat tightened her grip and Emma relaxed against her.

"And there's them hooks," Emma said bitterly.

"What?"

Emma looked up, eyes wide, and shook her head. She looked down again. "Nothing, please, it's just ... this is the only place for some of us."

"What do you mean? Emma, please tell me."

Emma shook her head again. "It's wrong. It'll all go wrong again if I do."

"What?"

"You'll hate me."

"Emma! I'll do no such thing — it's out now, whatever it is. Certainly, it's better I know than to wonder?"

Emma was silent for a long time and Cat could see her shoulders shaking.

"Please tell me?"

"There's none in this house don't have a story," Emma said finally, voice just above a whisper. "Mister Roffe, he ain't no proper gentleman, but we keep his secrets a'cause he keeps ours."

"What secrets, Emma?"

"Skiff," she said. "He were caught poaching and ran, but there's talk he were with a band of highwaymen, too. Nothing to be sure of, but the magistrate and lord took the chance Skiff gave them to be rid of him. He'll hang if he's ever caught off Mister Roffe's lands, I think." She sniffed and rubbed her eyes. "Mistress Singley, well, there was a man what beat her and he don't beat no one no more, if you understand."

Cat began to. A man like Roffe, a man with secrets of his own, would want those serving him to have no choice but to keep his counsel. The servants might not know the details, but they'd know something was off — better to have those who owed you their place and had nowhere else to go.

"And you?" Cat prompted, thinking, and me. Nowhere to go but back to starving on the streets.

Emma buried her face in her hands.

"You'll hate me, miss," she whispered.

"Emma, I won't, I — I have secrets of my own, you know. Before I came here, I was nothing but a gutter-rat, a common beggar and thief in the market."

"Nothing common about you, miss."

Cat smiled. "I note you don't argue the beggar and thief bits."

Emma flushed red and looked down at the water, which drew Cat's gaze there as well. The soap and salts made the water murky, but she could see the other girl's form beneath it and it stirred ... something, she didn't understand. Like a cramp, but not at all painful. Emma's body, where it touched hers, seemed to suddenly catch fire and burn her skin, and she found it oddly difficult to breathe.

"I'm sorry, miss, I —"

"It's Cat, Emma, haven't we said that?"

"Aye, Cat, but it's sore hard to keep it straight when Hinds is about. I fear slipping and her going all prune-faced about it."

"Hinds can go —" Cat broke off rather than use one of Clanton's favorite suggestions for what her tutor could go and do. She should, she supposed, take Emma's example and try to keep her own roles straight. At the manor she was a proper lady, after all — while at the townhouse, she was still —

"I *was* a thief you know. A beggar too, but earlier. Once I grew enough, there was more in the way of thieving."

After that, there was nothing for it but to tell Emma stories of her life on the streets. The girl seemed fascinated by it — thinking it more of an adventure than Cat ever had at the time, and Cat played into that. Something in her chest seemed to swell with every one of Emma's oh's and ah's at Cat's tales, and the girl's laugh was like the gift of a chest of coin, a tinkling that nearly brought tears of happiness to her eyes.

They were called to supper before she'd nearly run out of tales, but she kept them up while Emma dried her and helped her to dress, ending with her tale of that last day with the gang in the market, not mentioning that the mark was Roffe, but still going on about her mad dash away from the others in the gang, her leaps over market tables, and her last, desperate scramble up the drain pipe with Brandt close behind her.

"Loo," Emma breathed. "That were close. Yer like some hero in a story-tale!"

Cat couldn't help but grin. "Nothing like that."

"So, you made yer own way after that?" Emma asked. "With that fat purse?"

Cat's grin faltered. "No," she admitted finally. "The purse, it turned out, was worthless. Full of iron disks made to feel like coins." She laughed ruefully at the memory. "Rusted, too, so not even worth their weight in iron."

Emma gasped. "All that for nothing? Who'd carry such a thing?"

Cat sighed. "Someone with a very different plan, I suppose."

CHAPTER 19

After supper, Cat retired, and Emma came with her to help her ready for bed.

Cat intended to have Emma's secret, now that she'd told her own. She wanted to know what had brought the girl to Roffe's employ and what hold the man had over her.

She waited until she was in her nightgown, seated at her dressing table, with Emma behind her brushing her hair, then reminded the girl that their earlier talk was not complete.

"You never told me your secret, Emma."

Emma's hands stopped drawing the brush through Cat's hair and there was a long pause. Cat kept herself from looking at the girl in the dressing mirror, instead she busied herself with a bit of ribbon laid out there.

"It's nothing near as exciting as yours, miss, believe me."

"But I want to know," Cat said. "I want to know all there is about you."

There was a longer silence and Cat scarcely dared to breathe. She felt like she was in the garden, a bit of seed on her outstretched palm, holding still as stone so that a sparrow might alight there.

"You'll hate me, miss," Emma whispered.

"I could never hate you, Emma." Cat felt it was the truest thing she'd ever said.

She rose and took the hairbrush from Emma's hand to set it aside, then took the hand to guide Emma to the settee. They sat, Emma looking down at her lap, and Cat squeezed her hand.

"I will never hate you, Emma. Please tell me."

For a moment, Cat didn't think she would, then, the girl's breathing gave a little hitch and she squeezed Cat's hand in return — her grip growing tighter as she spoke.

"It weren't but a kiss," she whispered, voice barely audible.

Cat frowned, not understanding, but waited.

"We was just in the loft, playing like. And there were a bit of a kiss." She swallowed and went on in a rush as though the start of it had burst a dam and now the whole would have nothing but that it was voiced. "But my family's nothing in the village and her Da's the mayor and her brother saw, you see? An' her brother, he says he wants what he saw … an' more from me or he'll tell. But I won't, so's he does. Word spread there were more to it — gossiping, cackling biddies, the lot of them." Her voice turned bitter and angry. "What man'd have a girl there's such rumors about, eh? Not that I'd want a one of them!"

Cat frowned, confused. "A girl?"

She knew what kissing led men and women to — she'd seen it often enough in the alleys off the market. The older boys in the gang all claimed to have done such things, though she doubted that, as there were no girls around for them to practice on and no coin for food, let alone the whores. And there were enough oaths and insults and threats thrown about the gang that she understood some men did the same with men — or boys, for she'd seen more than one of the prettier ones go off with Brandt and come back crying, not wishing to speak of what had gone on. It was frowned on, made fun of, and at risk of gaol or a hanging at Newgate if found out, but it did happen. But both girls?

How ever would that even work?

She'd never had a real interest in that sort of thing — any thought of it had to be stamped down. To even begin to explore it would have meant revealing she was a girl to someone, and that simply wasn't an option. Besides, from what she'd observed in the alleys it was a thing men sought and women provided — if she didn't want to take herself to the buttock brokers herself, then why think about it?

And as for other girls, well, there were either the doxies or the older women of the market — Cat had, as near as she could figure, never spent any time in conversation with another girl for her entire life. Until now, under Roffe's roof.

Until Emma.

The girl's eyes were closed and her grip on Cat's hand was so tight as to be painful.

"Please say you don't hate me, Cat," she whispered.

"Girls?" Cat asked again, her mind still trying to make sense of it — and her own feelings.

She was keenly aware of her hand gripping Emma's, and both of them in the other girl's lap. Her hand, beneath the pain of the tight grip they both had on each other, seemed to burn with the same fire as her leg, which touched Emma's as they sat. It was also, suddenly, very hard to breathe and her head was filled with things — images of Emma in the bath, the feel of Emma brushing her hair, the touch of Emma's fingers brushing against her skin as she helped Cat dress.

Emma opened her eyes and met Cat's gaze.

"I know it's wrong," she said. Her eyes were full of unshed tears. "There were a whole sermon about hellfire the Sunday after, but —"

Cat raised her free hand to Emma's cheek. She wasn't sure why — wasn't sure she was thinking at all, come to that, except to wonder, as her thumb brushed Emma's lips, just how the girl's skin could be so hot without them both bursting into flames where they sat.

Emma's voice trailed off at the touch. She leaned toward Cat, barely an inch. Cat leaned toward her, no more.

Then who moved next, they'd never remember, only that their lips met somewhere in the middle.

CAT WOKE to find herself snuggled against Emma's side, her head nestled against the other girl's shoulder, with one leg over Emma and Emma's arm around her and her hand laid lightly on Cat's hip.

The morning sun filtered through the curtains. It lit a strand of Emma's hair, just in front of Cat's face, which moved with every breath Cat made.

It was, Cat thought, the most splendid morning ever.

More splendid, even, than her first morning waking in this house, when she'd been fed to fullness for the first time she could ever remember.

This morning satisfied a deeper hunger she hadn't even known was there, one which had left her, until now, emptier than she'd known.

A sudden pounding at the bedroom door and Hinds' shrill call of, "Miss Catherine, are you awake?" spoiled the moment, sending both Cat and Emma to bolt upright in the bed.

The bedclothes tumbled to their waists and they each flushed red — from seeing the other, from the other seeing her — which was suddenly very, very different from the times they'd seen each other in the past — and from the sudden knowledge of what Hinds would say if she barged in.

The proper progression of events would have been for Emma to wake Cat, bring her breakfast, help her dress, then Cat could go to her first lesson of the day with Hinds. A quick look at the amount of sunlight filling the room, though, made it clear they'd missed all of that.

Emma scurried from the bed and began rushing about the room, picking up and examining what was an astonishing amount of clothing tossed about with abandon.

"Where're me clothes?" Emma whispered. "Here!"

Cat's nightgown, which she'd never made it into the night before, struck her in the face. She shrugged it on and saw that Emma was no closer to collecting her own clothes. The girl had one leg in her drawers, holding them up with one hand, while she frantically searched the floor.

"There was the time we spent in the tub again," Cat suggested.

Emma froze, looked to her, then her eyes widened in horror.

"Oh, Lord, that's why me drawers're damp!"

The door rattled.

"Miss Catherine? Why is the door locked? Are you there?"

Emma rushed to the bathing room and her exit was followed by a wail of despair.

"Miss Catherine?" Hinds called from the hallway.

Emma reappeared holding her sodden gown before her. Cat nearly giggled, only holding it back for the look of horror on Emma's face. Yes, they had been in a bit of a hurry to get to the water and salt — the reminder that such would ease Emma's bruising being the thinnest of excuses at that point.

Emma was near tears now, though, and Cat understood why. Despite the humor of the situation, Hinds would certainly leap to the worst, correct, conclusion, and there was no telling what might happen then. Emma'd already had to flee her home once over such a thing.

"Miss Catherine, you're late for your lessons and I can't find that girl anywhere! Are you in there? Are you awake?"

"Toss that back," Cat whispered and left the bed, she opened her wardrobe and grabbed one of her poorer nightgowns, it was still better than a maid would have, but close enough. She gave that to Emma. "Put that on and come back to the bed."

"What?"

"Miss Catherine! I have sent Mistress Singley for the key and I shall enter!"

"Now!" Cat ordered, and Emma did, tossing her dripping gown back toward the tub where it made a sodden squish and eeling into the nightgown.

Cat knelt on the bed, gesturing urgently for Emma to join her.

"Cat, I don't understand —"

"Here," Cat said, tossing Emma a pillow and taking one up herself. "Now hit me."

"What?"

There was the sound of a key in the bedroom lock.

Cat drew her pillow back and struck Emma full in the face with it.

"Hit me!"

Emma stared at her wide-eyed for a moment, then tapped Cat on the shoulder with the pillow.

Cat ripped the end of her pillow and swung it hard, sending feathers in a white cascade across the room, the bed, and everywhere, covering both girls like fallen snow.

The door opened and Hinds entered with the feather flurry in full form, barely reaching the height of their arc to gently settle to every surface in the room, especially Cat and Emma.

"What is this nonsense?" Hinds yelled.

Behind her, Cat saw Singley first narrow her eyes, then chuckle.

Cat stared at Hinds, doing her very best to appear young and naughty, but not so very naughty as she'd actually been. There was an art to it, she'd learned in the markets — once caught, it's best to own up to *something,* just not what you were really about.

She set the empty pillowcase to the side, watching Hinds' eyes follow it.

"I'm terribly sorry, Mistress Hinds," Cat said. "We were playing and the time must have got away from us."

"Playing?"

Singley chortled, shook her head, and left the doorway.

"Yes," Cat said. "I couldn't sleep last night — it was very dark and I was having nightmares, you see, so I called Emma from her room to stay with me. And then this morning —" She took up a handful of feathers and let them fall through her fingers. "— the pillows were just there." Cat lowered her eyes. "I'm very sorry I was late for lessons."

Hinds' jaw clenched and she sighed heavily. "We will resume those lessons as soon as you are dressed."

"Yes, Mistress Hinds," Cat said, not raising her eyes.

Hinds' eyes narrowed and she looked about to say more, but she spun on her heel and stormed out, pulling the door shut behind her with a muttered, *"Children!"*

No sooner had the door clicked shut, than Emma's look of terror at being discovered gave way to hysterical giggles. She fell back on the bed, laughing, and Cat with her. The two rolled about, holding their sides, for a time. When the laughter began to subside, of course, one or the other of them, and who started it one couldn't tell, would poke or tickle the other, setting the whole thing off again. And one cannot, under any circumstances, have a bit of tickling that doesn't eventually become a full-on wrestling match.

Cat lost, as she intended to do, for she didn't feel it was fair to use any of what she'd learned of fighting against her friend.

She grinned and squirmed deliciously as Emma pinned her hands above her and used her full weight to try and keep her still — which, in truth, Emma didn't try very hard to do.

Their struggles both ceased and they sobered at the same time, as if by some mutual signal, with their faces very close, lips almost touching.

"I should get you dressed and to your lessons," Emma said, her voice rough.

"Yes, I suppose," Cat agreed. "Hinds may return if we're too long about it, and the door's not locked."

Reluctantly, but slowly and not without each darting little pecks and kisses to whatever part of the other happened to present itself, they disentangled themselves from the bedclothes and began to dress.

"Wear one of my dressing gowns to get to your room," Cat said. "Yours will never dry in time."

Emma nodded as she pulled Cat's stays tight and tied them.

"That was clever," Emma said, "with the pillows. I thought we was caught, sure."

"It's … well, it's like a setup in the market," Cat said. "One boy to let the baker see him fingering the buns while another pulls the till —" She gestured at the feathers strewn about. "— the lesser crime hides the larger."

CHAPTER 20

*R*offe's behavior, and what further secrets he might himself be hiding, nagged at Cat.

She watched him carefully the next few times he came to the townhouse. His answer when asked where he spent his nights was always to simply say his "club."

There were some times that Roffe came to the townhouse only for a brief visit — he'd go to his workshop, then leave again as though retrieving something, having Clanton drive the carriage for him instead of a hired coachman. It was around these occasions that Cat determined to follow him and learn more of his doings.

She waited until Roffe went to his workshop and Clanton left to ready the carriage, then retired to her room, but not to study or rest.

Instead, she quickly stripped off her restrictive dress and under-clothes and put on the looser, dark clothes in which she trained with Clanton, then skinnied through her window. The bars had never been repaired from when she'd escaped after Clanton locked her in, almost as if Roffe were daring her to leave.

As if she would. The taste of this luxury, just the luxury of enough food at every meal, was enough for her to know she'd never give it up, no matter the cost. If it meant learning all Clanton and the others chose to teach, in the manner they chose to teach it — well, she'd accept the bruises with as much grace as she could muster. Those were skills that would keep her safe and fed her whole life long.

It was more difficult to squeeze through the bars than she remembered, she'd grown some, and in awkward places, but she made it. Then twisted to grasp the little ledge above the window and pull herself out and up. Another handhold a bit higher, a scramble to find purchase for her soft shoes, and she was climbing up the wall. Past Roffe's workspaces and onto the roof.

She'd barely cleared the edge of the roof when she heard the rattle of a carriage and Clanton pulled around onto the street.

Cat looked around and judged the night. There was little fog yet, though that might change, so she'd have a good view of the carriage for a long way, and the roof was dry, for a wonder. The streetlights were lit, as well, adding to her advantage, and she knew these rooftops well, thanks to Clanton's little tasks.

She heard, rather than saw, Roffe leave the townhouse and enter the carriage. She knew well enough to follow by ear for a time, as she knew how Clanton was so aware of his surroundings.

As the carriage started off, she rose and followed along the roof, keeping well back from the edge to be out of sight.

It was as though a great weight had been lifted from her shoulders — she hadn't felt this free in quite some time, even when running the rooftops. Those sojourns had been at Clanton's direction, not her own will, so this was very different.

The carriage turned and she had to leave the roof for the street, darting through an alleyway to catch it at the next street over. Her breath came easily as she ran, keeping to the shadows.

Through the city they went, Cat sometimes taking to the rooftops again, sometimes alleyways, and sometimes simply walking hurriedly if the street was crowded and the carriage slowed. To those around her, her clothes were enough like those of the poor that they paid no heed other than the occasional look of distaste.

Eventually their destination became clear — one of the larger estates on the outskirts of the city. Not townhomes set on the street, but large manors on open lands, set about with walls to keep the Mob at bay. It was an area of enough wealth that Cat began to worry she'd stand out too much with her dress. The rooftop garb would work well enough, with the skirts down, in most areas, but not the very wealthy.

Roffe's carriage joined a line of others and when it reached the gate, Cat dashed around a corner of the wall.

She set her sights on a bit of tree branch overhanging the wall, one of many in a small copse set along it, and ran hard. She launched herself up the wall as Clanton had taught her, hands and feet scraping on the rough stone to find just enough purchase to propel her the tiniest bit higher, stretched out her arms, and gave one last push with her feet.

The branch slapped into her palms, bowing a bit under her weight, but she swung herself up enough to clear the wall and drop to the other side. Her foot came down on log or stone and she let that leg collapse to avoid turning her ankle, letting herself fall to the ground and roll instead of landing upright.

It was more noise than she'd like, though she didn't think anyone, even out on the grounds, would hear over the noises from the house.

Carriages clattered up the drive, then edged forward as the ones ahead dropped their occupants at the front. Music, voices, and laughter, spilled out of the house and sounded through the grounds, as did the lights.

Cat made her way to the edge of the copse of trees and settled into the shadows. She was in time to see Roffe exit his carriage, greet a man still on the steps of the house, and enter with him. Clanton pulled the carriage away with the others, presumably to wait upon Roffe.

She frowned. This was not at all what she'd imagined Roffe was up to on those evenings he didn't have her accompany him. She'd thought these were the times when he went about his business of theft and burglary. She'd wanted to show him that she was ready to join him in that, to expand her training. But this? Yet another dinner party? Then why shouldn't she attend? Why would he go alone?

No, there was something more to it than appeared.

She watched more guests arrive; then the line of carriages became shorter and shorter until the last clattered away to wait upon its master. The last guest climbed the stairs and entered the house. The servants who'd been assisting with the carriages and the guests dispersed to other duties as well, leaving a lonely pair of footmen to wait upon any late arrivals.

The music and noise from the house increased and Cat was tempted to approach to look in the windows.

Instead she pondered the mystery of why Roffe was here without her. She was still convinced that these excursions were when he plied his trade. She supposed being an invited guest was a fine cover for a thief, but what could he really make off with? Whatever could fit in his pockets? Jewelry, she supposed, would make a fine haul and be easy to find if one were already in the house.

She glared at the house as though it were responsible for her confusion, then took a deep breath.

She'd wait, she'd watch, and see what there was to see. If not this time, then the next she'd discover what Roffe was up to.

CHAPTER 21

The night dragged on and Cat kept to her place, resisting the urge to sneak up to the house and peer in the windows. There was no one on the grounds and the lights inside would keep her hidden, but she felt it unlikely she'd catch sight of Roffe there. Instead, her eyes scanned the whole of the house, looking for anything out of the ordinary.

After some time, surely after the dinner itself was over and the guests had moved on to whatever entertainment was being offered, she saw something that seemed odd.

A light shone in one of the upper windows — door, really, as it opened onto a balcony — but not the bright light of a well-lit room — this was the flickering of a single candle, only dimmer and it came and went as though being repeatedly extinguished and relit.

That's odd enough for a look.

She scanned the grounds to be sure no one was about. A bit of mist was rising — still not a great deal, though she suspected there'd be more in the city itself.

The bare sliver of a moon crept behind a cloud and Cat moved, scurrying from shadow to shadow, bush to tree, and finally into the deeper shadows beside the house itself.

From a distance the wall looked smooth, but up close it presented Cat with all the handholds she needed. Window sills, overhangs, decorative work, and the odd bit of mortar crumbled away from a gap between stones, were her pathway up — past the ground floor, then the first, to the edge of the rail around the second-floor balcony behind which she'd spotted the light.

She lowered herself out of sight again, hanging onto the rail with just her fingertips, and edged her way around the balcony to the other side where there were more shadows to hide in. A thick drape obscured the glass doorway on that side. Once there, she pulled herself over the rail and crouched in the shadows — still for the moment as she waited for any outcry or other sign she'd been noticed.

The light in the room still shone periodically.

After a moment, Cat peeked her head along the glass of the door until she could see around the drapery.

She found she'd been right in her assumption that any odd happening would be Roffe, for it was him she saw within the room. He held a candle, but it was shrouded in a thin, metal tube that let its light out in only one direction, and only a bit at that. The bottom of the shroud was bound in leather to protect the holder's hand from the metal heating up, and Cat could immediately see how useful such a thing would be in keeping the light less visible to others.

As she watched, Roffe opened a drawer in a large standing chest and shone the light within. He reached a hand in and shifted the drawer's contents, frowning down at it.

Well he's a bold one, burgling the house after eating their dinner.

Roffe moved on to the next drawer and then the next, taking the time to feel under and behind each drawer before closing it.

Cat took a moment to examine the room. It was clearly a man's bedroom, with large, heavy furniture, intricately carved, but evoking images of solidity and the trunks of the trees it had come from. A desk sat against the wall nearest the balcony, as heavy as the rest, and full of drawers and cubby holes — not the delicate sort of writing table one might find in a lady's chamber. Cat frowned.

I'd think he'd have more luck in the lady of the house's rooms, if he's after valuables.

That was where the jewels would be, she was certain, but Roffe seemed intent on rifling every nook and cranny of this room. Moreover, Cat could clearly see a box on top of the chest which must certainly contain the man's cuff links and other items of value, yet Roffe ignored it in favor of rifling drawers and an apparent search for secret compartments.

Roffe froze and cocked his head as though listening for something, then turned quickly, casting his light and scanning all about the room.

Cat ducked back out of sight, her heart pounding. Had he seen her? And, if he had, would this be more cause for him to punish her or Emma? That thought chilled her and she regretted following Roffe, but her curiosity still had hold of her.

The light no longer shone through the glass of the balcony door, so Cat crept to the drapery's edge again and peered around it. Roffe was standing where he had before, candle set to cast its glow away from the balcony, but he seemed to be looking at her in the darkness.

Well, if he'd seen her, he gave no sign, and soon smiled and went back about his business of rifling drawers. If he had — she was in it anyway and might as well watch.

Finally, he seemed to find what he'd been searching for as he pulled a bundle from behind one of the drawers.

Cat strained to see and Roffe accommodated her by taking the bundle to the desk and seating himself. She edged back into the shadows so that a casual turn of his head wouldn't allow him to catch sight of her, but also rose a little so that she could see the desk's top.

All of this for a bundle of papers?

For that was what Roffe was leafing through. And not the new banknotes or something else of value, so far as she could tell, but simple letters and leather-bound, handwritten volumes. She wished the light from Roffe's muted candle were brighter, so she could better see what he found so engrossing about the papers. She could see, though, that the papers were not uniform — they came in a number of types of paper and different hands, some grouped together and bound with ribbons, others inside folded pieces of heavier stock.

Whatever they were, Roffe was apparently satisfied with them. He rose from the desk, tucked the various papers and volumes into his pockets, and looked around the room.

Roffe's head came up and he cocked it to one side, then he hurriedly extinguished his candle and rushed to the bedside where he dropped to the floor and slid himself under the bed just as the room's door opened, spilling in light from the hall outside.

A man entered, presumably the lord's valet. Cat pressed herself into the deepest shadows, wondering what Roffe would do now — he was on the verge of being caught red-handed rifling through the lord's bed chamber. All it would take was one look under the bed or a single dropped item. She readied herself to make some noise as a distraction to draw the valet's attention and allow Roffe to make his escape.

The valet began arranging the room, turning down the bed, and pulling clothing from various places. Cat realized that it must now be later than she'd thought — that she'd been waiting and watching Roffe for longer, and the party was now over with the household readying for sleep. Roffe's absence at the end must not have been noted — they'd likely assumed he left without taking his leave. She wondered at that, as his host might think ill of him for it and word might get around to others. It seemed a poor burglar who'd let himself stand out like that on the same night he looted his host's bedchamber.

Still she waited, for if the lord of this house was about to be in his bed with Roffe underneath it, then her mentor would have even more need of a distraction to make his escape.

After a few more minutes, another man entered the bed chamber. This one well-dressed and Cat assumed he was the lord — an assumption proved out as the valet assisted him in changing into bed clothes.

She heard the murmur of voices and edged closer to the glass of the doors, straining to hear.

"That will be all, Franklin," the man said. "I've some work to do, but you needn't attend me."

"As you wish, m'lord," the valet said, but still took the time to pour a small glass of dark red wine from a decanter he'd placed on the desk.

The valet left and the man in the dressing gown sat at the desk, took a sip of the wine, and pulled a bundle of papers from a drawer. He began leafing through them, his forehead creased with concentration.

There was movement deeper in the room and she saw Roffe's leg come out from under the bed. She ducked down further and hoped to become visible to him from his position, fearing that he believed the man had left the room with the valet, though why he might, when the room was still well-lit, she couldn't tell.

Is he a fool?

She'd thought, hoped, that Roffe had more sense than this — instead, she watched in bewilderment as Roffe not only slid from beneath the bed, but stood and made his way toward the man at the desk, then further bewildered as he spoke.

"Lord Harrington."

The man at the desk spun around.

"What!" His expression went from startled to puzzlement to anger. "Roffe? What are you doing in my chambers, man!"

"I'm afraid, my lord, that we have some business to attend to." Roffe almost sounded regretful.

"Business? Why didn't you say so earlier? And where did you disappear to? And why, again, are you in my chambers?" Lord Harrington shook his head. "Never mind that, in fact. I think we have no business at all to discuss. Now I'll ask you to leave!"

Roffe smiled and moved closer to him. "You may ask, my lord, but still there's a bit of business."

Cat thought that though he called the man "my lord" it didn't sound respectful at all, he said it with a mocking tone that she could hear even through the glass.

"You impertinent cur! I'll have you whipped into the street!"

Harrington took a deep breath as though to call for his servants to do just that, but Roffe moved quickly, more quickly than Cat expected and possibly more quickly than she'd seen Clanton do. In the moment of Harrington drawing breath, Roffe was at his side, one hand behind the man's head at the nape of his neck and the other pressing a blade to his throat.

Harrington froze, first from surprise, then a look of fear crossed his face. The blade winked in the room's light as Roffe twisted it against the man's neck.

"Think on what you do next, my lord," Roffe said. "Who will come first if you cry out? Your valet? He's quite old, I think, and not so very fit. He'll fall first, but who will come next in response to your cry? Your wife's rooms are near, are they not? Your daughter? Your son? Will they come to see what causes their dear papa to yell in the night?" Roffe leaned close and stared into Harrington's eyes. "We have business, my lord, best kept between our two selves. Please nod if you agree this is the case."

Harrington nodded slowly, wincing as the blade at his throat pressed tighter. A thin trickle of blood ran down to stain his dressing gown.

Roffe removed his hand from Harrington's mouth, but kept the blade in place. With quick motions he pulled leather cords from his pocket, looped them around the man's arms and the chair, and pulled them tight.

"I'll step back now, my lord, for our discussion. Have no doubt I'll take what steps I must to keep our business between us."

Roffe stepped back, the blade disappearing into some pocket of his evening clothes. He grasped the decanter of wine as he did so.

Harrington seemed to recover his courage with the disappearance of the blade.

"What is it you want, Roffe? What's the meaning of all this? You can't think to get away with it."

"I wish to speak to you of your investments, my lord, and do you a service."

"What? Investments and a service?" Harrington scowled at him. "You have some scheme you want money for and think this is the way to get it?"

Roffe shook his head and raised the wine decanter to his lips. He took a long drink.

"You vulgar little —"

"I'm afraid you misunderstand me all entire, my lord," Roffe said, the courtesy of his words offset by his interrupting Harrington. "The investment and service are unrelated matters — or, rather, the acquisition of the investment allows me the opportunity to offer you the service, you see?"

"No, I do not."

Roffe drank again. "Are you acquainted with Chatwin Aubert?"

"Of course I am, man, that's a silly question!"

Roffe nodded. "Indeed. One would assume you are acquainted with the man when you've made such an investment in him."

"Aubert and I have no joint dealings, what are you —"

Roffe pulled the bundle of papers and notebooks from a pocket and began leafing through them. As he did so, Harrington broke off speaking and turned quite pale. His eyes darted to the place Roffe had found the papers, then to another drawer, then back to Roffe.

Roffe raised an eyebrow. "An investment is not always monetary, is it, my lord? An investment of time, of information, of knowledge — all may show returns, yes?"

He stood and made his way to the standing chest. He set the bundle of papers on its top and slid the drawer Harrington had glanced at from its place.

"This one, my lord?" he asked. "I missed something, yes?" He felt at the sides and back of the drawer, then held a hand below it and the other inside. "Ah, yes, a false bottom, I see." He threw the drawers contents to the floor and pried up the thin bottom to remove yet another sheaf of papers. "Clever you, to use more than one device." Roffe leafed through the papers, murmuring to himself, his eyebrows raised. "So many men attached to your strings, my lord. Debts, indiscretions, peccadilloes ..." He rifled through one of the bound journals. "Oh, my, this one's been a naughty lad with the books, hasn't he?"

Harrington swallowed. "So, Aubert hired you to get back the evidence of his indiscretions? You're some kind of thief, is that it?"

"Not exactly, my lord, though I'm known to take a thing or two which isn't strictly mine."

Roffe placed the new bundle and those he'd found before onto the bed. He stepped over to Harrington, one hand in his pocket. In a single motion, he clapped a hand over Harrington's mouth, and knelt, taking his other hand from his pocket and slapping it down on the man's thigh.

Harrington jerked in place, his eyes went wide, and Cat heard a muffled scream. He was struggling to get away, but Roffe kept him in his seat. Cat edged forward to see what Roffe was doing that pained the man so, but so far as she could tell, he only gripped the leg tightly. That grip, though, must be excruciatingly painful for the lord. His leg shook with tremors and his face gleamed with sweat.

After a moment, Harrington's struggles ceased. He was breathing heavily, as though still in pain but the worst of it having eased.

"I'll free your mouth now, my lord, so that we may continue our chat, but you mustn't scream, you understand? There'll be more if you scream."

Harrington's Adam's apple bobbed up and down. His eyes were still wide, but he nodded.

"Very good, my lord."

Roffe slowly took his hand from Harrington's mouth and when the man remained silent he stood and backed a pace away, leaving an odd, brass disk nearly an inch thick on Harrington's leg.

"Who are you?" Harrington asked, his voice raspy.

"You know who I am, what will happen next, and you know, though you haven't quite accepted it yet, that there is nothing you can do to stop me." Roffe nodded at the disk. "I have a great many more of those, should they prove necessary to convince you, and each will be more painful than the last."

Harrington licked his lips. "Some of those men'll not thank you for the documents' return. They'll turn on you, fearing what you know. I can make it worth your while — safely worth your while, understand?" He swallowed. "What do you want? Let me be and I'll get it for you, I swear."

"I'm sorry, my lord, but I do have a contract to fulfill. You understand, reputation is all in my business, yes? You needn't worry about me, though, I have no intention of attempting to turn these over to their proper owners — none other than those belonging to the gentleman I'm contracted with, that is."

Harrington chuckled, winced, tried to ease his leg's position, and winced more. "You'll use them yourself, then?" He snorted derision.

"As necessary, my lord, and your dogs will find me a far easier master than yourself. That was your error, you know? You pushed too hard — made it a better bet for a man to come to me than simply do as you bid." Roffe smiled. "It's grown quite late, I'm afraid I must be off, but I do wish to offer you a service before I go."

"A service?"

Roffe nodded. "An exchange might be a better term." He eyed the bundles of papers. "I don't believe this is the whole of what you have, nor the best of it, and it would be a shame for your hard work to end with you. Tell me where the other documents are and you will gain my services for one name. Name the man, whisper it in my ear, and he will meet me." Harrington's eyes narrowed and Roffe sighed. "No, my lord, I'm afraid that won't work at all. You may not name me, nor my principal, nor some far off Oriental you imagine I'll waste my time pursuing to give you a bit of vengeance on me. This is a … a personal service, you understand? Someone known to you. Someone you may wish to have follow you close behind on your coming journey."

Harrington looked around the room. He attempted to straighten his leg again, but winced. He closed his eyes, shoulders slumped, as though resigned.

"Is it a bargain, my lord?" Roffe asked. "Or must I be on my way without a name."

"Lady Winthrope," Harrington said, eyes still closed.

For the first time, Roffe looked genuinely surprised.

"A lady? That is novel. She must have truly angered you in some way — no, I have no need of the reason. The name is sufficient. And the location of the remaining papers, my lord?"

"Albert Brecht. A solicitor. He has a sealed box in his keeping."

"A solicitor? Interesting."

"There are some things one doesn't wish found, if they're found, in one's own keeping."

Roffe nodded understanding.

Harrington's eyes were still closed. He clenched his teeth. "Be about it man. Be done. Only make it quick, will you?"

Roffe moved again, clamping his hand to Harrington's mouth and pulling his other from a pocket. Cat caught a glimpse of another bronze disk in it before he clapped it to Harrington's abdomen.

The muffled scream came to her even through the door's glass. Harrington's whole body tensed, lifting him off the chair, but Roffe stayed with him. The lord writhed and twisted, trying to escape from whatever the disk did to him, but Roffe held him tight. Cat wanted to look away, but she seemed frozen and unable to move. Harrington's agony seemed to last forever, until he finally sagged to the chair, his head lolling to the side. A thin trickle blood ran from his lips.

"I'm sorry, my lord," Roffe said softly, retrieving the leather thongs binding Harrington's body to the chair, "but my contract specified otherwise."

Roffe looked around the room. He secreted the bundles of papers and journals in various pockets, returned the removed drawer to the chest along with the false bottom and its former contents. The decanter of wine he returned to the desk.

He grasped the brass disk on Harrington's leg and gave the casing a twist. Cat could hear, now that there were no muffled screams, an odd buzzing *whir*, and then Roffe lifted the disk and placed it back in his pocket. He repeated this with the disk on Harrington's abdomen.

Finally, he spun Harrington's chair around so that it faced the desk and arranged the man's arms and head to appear as if he'd been working and then slumped forward onto the desk's surface.

He stepped back and regarded the scene with a frown, then shook his head and moved Harrington's glass of wine just next to one outstretched hand. With a fingertip, he gently toppled the glass, sending a spill of wine across the desk.

Roffe stepped back, turned full circle to take in the entire room, and gave a satisfied nod.

"Run along home now, Catherine," he said. "I'll join you there shortly."

CHAPTER 22

t first Cat froze as Roffe spoke to her — or, perhaps, she was already frozen in place from the horror of watching him kill Lord Harrington. Then she fled — from being found out, from what she'd seen, and from the chilling implications of what she'd heard.

She leapt up, flung herself over the balcony rail, and barely felt the stones of the manor wall as she descended. Later she'd remember it almost as a fall, where she'd only grasp a foot or hand hold briefly to slow herself.

Once on the ground, she ran swiftly for the wall, making no attempt at stealth or concealment. It was by luck, more than design, that she found the tree with the overhanging branch, clambered up it oblivious to the scraping of the bark her haste caused, and dropped to the other side of the wall.

She paused then, back to the wall, a bit out of breath from her run. The street was deserted, it being so late, but she could hear the *clop-clop-clop* of a horse in the distance. The fog had thickened, leaving a yellowish globe of light around each streetlamp, but much of the rest in shadows as the mist seemed to eat the lamplight.

Cat took a moment, trying to think. Roffe was not what he'd said — not a thief at all, but some sort of hired killer.

It wasn't the death that bothered her, she'd seen death before. Waking up to a dead beggar on the street outside wasn't uncommon; she'd seen men and boys beaten to death by her gang and others, even a pair of her own gang, older then, but remembered, taken up and hanged at Newgate — and hadn't that been the last joke for them to see their old mates picking pockets in the crowd as they were set to do the dance.

No, it wasn't the death.

It was the coldness of it. And, truth to tell, the hiring of it. There was something about that which frightened her far more than the bloodiest brawl she'd ever witnessed.

The *crack* of a branch sounded from within the walls and Cat was off again.

Roffe hadn't sounded angry, not as he had in the Mechanicals Room, but she didn't want to see him — not until she'd had time to think, that is. Perhaps not ever again.

She ran, not really knowing where, until a pain in her side made her come panting to a stop.

One hand clutching her side, the other bracing herself against the wall of an alley, she felt she'd finally had distance enough, or was exhausted enough, to stop. She looked around, finding something familiar about the place, and realized with a start that she must have run instinctively to someplace she felt safe — the alley behind her old gang's hidey-hole.

Some part of her must have been guiding her path, thinking to take her someplace safe. This alley, and their flop in the abandoned building, had been such a place — safe … once. No longer though. She wasn't safe here or from her former gang — if they recognized her, Brandt had sworn to kill her; if they didn't, then she was an interloper and they'd deal with that. Either way this was no safe place for her any longer.

"Told you I heard a noise."

The voice behind her made Cat spin around.

Brandt was there. A year older, and bigger — Cat was surprised he was still part of the gang and hadn't moved up to run with the older boys. But then Brandt had always liked to be in charge. It wasn't surprising that he'd hang on to the place where he was the biggest and strongest and could be the leader for as long as possible.

"Get him," Brandt said.

In the shadows of the alley, Brandt must not have recognized her. She was taller now, and with longer hair than she'd kept while in the gang, and she had the skirts of her rooftop garb bound up so that she must appear to be a boy of about Brandt's age in the darkness.

The shadows moved all around her. Cat had been so lost in her thoughts that she hadn't noticed Brandt and the others approach. Now the gang came out of the alley's shadows — all the little dark places made by the abandoned boxes and barrels and other trash. They surrounded her and hands grabbed at her. She struggled, but she was tired from her run and confused by what she'd seen, so her heart wasn't in it.

"Hey!" Osraed called as his hands grasped at something he recognized despite Cat having little of it. "It's a girl!"

Cat's mind focused then and she struggled for real. She'd seen what happened to girls caught out by one of the gangs, even her own. The younger members wouldn't take part, but those who'd gotten older — Brandt, Dome, and even Osraed — would.

"Hold her!" Dome yelled.

She almost broke free of Osraed, but Dome's grip on her other arm tightened and he jerked her about. Other boys from the gang rushed in and grasped at her as well. There were simply too many of them for her to break their grip and escape.

"Brandt, it's me!" she tried, hoping that the surprise of seeing their old mate once again might get her freed. "It's Cat, don't do this!"

"Cat?" Brandt stepped in front of her, squinting at her face in the dim light.

Osraed and Dome held her arms tightly, not letting go at all, and someone had a hold of her from behind, his arm snaked around her neck. Even with what Clanton had taught her of rough and tumble fighting and what Roffe had shown her of his own methods, they were too many and had too tight a grip for her to break free.

"Runt?" Brandt asked, looking closer. His face grew puzzled, then he reached out to grasp her chest, probing and squeezing cruelly. "*Why you —*" His hand moved to between her legs, grasping there, but finding nothing.

"A girl all them years?" he asked. He lashed out to slap her across the face. "You lying *bitch.*"

"Cat?" Osraed murmured.

"It's me, Osraed," Cat whispered back. "Please don't do this, I can explain. I —"

"Thievin' and lyin'?" Osraed's voice was soft and full of hurt. "All them years you were a girl and lyin' to your mates like that?"

"Put her on the ground, lads. She lied and kept me from havin' a taste while she ran with us, I'll have it now," Brandt said, stepping back. His hands went to his breeches. "On the ground now."

HANDS PAWED AT HER, feet kicked her legs out from under her, and she went to the hard cobbles of the alleyway. Then there were more hands pulling at her clothes, exposing her to the chill, damp air. She struggled and might have got in a few good blows, but there were too many for her to fight off. There was pain everywhere as they struck at her in return — a blow to her head that dazed her, the sharp piecing of a bit of glass underneath her.

She screamed — not that she thought anyone would come to help, that sort of thing didn't happen in this neighborhood, but because she had to.

A hand covered her mouth and she managed to bite it, but then it was replaced with a bit of cloth, stuffed in and held in place.

Brandt's weight came on top of her, his face near hers and his breath rank and hot against her cheek.

He grunted, shifting atop her as she struggled. His knees forced her legs apart and she felt the slimy water of the alley's floor on her bare skin.

"Stay still, damn you!"

Brandt rose up and struck her in the face, knocking her head back against the cobbles and dazing her.

Cat struggled against the haze to open her eyes, struggled against leaden limbs to strike out at her attackers, struggled to twist herself away from his probing weight, but her vision blurred and her eyelids drooped. She forced them open, saw Brandt smile as she stilled, then saw him look up, past her down the alleyway, and frown.

CHAPTER 23

*C*at jerked awake, heart pounding in her chest. She flung herself from her bed to put her back to the wall, eyes taking in the room — her room. Her room at the townhouse.

She took a deep breath, calming herself. Memories of the night before coming back in fits and jerks. Her head pounded and ached, and her body was bruised and battered, but she did remember bits of it after Brandt's last blow.

Brandt looking up and then something striking him and knocking him away. The other boys, as well, scrambling to their feet. They released her, but she could do no more than roll to her side and try to crawl through the chill muck of the alley toward the nearest wall and some sort of shelter.

Then there were new hands on her and she batted them away, but they persisted. Lifted her, flung her over a shoulder with less care than would be given a sack of potatoes, and carried her away.

It must have been Clanton, she decided. *Followed me and came to rescue.*

That made sense.

She was still dressed in the clothes from last night, her roof-running garb of green and grey. The trousers were pulled up, but

162

loosely tied. They'd slid down to her hips as she left the bed, so she pulled them up and tied them tighter, then straightened from the half-crouch she'd taken in her initial fright.

Another deep breath calmed her, then another and she was almost able to think straight.

There was what she should do, now that she knew Roffe's true calling — and what he would do, now that he knew she knew.

Cat considered that.

He might throw her out. She should run, herself.

She wanted no part of that game, killing for hire, no matter the wealth it might have brought Roffe, but where was she to go? She had nothing save what he provided.

No, that wasn't quite true — she had the skills she'd learned. He might have provided them, but he couldn't take them away. The lock-picking, the woodcraft, the fighting skills —

Which would have stood her in good stead last night if only she'd kept her wits about her and not been grabbed so unawares, something she vowed to never allow again.

Even Hinds' teachings were valuable. She could move, at least for a time, in nearly any level of society thanks to that.

All of those were hers now and she could make a decent life as a thief, no matter if she fled Roffe.

She frowned.

What would Roffe do, though, now she knew his secret?

He wouldn't just let her go — he had some plan for her, she was certain — but, neither, did she think he'd harm her. He'd not seemed angry at her being outside the window where he'd killed that man — only … amused? Amused, and told her to run along home.

So, she might still have a place here, if she wanted it — which she didn't. But she didn't think she was in any immediate danger from Roffe.

There was a noise from elsewhere in the house, so Clanton must be at home. That and the sudden rumbling of her stomach decided her — whatever she did, even run, she'd want a full stomach for it.

She left her room — changing to other clothing could wait.

Clanton wouldn't be offended by the faint stench of alley still on her, and she was too hungry to care. The teachings of her time on the streets were still with her, at least in that — food first, if you can, and all else can wait.

Downstairs, though, was no Clanton, and neither in the kitchen. No food, either, as though he'd not made or not yet returned from his morning trip to the local pub. She checked the time and found it not so late that she should be certain he'd have returned, so perhaps the noise she'd heard had been him going out for it.

Then the noise came again — from upstairs.

"Clanton?" she called.

He didn't often go upstairs, save to her rooms, so she should have passed him on her way down.

Another sound, a dull *thump*, and this from up the stairs again — which would make it from Roffe's rooms, where Clanton never went at all if Roffe was not about.

"Clanton?"

No answer and that settled Cat on the source of the noises. It must be Roffe, decided to stay the night in his rooms and deal with her.

"Mister Roffe?"

There was no answer, so Cat climbed the stairs. She might as well face him now as later, and see what he had in mind for her.

The door to Roffe's room was open. The curtains were pulled tight against the morning sun, but a fire burned in the hearth, casting light and shadows equally throughout the room.

"Mister Roffe?" she tried again.

No answer, so she went to the doorway.

The thumping must have been Roffe moving the furniture about. The two wing-backed chairs and their round table, which normally sat against the wall, had been moved to the foot of the bed facing the portrait. A bottle and glasses sat on the table and Roffe, face hidden by the deep wings, but recognizable by the same clothes he'd worn the night before, sat in the far chair.

"Come in and have a seat, Catherine, I'm certain you have questions."

Cat entered the room. She walked to where she could see Roffe's face, but didn't sit. He didn't seem angry — only still amused, with a wry grin, but also melancholy, as shown by the set of his eyes.

"A seat, I said, and a drink if you like."

"It's a bit early," Cat said.

She sat, but kept to the edge of her seat. The chairs were positioned so that she couldn't see Roffe without leaning forward and turning her head, the chairs' wings blocked him from view, but she could see the portrait quite well right in front of her.

"There are some mornings it's never too early, don't you think?" Roffe asked. He raised his own glass and sipped at it. "It'll settle your nerves after last night — and I don't offer this brandy often, so you'll not wish to miss your chance."

Cat took up the empty glass and the decanter to pour herself a bit. She set the decanter down and sniffed, wrinkling her nose at the burn.

This is somehow special?

The first sip burned at a cut on her lip from the night before, and another inside her cheek, and she almost spit it out, but it traced a line of fire down her chest and settled in her stomach where it kindled a deeper warmth. She took a long breath. The drink did relax her, so she took another sip.

"She ran too, you know," Roffe said, gesturing to the portrait with his glass.

"Your brother's wife?"

"Oh, now, Catherine, you're more perceptive than that — don't disappoint me so."

Cat nodded. She settled further back in the chair, allowing herself to relax. Roffe seemed in a talkative mood, not angry at all, so she might find out enough of his plans for her now to make her own plans to leave. Perhaps even not right away — there was food enough here, after all, and a place to sleep. More to learn, she was certain, if she could stomach being around Roffe for the time it took, and all she could learn might help her make her own way.

And there was Emma.

That thought surprised her, and Cat struggled for a moment with the implications. Could she leave the other girl behind? No, she couldn't — she had to admit, at least to herself, that she truly did love her.

That … complicated things.

Roffe seemed to be awaiting an answer, so Cat studied the portrait. She'd wondered more than once why a man might keep a portrait of his brother's family in so prominent a place. Roffe's admission that there was more to it made her think.

Perhaps Roffe himself had been in love with the woman but she'd chosen his brother? That had an appropriately tragic ring to it, given Roffe's line of work. Some conflict where the brother died, perhaps at Roffe's hand …

But, no, she thought it must be simpler than that. Roffe was not, in her experience, so convoluted as all that. The man simply lied when it suited him, and this bit about the brother's family seemed like such a time.

"Not your brother's," Cat said.

"There you go," Roffe said.

"She ran, you said?"

"I met her in Dublin. There on business. Aideen — it means little fire, and she certainly was." Roffe sighed. "I never had any bloody intention of marrying, you understand, it's … not recommended in my line of work."

Cat could hear the wry grin in his words despite not being able to see his face. She remained silent through a long pause, waiting for Roffe to say more.

"She stole my heart," Roffe said, "much as I stole her father's life. She never learned that, of course. Might have suspected it in the end, but I never leave any proof behind, so …"

Roffe leaned forward to take up the bottle and refill his glass.

"Don't put the bottle so far back," he said.

"You killed her father?" Cat asked.

"Oh, all right, let's get to that." Roffe sat back again. "As you discovered last evening, I kill people." He paused for a moment. "For money, if you were at all uncertain."

The blunt and unashamed statement of it took Cat by surprise, though, on reflection, she wasn't sure why it should. Roffe had never shown her a bit of shame or embarrassment at any of his actions, so why should this be any different?

"Before you go on with some sort of judgment of it," Roffe went on, "I'll remind you that you were quite all right, enthusiastic even, about the prospect of joining me when you thought it was thievery I was about."

"That's —"

"A life is just another form of property, Catherine, there for the taking. Do you honestly suppose that a man whose name makes it to my ear is not deserving of what I'll bring to him? Would you suggest that the world is somehow made *lesser*, being now bereft of Lord Harrington? The man was a vile, foul villain — a blackmailer and worse. There're a dozen or more fine citizens of our city cheering his demise at this very moment. They wake to learn that they are free of his depredations and rejoice."

"And yet, she ran," Cat said.

Roffe sighed, a long, drawn out affair.

"She ran," he allowed. "I had a mere two years with my little fire, then the babe was born. She changed after that — became more … cautious, is perhaps the term. I was blind to her suspicions and careless. She confronted me not long after this portrait was completed. I denied it, of course, but I could see her suspicions were not allayed." Roffe paused and Cat could hear him drink. "Ah, Aideen, my little fire … she was gone within the year along with the babe."

Cat studied the portrait as Roffe remained silent. There was, she thought, a bit of a resemblance between her and the woman. Now that her hair was longer and allowed to take its natural curl, she could note that. The new knowledge sent a chill through her.

Is that what he wanted her for? Because she resembled his vanished wife? But how could he have known that when he took her off the streets? She'd been grubby then, her face half covered in dirt and grime most days, with her hair hacked short and dressed as a boy.

She'd not noted the resemblance herself until now. But could he have seen it, somehow, and wanted her for that?

She shuddered at the thought and the memory of Brandt the night before came to her. His weight on her and his fumbling as he forced her legs apart. The thought that Roffe might want the same made her stomach churn.

"I searched for her, of course," Roffe said finally. He chuckled. "I sent men to Ireland — a dozen of them, thinking that's where she would go. There was some distant family still and I couldn't think where else she might find help. I misjudged her. I do not often misjudge people so."

He filled his glass again and Cat, when he was done, filled her own. The brandy was working to numb her, both the physical hurts from the night before and her worries about Roffe.

"Would you believe she stayed in London?" Roffe barked laughter. "Months, nearly a year, my men scoured Ireland for her — turned over every stone and turned out every croft that might hold her — and all that time she was here, never more than ten leagues from where we sit right now. I might not have found her at all, save that something spooked her and she fled again. She thought, I presume, that my men were closing in, but they weren't — not until she bought passage for America."

Roffe fell silent for a long time and Cat wondered if he'd tired of talk before he spoke again.

"She died en route," he said.

That led her to wonder how, but she didn't ask. She didn't want to know if Roffe had killed his wife for running.

"The babe?" Cat asked in a whisper.

"Left behind," Roffe said, "to be sent for later, once she was safe and stable. It took me more years of searching to find where. Left behind with a damned old servant woman she'd brought from Ireland when we wed, and I'd dismissed as soon as I could. I'd forgotten about the hag entirely until my hired men uncovered word — by then it was too late, again, though. The old bitch Agnes was dead and my little Kathleen was nowhere to be found."

$\mathcal{C}$at froze at Roffe's words.

Her limbs went weak and tingled with more than the brandy.

Agnes.

Mother Agnes.

Cat, her name taken from her last, only memory of her mother — not even a face to recall, only the brush of lips upon her forehead, the scent of safety and love, and the whispered words,

I love you, catling, never forget.

I love you, Kathleen, never forget.

Cat's hand rose slowly to her breast and clasped her locket through her blouse. The little scrap of thong-bound hair. Hair the color of fire, the color of her own, the color of the woman's in the portrait Cat suddenly couldn't tear her eyes from. Her eyes burned with tears and her throat tightened so that she raised her glass to her lips, rim *tinking* off her teeth, and gulped to ease herself. The liquor helped, spreading warmth through her.

Her mother.

And that meant that Roffe ...

"You do see it, don't you?" Roffe said. "Or must I be more explicit?"

"I'm … she was my mother?"

"Indeed."

"And you …"

"You are my daughter, Kathleen Roffe … though I'm afraid it must remain niece and Catherine. Kathleen Roffe, you see, perished along with her mother aboard that ship — so far as all official records are concerned, that is. It would be beyond even Clanton's skill with documents to bring you back from the bureaucratic grave."

Cat stared at the portrait. It was somehow easier to think of the woman pictured there as her mother than it was to think of Roffe as her father. A father her mother had run and hid from when she'd found the truth, taking Cat with her. A father, nevertheless, who'd found her at last and taken her in, even if the manner was —

"Why?" she demanded, suddenly angry. "Why that farce in the market with your purse? Why the stalking of me, hounding me to ground through the city? Why not just tell me? Damn you!"

Roffe laughed. "Oh, yes, I should have stopped the urchin you were in the market there and said, 'Hello, girl, I'm your long-lost father — come along with your daddy, now?'" He laughed again. "I can picture that, can you not?" He sobered. "No, I had to give you a reason you'd believe for my interest — and one you'd accept."

Cat's anger deflated, as she had to agree. There was no way he could have approached her then, not without her thinking he was after, well, what the men who approached the street boys and girls were typically after.

Her mind was awhirl with this new information.

"But — to kill? To kill for money?"

"As I said, girl, do you think a man's name comes to my ear without there's a reason?" Roffe laughed, then he stood. "Come. I have a gift for you."

CHAPTER 25

*R*offe led her down the stairs, his grip on her arm verging on painful.

Past the first floor, then the ground floor, and down to the kitchen.

There were further stairs there, near the stillroom, that led down to the cellar, but Cat had explored and found them empty.

"Where are we going?" she asked.

"I told you I've a gift for you, girl," Roffe said.

He took up a lantern near the stillroom, released her for a moment to light it with a taper lit from the gas lamp, and then took her arm again. The lantern cast wild shadows on the stairs as they descended, made all the more frightening by the rough-hewn blocks of the walls. The walls of the cellar were all large blocks of stone, tool marks from the mining clear on their surface, with jagged edges and hollows. The cellar space was filled with the brick columns and arches that supported the ceiling, with only a few empty bags and broken crates strewn about.

At least that was how Cat remembered it from her explorations.

"Who's there?" a voice called, muffled and echoing through the dark, empty space. "What's this about?"

Cat heard the jangle of metal on metal.

"Let me loose, please! Oh, God, make it stop!"

"What's going on?" Cat asked.

"Do you not recognize the voice?" Roffe asked.

He raised the lantern high above his head so that its light would be cast farther.

Beneath one of the support arches stood a figure, his arms held above his head by chains from his wrists to the arch's peak. His head was covered with a rough bag and he cast about as though to try and catch a glimpse through it. His right sleeve had been cut open along its length, baring his extended arm, and his left trouser leg had been similarly treated, exposing his thigh. Both had attached to them the odd, four-legged, brass disks Cat had seen Roffe use on Lord Harrington.

"What is this? What have you done to him?" Cat asked.

The figure's head jerked up. "Who — Runt, is that you? Damn you, I'll —"

He jerked against his chains, then broke off in a scream of agony as he moved his arms and legs to get at her. What he said, closer now, was enough for her to identify him.

"Brandt," she whispered, then turned to Roffe and asked again, "What have you done to him? What are those ... things?"

Brandt continued to scream as he moved in the chains, seeming to seek a position that didn't cause him agony. He finally settled again with most of his weight on his uninjured leg and his arm hanging loosely from the chains. Blood trailed from the disks and down his arm and leg to soak his clothing.

"Make it stop," he whimpered. "Please, Runt — Cat, please, make it stop."

Roffe stepped to a nearby table and set the lantern down, illuminating its contents. A half dozen more of the devices lay on its top along with a thin-bladed knife. Roffe picked up one of the disks and held it to the light so Cat could see.

"These? My own invention."

Roffe held it carefully and pressed its side.

There was a muted click, then the tinkling of metal against metal. Brandt began screaming again at the sound.

The four legs of the disk Roffe held came together like a claw and a thin, razor-sharp blade corkscrewed from its bottom. The blade twisted and turned until it extended some few inches from the disk, then stopped.

Brandt screamed the entire time.

"Oh, shut up!" Roffe commanded. "This one's not even touching you! Quiet, or I'll give you another!"

Brandt's screams trailed off into helpless, muffled sniffles.

Roffe smiled. "It's the sound, you see. They come to associate it with the pain and one can get the most interesting reactions thereafter." He looked at Brandt. "Some are only annoying, though."

He pressed the thing's side again and, after the click, the blade twisted its way back into the case and the legs unfolded.

Brandt tensed, but uttered only a muffled yelp at the sound.

"Do you see?" Roffe asked.

Cat's stomach churned at it, but she did. The legs would grip the victim's flesh, holding the device in place, then the blade would enter, chewing its way through the body. She felt sick at the thought of it, both for its use and the evil perversion of the mechanical arts she'd begun to love.

Roffe grabbed a wet cloth from a bucket near the table and wiped it across Brandt's thigh near the disk. Brandt whimpered, but held his screams.

"See here?" Roffe said.

The blood smeared, but even in the dim light of the lantern Cat could see five holes where Roffe must have once removed another of the disks. They oozed blood a bit, but were remarkably small.

"If properly placed, there's less blood," Roffe said. "A few drops only — and those stop once a man's dead, of course."

Brandt sobbed.

"The damage, you see, is all internal — slices the muscles with every movement. And if it hits bone, well." Roffe smiled at Brandt's leg and tapped the disk there, causing Brandt to scream. "That's where this one's set itself."

Roffe stood, tossed the cloth into the bucket and set the device on the table, then wiped his hands clean with a fresh cloth.

"The pain will make a man give you his secrets, as you saw last night, and the marks remain unnoticed if the death seems to be of natural causes." He waved at Brandt. "There'll be no need of such precautions with this one, of course. No one will remark on one more bloodied corpse where he's from."

Brandt began begging then, a long litany of promises and pleas, muffled by the sack and made nearly incoherent by fear.

Roffe pulled the sack from his head and grasped Brandt's hair, yanking his head back. He put his face close to the boy's ear and hissed.

"Do you think you'll find mercy here?" Roffe asked. "After what you did? What you tried?"

"I'm sorry!" Brandt wailed.

"She is *mine*, boy. Mine alone and you'll suffer the same as any who try to take what's mine. Catherine, come here."

She moved as though in a daze. The blow to her head, the drink, the revelations of her mother's death and that Roffe — this vile, certainly mad creature she watched torture Brandt — was her father … all of it had fogged her mind to such a state that she couldn't think straight.

Roffe grasped her arm and dragged her before Brandt so that they were nearly touching.

"Please," Brandt whispered. Tears and snot streaked his face. "Please let me go, Cat, I'm sorry, I am."

Something was pressed into her hand and raised between them. Cat looked down and found she held the thin-bladed knife she'd seen on the table.

Roffe stood close behind her, his body pressed to her back, arms to either side. He blocked her from turning aside or stepping back and his breath was hot on her neck as he whispered to her.

"End him," Roffe said.

"*No!*" Brandt cried. "Please, Cat, we were mates — we were —"

"Think of what he tried to do to you," Roffe whispered. Cat could smell the brandy on his breath as it wafted over her cheek. His face rubbed against her hair and his body pressed harder against her. "Bully. How often did he strike the younger boys?"

"Cat —"

It was as though Roffe's words called up the memories. Brandt keeping the gang in line with fists and feet, boys crying themselves to sleep all bruised and bloodied, as Cat had more than once for mouthing off to him or not bringing back enough coin.

"Murderer — there're bodies enough to his credit, are there not?"

Roffe's hand on her arm helped her raise the blade to barely touch Brandt.

"Please —"

There weren't many, but there were some — bodies carried hurriedly through the alleys to be left or dumped in the river.

"Buggerer — he took the younger boys aside from time to time, didn't he? Thought to take you when you pretended, but you avoided him."

"*No*, I didn't! Never! I —"

Oh, yes, Cat thought. Taken aside, walked away from the group by the older boys, Brandt most of all, then sniveling the night away when they returned and not a word said about what happened.

"Rapist —" Roffe whispered.

"Cat, *please!*"

Cat's throat closed off and she couldn't breathe. The feel of Roffe's body against hers reminded her too much of the night before. Brandt's weight on top of her, the others pawing at her clothes.

Roffe grasped her about the middle, hands low on her belly, and she gasped. His thigh pressed hard against the back of hers, parting them.

The blade slid in with deceptive ease, slicing through the cloth of Brandt's shirt as cleanly as his flesh. Brandt's eyes widened and Roffe sighed, a long, low, exhalation that ran hot along Cat's neck, making her shiver despite its heat.

"No," Cat whispered, coming back to herself from whatever state she'd been in. She tried to pull the knife away, to take it back, but her movement was jerky and the razor-sharp blade slid through Brandt's flesh.

Hot blood washed her hand, cooling and feeling chill in an instant from the cold air of the cellar. Brandt screamed.

"I didn't!" Cat yelled. She stepped back, Roffe moving with her, his body still tightly pressed to hers. "You did it! You moved my arm!"

But Roffe's hands were still on her belly, so she knew that wasn't the truth. She flung the blade from her to clatter in the cellar's shadows and stared at Brandt in horror.

He screamed more and thrashed against the chains, every movement causing him more pain, but he couldn't seem to help it. Blood soaked his shirt, the stain growing larger as she watched, and glistened on his flesh in the lantern's light.

Roffe released her and stepped away.

"Good girl," he said.

"*Damn you!* I never meant to —"

"But you did, Catherine."

"Get him down! Call a surgeon!"

Roffe examined Brandt with narrowed eyes.

"Oh, no, you've done for him."

Brandt's screams redoubled.

"That's a gut wound," Roffe said. "He'll be a long time in the dying, but it'll come. You should end it now, if you're so tender-hearted."

Cat backed away, unable to tear her eyes from the blood covering Brandt's midsection.

It was only dimly that she heard Roffe's next words.

"I'll return when he's done with screaming. Hurry him along if you've a mind."

The grating of the cellar door's lock came in a pause between Brandt's screams and was quite loud to her.

CHAPTER 26

Cat was able to get Brandt down from the chains, though it was no kindness in the doing.

She needed the thin-bladed knife and the leg of one of the disks to pick the crude mechanism of the manacles, and the boy redoubled his screams when she approached. He screamed and thrashed away at every movement and she was unable to both support him and pick the locks, so in the end he collapsed to the cellar floor in a bloody heap.

Cat tried to make him comfortable, but there was little she could do. Not even offer water, for the only water in the cellar was the bucket soiled with the boy's own blood.

She finally whispered, "I'll bring a surgeon," and took her crude tools up the stairs to the cellar door.

That lock yielded quickly, it being no more complex than needed to keep servants out of the household's goods, and Cat had a moment's spark of hope as the lock *clicked* and turned under her hands.

That hope was dashed as she discovered the door was barred from the other side.

Try as she might, the bar wouldn't yield — neither to her shoulder *thumping* against the door nor to any of the implements she slid between door and frame in an attempt to lift it.

An exploration of the cellar walls revealed no other way out, only a few narrow drains no bigger around than her arm. She returned the lantern to the table after her search and made her way back to the door, not wanting to be near Brandt and his screams.

Perhaps it would be kinder to end it for him, she thought.

She settled with her back to the cellar door, arms hugging her knees to her chest, and let her eyes fill with the tears she'd been holding back.

She hadn't wanted this. Hadn't *wanted* to kill Brandt, but the knife had moved almost of its own volition. She didn't even remember the moment, only the realization afterward that it had.

It must have been Roffe, moving her arm somehow, mustn't it?

How could he have done this to her? Was he not her father?

His rant to Brandt had been frightening — the worst she'd seen from him, even more so than when he'd beaten her for touching his mechanicals.

And the words …

Speaking of her being his, like a possession of some sort, and punishing those who'd take her from him.

Her mother had taken her in such a way, hadn't she? Seen something in the man she'd married that frightened her enough to flee the luxury of Roffe's home and seek shelter in the slums, then risk the unknowns of the colonies.

What might Roffe — the Roffe revealed to her in this cellar — do in such a case?

He'd given little detail about her mother's death — might he have turned that rage and violence against her as he had against Brandt? Roffe might say he sent his men, but Cat believed that less and less now. He would have wanted to confront her.

The lantern's light lasted for some time.

Cat's thoughts in the darkness that followed, and Brandt's screams, lasted somewhat longer.

IT WAS CLANTON, not Roffe, who finally opened the cellar door.

Cat looked up, blinking against light of the downstairs lamps the opening door let in, which seemed much brighter after all her time in the dark. She edged away from the opening, as much as the narrow stairtop would allow, not bothering to rise.

She wondered how long she'd sat there, lost in the darkness of her thoughts and Brandt's screams.

Long enough for her mouth to grow parched with thirst and her belly to ache with hunger, though the thought of food now turned her stomach.

Clanton knelt and offered her a mug.

She sipped, cool water slipping easily down her throat. The mug was only a quarter full and Clanton accepted it back from her once it was empty.

"More in a bit," Clanton said. "Let that settle." He took a lantern from beside the cellar door and started down the stairs. "Come on, then."

Reluctantly, Cat rose and followed, though she longed to run. Her mind still felt clouded and it was easier to do as Clanton said. She swallowed hard and stopped, looking away, when the light reached Brandt, but Clanton called her closer. Docilely, she obeyed.

Brandt's body lay in a wide, sticky pool of blood. Here and there it had not been enough to cover the cellar's cobbles, so it traced a dark path between them. The boy's face was set in a rictus of pain and horror, not relaxed in any final peace as she might have hoped.

Clanton sighed.

"There's less to clean up, y'do 'em quick."

CLANTON GAVE HER NO RESPITE, nor time for any but a few sips more water, then it was to work.

There were several barrels waiting in the kitchen near the cellar door.

Cat had to drag one down, empty, and help him with the body. She balked at that, but Clanton's look cowed her.

"Easier —" Clanton grunted as he threw his weight against Brandt's leg to bend it. "— do you not wait —" Another grunt and a sickening sound from within Brandt, accompanied by a fresh wave of the horrid smells filling the cellar. "— too long after he's dead."

Cat sat back from trying to bend Brandt's elbow in a similar fashion. It was remarkable how quickly some of Clanton's casualness with the work had affected her. She studied Brandt's face for a moment.

Was she unhappy he was dead?

No, the boy'd made her life a living hell in her time amongst the gang, singling her out for a beating more than most. Brandt, she knew, would have left her laying gutted in an alleyway without a second thought if it would gain him a tuppence — or a moment's pleasure from her body, willing or no.

No, she wasn't unhappy he was dead — and she might have reveled in killing him herself if the circumstances had been different.

The gruff, workmanlike efforts of Clanton had greatly calmed her and she was now able to think a bit more clearly than while she was trapped in the cellar with Brandt's screams.

"I was not in control of that," she said, "if you'll remember."

"'Course y'were," Clanton grumbled. "Y'call out 'Oy! I just slit his throat for him!' An' that cellar door opens, bang! Y'knew that. Somewhere in ya, y'knew that." He pointed at Brandt's elbow. "That arm won't fold itself, girl. Back to work."

Cat sighed and resumed her efforts.

She supposed he was correct. She'd known what Roffe wanted of her, after all, but had simply been unwilling to do it.

"Easier, too," Clanton went on, "do you wait 'til this eases, but you'll rarely have the days that takes — an' the cleanup's worse. Best if you act quicker in future."

"There won't be a future," Cat muttered.

Clanton paused again and stared at her, then he grinned and chuckled.

"Roffe told me y'know who he is now — what he does, too?"

Cat nodded.

"Well, then I'm free to say it — y'have his look in your eyes, girl. Whatever else y'do —" He nodded to Brandt's body. "— there'll be more o'this."

BRANDT'S BODY went into the barrel.

It was heavy work, even with the use of a wheeled handcart, to get him up the cellar stairs to the kitchen. Once there, Clanton had her fill the barrel with the harshest spirits Cat had ever smelled.

"Not for drinking, at all," Clanton informed her, handing over another jug.

"What will you do with him?" Cat asked.

"None of this," Clanton said, handing her another jug to pour, "and an alley, if we were hurried. His lot's expected to end there with an opened gut. The river's good a'times. Plan the tides right and there's merry hell to figure where he might've gone in. *This* one, though —" He held the barrel's top in place now that it was filled and set it with a cloth-wrapped hammer. "I know a man what knows a man what knows a doctor, y'see?"

"A doctor?"

"Always wantin' to poke about a man's insides."

Cat swallowed hard, her stomach churning again at the thought.

"Now," Clanton said. "I'll be taking *this* —" He knocked knuckles on the barrel's top. "— to my man. *You* —" He pointed to the cellar. "— clean up the mess. There's three barrels there I filled for you. Dump them down and scrub up the bits. Fill 'em again from the kitchen pump and rinse it all good."

CAT SCRUBBED the cellar and finished well before Clanton returned.

There was something cathartic about removing every trace of what happened there. Kneeling on the damp cobbles, scraping brushes against the stone, she felt satisfaction as the last of the red-tinged water went down the drains under the lamplight and the next sluicing of the cobbles showed clear and pure.

Clanton gathered up the brushes she'd used, then ordered her to strip off her clothes. This set of the grey and green patterned garb was nearly done for, she thought, what with the rips and tears from her struggle with the gang, being flung to the alley's cobbles, and then soaked with blood-tinged water as she cleaned the cellar floor.

Clanton's brusque, businesslike attitude left her oddly unembarrassed to strip so in front of him. He seemed to treat it as nothing of note, so she did as well. His acceptance of her in the aftermath of Brandt's death was comforting.

"You'll want a bath, I imagine," he said as he bundled her clothes up. "Kitchen fire's lit, so there'll be hot water upstairs for you."

That he'd lit the fire to burn those brushes and clothes, along with the last remnants of Brandt's blood in the house, went without saying.

Cat was kept at the townhouse for nearly a month after discovering Roffe's true occupation and Brandt's death, and never far from Clanton's watchful eye. Being always watched was bad, but the forced separation from Emma was worse for her.

Roffe watched her closer, too, spending more time at the townhouse than was his wont before, though he still dined and slept at his club. He didn't spend that time with Cat in any way, but watched her instead – at least at first.

After a fortnight, Roffe began spending time in his Mechanicals Room and invited Cat to join him, but even this left her wary.

"You seem unusually pensive," Roffe said, head buried in some device.

Cat longed to move closer and get a look, but she'd not been invited to. These invitations, which she might have welcomed before, left her wishing Roffe would return to his old habits. Even the occasional explanation he offered as he worked only brought to mind the violent outburst he'd had when she had the audacity to work on the little cleaning device – which, even now, sat in a shattered heap in the room's corner.

"I'm sorry," Cat said.

Roffe paused in his work and looked up, a jeweler's loupe at his right eye making him look almost comical – if she didn't think about the violence and murders he was capable of.

"You're afraid," Roffe said.

"I'm uncertain," Cat allowed.

Roffe grunted and returned to his work, making minute adjustments to the device's insides – with, if Cat were any judge, entirely the wrong tool for the job.

"Do as you're told and there'll be no cause for either," Roffe said, jabbing forcefully at the device.

"Will that include more murder?" Cat asked before she could stop herself.

Roffe went still and silent, causing Cat to freeze as well, for fear of which way his mercurial moods might take him.

"Of course, it will," Roffe said, finally, not looking at her. "That is, after all, our family business."

Cat stayed silent. There was little she could say to that.

"You should call me 'father', I think," Roffe said after a few minutes, "now that it's all out in the open."

Cat's stomach turned at that, but she thought it not the time to argue.

"As you wish, father."

"I sense you're troubled," Roffe said, looking up from the device. He pulled the loupe from his eye and frowned at her. "It would truly be best if you'd accept –"

The mechanism he'd been working on emitted a low whirring sound that grew in pitch. Roffe rose and made to step back, but not before there was a sharp *clang* and bits of brass flew from the case.

Cat jumped at the sound, but she was far enough away to escape injury. Roffe was not so lucky – a piece of brass caught his cheek, leaving a shallow cut that bled freely.

"*Damnable* –" Roffe broke off, glaring from the workbench to Cat, as though she might be the cause of the trouble, then he dabbed at his cheek with one hand and left the room.

~

Despite Clanton's demands of her on their outings – the need to stay in whatever character he set her, no matter the circumstances – Cat now found them a welcome respite from the oppression of Roffe's tenure at the townhouse.

They returned one afternoon from such an outing, Cat dressed as the *Flowergirl*, so having to come in through the alley and carriage house, to find a note on the kitchen table.

Clanton grunted as he read it.

"Mister Roffe's out," he said, then immediately crushed Cat's relief with, "Be back presently. You're to change to proper clothes for him to escort you out."

"Out where?"

Roffe's schedule of events he planned to escort her to was usually better set than to give so little notice.

"Don't say," Clanton said.

Cat had barely time to change her clothes before the townhouse door opened again and Roffe arrived.

He looked Cat over without a word, then nodded as though she'd somehow satisfied him and told her to come with him.

They went to a hired carriage waiting outside and started off, neither speaking.

The carriage came to a stop and Roffe stepped out, holding out a hand for Cat. She stepped down and looked around, shocked to her core. She recognized the place, of course, one could hardly move about the city and not know it, but what did Roffe mean bringing her here on such a day?

The square at Newgate Prison was crowded with people, the carriage had barely made it to the edges, and Roffe grabbed her arm roughly to guide her closer to the gibbets at the far end.

"Why are we here?"

"I told you, to see a show," Roffe said.

Cat looked around. The crowd was loud and boisterous, but Roffe made his way through with ease. A poke with his walking stick, an icy glare as someone turned around, and the way parted. They were soon at the front, the very best place to view the show, if one cared for such things.

Cat didn't. She'd had no qualms about picking any pocket in this crowd when her gang had come here, rich or poor. The people who came to view a hanging were feeding on the misery and misfortune of others, in her opinion, perhaps colored by the knowledge that she might one day be the object of their attentions if she were caught out.

"Mister Roffe, I'd prefer to leave."

"No, you'll watch. We've a special treat today, and a lesson for you — wonderful timing, I couldn't have planned better. You've been surly again, and I can see thoughts churning in your little mind like the gears of some device."

Cat pulled her arm free of his grasp. "If you wish me to learn that there's a price for being caught in our endeavors, I'm well aware of that."

Roffe smiled and Cat felt the little chill she always did at that expression.

Two men, their hands tied behind their backs, were led up onto the platform and the crowd greeted them with boos and hisses — both were young, one little more than a boy, Cat thought.

Roffe moved behind her and grasped her shoulders, forcing her to face the platform squarely. "Watch now," he hissed in her ear.

It wasn't quick. The nooses went around the men's necks and the charges were read. Cat couldn't hear because of the noise of the crowd. Someone threw the first bit, possibly a potato, and then more followed — rotten fruits and vegetables pelting the two men as they stood helplessly bound.

Cat felt Roffe move closer. His body pressed against hers and he put his lips very near her ear.

"Did you hear what they're charged with?"

Cat shook her head. "No, and I don't wish to. Can we not go home?"

"They're sodomites."

Cat frowned. Roffe seemed to think this was important for her to see, but what was his purpose? Then the word registered and she stiffened.

"Yes," Roffe whispered. "Of course I know. Do you think aught happens in my household I'm not aware of?" He shook her roughly. "You've chosen a dangerous pleasure with your little maid, girl, so know this." He released one of her arms to point at the gibbet. The crowd had tired of throwing things and the hangman was at his lever. "It's as much a crime for you as for them. Cross me, and you'll be denounced. It'll be you and your Emma up there. Perhaps, if I've reason to think you still have value I'll get you loose, but your little plaything will dance at Bellby's ball, have no doubt of that."

The hangman pulled the lever and the two men dropped. The ropes brought them up short, but it appeared there were no friends, or none who'd acknowledge it publicly, to pull their legs and hasten them along. They twitched and jerked at the end of the ropes for what Cat thought was a horribly long time.

What filled her mind was the thought of Emma up there — sweet, gentle Emma being pelted by the crowd and set to dancing at the end of the hangman's rope.

Her jaw clenched and she swallowed hard.

"Do we understand each other?" Roffe asked.

Cat nodded. "I understand you."

"Good." Roffe jerked her around and started making his way through the crowd.

Cat remained silent, staring straight ahead. She understood Roffe well enough, but thought he didn't understand her. He thought by showing her this he'd cowed her — that her fear for Emma or herself would keep her to his line.

She'd do that well enough, to keep Emma safe, but knew the only true safety would be if Roffe could no longer reach them. He might think her cowed, but she'd simply determined that they must escape him.

Cat waited until Roffe off to his club for the night and she was certain Clanton was asleep, his rumbling snores audible in the kitchen even from his distant room.

She gathered her things quickly, then went up the stairs to Roffe's rooms. She looted those as if she were burgling the last house she ever would.

A few coins long abandoned on a table, more coin and some of the new folding paper pounds favored by the banks, cufflinks, fancy handkerchiefs, an old shaving kit, anything at all of value and small enough size went into her bags. Then those bags down the stairs to the stables and into the coach. She made short work of the butler's pantry, folding the silver she and Clanton never used into the linens so they'd not make a sound, then those, too, into the coach.

She harnessed the horses as Skiff taught her, then led them out into the misty darkness of the alleyway. The traces and tack jingled and she could do nothing about the sound of hooves and wheels on the cobbles, but she hoped it was not enough to wake Clanton.

Once away from the house, she clambered up to the coach's bench and took up the reins. She'd not driven the coach often, mostly the manor's cart, but it was little different. The city streets were empty for the most part and she was out onto even emptier roads before the first of the inhabitants truly started stirring.

She drove the horses through the night, pausing only at the crossroads to hold her lantern close to signs and be sure of her way, then on again.

It lacked an hour or so until dawn, she thought, and she could see lights in the manor's kitchen, when the coach finally clattered into the courtyard and she drew the team to a stop. Mistress Singley would be up, setting the bread in the ovens and preparing for the day's meals. Skiff, as well, to care for the animals. Emma would be soon to work at cleaning the house, so at least Cat had no need to fear dragging the girl out of bed.

Skiff came out to meet her, a puzzled look on his face at the sight of her atop the coach's bench instead of Clanton or a hired driver.

"I've no time to explain," Cat said, hopping down from the bench and handing Skiff the reins. "Will you see they're watered? I've driven them hard."

"Aye, miss," Skiff said, "but —"

"No *time*," Cat said. She started for the kitchen to find Emma — the girl would be up and about, she was sure, even though Cat wasn't in residence. She still had the duties of cleaning, even with working at being Cat's maid, and more of them when Cat was in town.

She made it only a few steps before she stopped, mind whirling furiously over what came next.

They couldn't take the coach on from here. Two girls driving so large a coach would be noted — they might even be stopped and questioned. Such a conveyance should have a proper driver, and a man for that, not a girl. It simply wasn't done.

She turned back and grasped Skiff's arm.

"Skiff, make the cart ready for me, will you? The market cart — and the two sturdiest horses. Will you do that?"

A cart would make more sense. Two girls from a farm heading to market. They'd be unremarkable in that, she thought, and could find some better excuse for traveling farther.

Skiff frowned. "What's this about, miss?"

"I — I can't explain, but it's important and I've little time. Please, I must get Emma. Will you do this for me?"

The groundskeeper looked from Cat to the coach, then to the manor. His brow wrinkled and she could see his mind working, then he nodded.

"Aye, miss, you see to your girl. I'll see to the cart."

"Thank you!"

Cat ran for the kitchen door where Singley was silhouetted against the light.

"What is this about?"

"Is Emma up?" Cat asked, then brushed past the woman not waiting for an answer. *"Emma?"*

The kitchen smelled of the bread baking in the oven and the herbs set to drying above it. Cat's eyes filled at the thought of how happy she'd been here, for so short a time, and at having to flee now and might never have this again.

Emma rushed into the kitchen, followed closely by Hinds, who was still in her nightdress and scowling at the fuss.

"What is it?" Emma asked.

Cat rushed to her and wrapped her arms around her. She squeezed tight, every bit of fear she'd had since Roffe's words at Newgate making her want to pull the girl inside herself and never let her loose.

"What —"

Cat released her, but only to grasp her face and pull her into a kiss — long and deep and full of love. She pulled back only a bit and stared into Emma's eyes.

"Do you love me?" she asked, ignoring the gasp of outrage from Hinds.

"Miss, what —"

"Enough of that! No playacting for the watchers, Emma, do you love me?"

Emma's eyes darted about, wide and not understanding, but Cat's urgency must have convinced her.

"Aye, Cat, I do — with all my heart, you know it."

"Then trust me, please," Cat said, her voice rushed. "You're in danger and we must leave. Leave now, for we haven't much time."

"Danger?" Emma shook her head. "I don't understand."

"He knows," Cat said. "He knows about us and he'll hurt you to control me, do you understand? He'll see you dead if he must — he told me so. The man's insane. We must leave. *Now*, please!"

Hinds stepped forward and roughly shoved Cat and Emma apart.

"*What* have the two of you been up to? What … what *ghastly*, unnatural —"

"Shut *up*, damn you!" Cat yelled and shoved Hinds away. Her hand went to the knife hilt tucked into her stays. If the screeching harridan delayed her, there'd be another body for Clanton to barrel up.

"I suspected, but didn't believe it," Hinds said, her face twisting in disgust. "Well, neither of you is going anywhere! I shall fetch the vicar and then the constable, and —"

Cat's fist closed on the hilt, but Singley laid a hand there and then stepped between her and Hinds.

"Now, now," Singley said. Her hand gripped Cat's tightly, keeping it in place. Her other held a teacup out to Hinds. "Let's all settle down and see what this is about, shall we?"

Hinds took the cup automatically, but her scowl didn't lessen.

"I see quite well what this is about," she said. "These two vile creatures and their unnatural acts have been found out and wish to flee!"

"As may be," Singley said, her voice calm. "As may be, but there's t'be no talk of vicar's and constables and such — not in Master Roffe's house, you know. Once one secret's out, there's no telling where it stops, right?"

Hinds' scowl lessened and she looked uncertain.

"I'm certain Master Roffe made as much clear to you on your hiring, Mistress Hinds. Secrets kept for secrets kept is the bargain, yes?"

"I —"

"Drink your tea, dear, and settle a bit. We'll work this out ourselves, won't we? That's best for all."

"I — yes, you're right, I suppose." Hinds raised the cup and drained half of it at one go in her distress. "It was only that …" She looked at Emma and Cat, who'd drawn closer to each other as she spoke. "To see them so —" Hinds scowled again and took another sip of tea. She took a deep breath and her shoulders eased. "We must contact Master Roffe, of course, and let him decide what's —"

Hinds broke off and frowned.

"Of course, dear," Singley said. "We'll send for Master Roffe at once."

"Yes," Hinds said. She blinked rapidly, her eyes rolling slowly and her head soon following suit. "We must send for Master … Roffe, and tell him of these …" She began to sway, but with some effort fixed her gaze on Cat and Emma. "… dirty girls."

Singley reached out and plucked the teacup from her hands as Hinds collapsed in a heap. She tilted the cup to the light, examining its contents.

"You've three hours, I think, before she's awake and sends for Roffe," Singley said.

At the kitchen door, Skiff stepped into the light and tapped the wood cudgel he held against his palm, his eyes on Hinds.

"Always the pigs," he said, "if'n y'need more time."

CHAPTER 29

"I don't know how to thank you," Cat said from the cart's bench.

The sun was halfway over the horizon, but blocked by the manor's bulk, so the kitchen courtyard was still dark.

Skiff heaved a last sack into the cart's bed and Singley handed up a basket for Cat to set beneath the bench. They'd looted the manor of nearly every bit of portable value — at least what could be easily disposed of — including a cache of guinea coins from a hidden compartment in Roffe's desk.

All of it was in the burlap bags covering the wagon bed, their upper halves filled with all manner of produce from the kitchen and household stores. If Cat and Emma were stopped, they could show a cart full of produce for market and be on their way.

"No thanks," Singley said. "I've no thought what the master's plans for you were, but I always suspected they were darker than I bargained for when I came here. There may be no other place for me, but you two could make a go of it."

Skiff shook his head. "Yer good girls," was all he said.

"What will happen to the two of you?" Cat asked. "When Roffe finds out —"

Singley laughed. "Skiff and I'll sit down and enjoy a cup of tea," she said. "Roffe had me teach you what I know, didn't he? Why should he be surprised if you were to use it?"

"But Hinds —"

"I've a thing or two will make her lose the last few hours, you know. By the time Master Roffe arrives, her memory'll be the same as ours."

Cat nodded. With Hinds unconscious, Singley could dose the woman with anything she wished.

"Best be off," Singley said.

CAT PULLED the wagon to the roadside and paused to think.

"What is it?" Emma asked.

"A moment."

No, she'd watched the few other carts on the road so far, and there was something wrong. They were getting odd looks, though no questions.

She examined the cart and found no flaws with it — it was common enough to be from a farm. She and Emma were dressed much as the few girls she'd seen on the other carts. The bags of produce in the back were not so many as in the other carts, but that could be explained by their having a poor farm — why were they being noted?

She stood on the cart's bench and looked around.

They were in an area where farms were plentiful, far enough from the city and the manor's village behind them —

"Damn me," Cat muttered.

"What?" Emma asked.

"We're in a bloody cart hauling potatoes *away* from the nearest markets," Cat muttered. "Clanton'd have my backside raw if he could see me now."

Emma looked confused, but Cat wanted to take no time to explain further. They needed to be on their way, but not noted as they had been.

There was a woodcutter's track ahead, so she clucked to the horses and guided the cart down it until they were sheltered from view of the road, then she hopped off and motioned for Emma to do likewise.

"We'll need to change," Cat said, "and you will need to put on your lady's maid's voice, though you'll be no maid."

"What d'you mean?" Emma asked.

Cat dug through the wagon bed until she found her bags from the townhouse. She thought for a moment — had she packed enough? Yes, there'd be something appropriate for each of them. She pulled two sets of clothes from the bag — *Merchant's Niece* and *Parson's Daughter* would do.

Or was it the Merchant's Daughter *and the* Parson's Niece? she wondered.

No matter, the point was the two dresses were the proper class for what she had in mind and the *Merchant's Whatever* fit a bit loosely on her, so it might fit Emma.

"Put this on instead," Cat ordered, then saw the look of confusion on Emma's face and sighed. "Look, we can't be two farmgirls with a wagon for market — it will never work. All the folk heading for market around here know each other and know where the markets are. We've been going against the flow of goods all morning and everyone who sees us is asking, 'Say, why are those two girls we don't know at all hauling cabbages away from the market?' Do you see?"

"Oh —" Emma nodded tentatively.

"So that's not what we are now. We are sisters, daughters of a shopowner who's recently died. We have family in ..." She thought for another moment, picturing Clanton's map. "No, *near*, Bristol, but not in it. Unfortunately, they are not well off — nor are we, for Father had debts —"

"Oh, dear."

"— and we have nothing left but a few personal possessions, not even household goods. We are forced to make our own way there to find our new home. You must speak as Hinds taught you for acting the part of a lady's maid — it will do for a certain class of merchant, such as our father was. Do you have that?"

Emma nodded.

"Tell me," Cat said.

Emma cleared her throat and spoke slowly as she always did when trying to keep the accent Hinds had taught her. "Our father's died and left us nothing and we must make our way to family in … near Bristol on our own."

"Good," Cat said. "We'll get the rest of the bits right on the road. Change your dress now."

Emma stripped off her things and Cat helped her into the *Merchant's Daughter* dress, then stripped herself and Emma assisted her in becoming the *Parson's Niece.*

Or, I suppose, we're now the Orphaned Daughters.

She eyed the cart and decided to unload some of the produce. It would do them no good in hiding what they'd looted from Roffe and the bulky bags visible over the top of the wagon would do their new roles no credit. No, they were the *Poor* Orphaned Girls, left in dire straits — traveling with no more than this rough cart and a few, meager possessions. Provided one didn't look too closely at the baggage and see the possessions were two households' worth of silver and plate.

"Help me unload these turnips."

With the work done, and pounds of Mistress Singley's ready produce left to rot in piles, Cat couldn't help but worry at the small bit of baggage they actually had left. There was a great deal of value there, but it was all they had to establish and keep themselves.

Cat couldn't help wondering if it would be enough. What sort of life would she and Emma be able to lead, and how would they keep themselves?

THEY TRAVELED for three days that way, then Cat turned the cart back the way they'd come and north at the first crossroads.

"I thought we were to go to Bristol?" Emma asked.

"Near Bristol," Cat said, "and that's the story we've told at the inns the last three nights. Now we will change our direction and our father's shop was in Southampton and the relatives who'll take us in are near Derby."

Emma frowned.

"Look, we're not exactly unremarkable," Cat said. "Two girls, traveling alone — that's something folk will remember, no matter our story. And my hair's like a bloody beacon — I'll have to find some dye soon." She ignored the look on Emma's face at the thought of dying her hair. "So, we've laid a trail from London toward Bristol. Anyone following us will move on that way from that last inn, but we've come back and headed north. In fact, we'll ride on through the night tonight, so there'll be no innkeeper to remember us within a day's ride of that last. We'll do the same short of Derby and head some other direction for a time."

"Y'think Master Roffe'll come for us?" Emma asked.

"Accent," Cat prompted, causing Emma to huff. It was work to keep up such a role.

"There's no one about but us," she said.

"You must have the habit, or people will remark on any slip," Cat said. "It's no more than you'd have to do if you got the place of lady's maid you wanted."

"Thought it were you I'd —"

"Emma."

The other girl huffed. "I thought it would be you I'd serve as maid, when Mistress Hinds was teaching me — and I could be myself in private."

"Perhaps later," Cat said, "once we're settled somewhere. But for now, it's best to be used to it."

Emma settled back on the cart bench, arms crossed. "Like t'break my teeth on them words."

CHAPTER 30

They made their way for days, then weeks, doubling back
and turning, changing the location of the father's store and
their distant relatives each time until Emma despaired of ever remembering what it was today.

Three times Cat left Emma and the cart at a village inn to go on
ahead to a larger town or city with a bag over her shoulder and the
Flowergirl's clothes — the *Flowergirl* could pass for a poor girl traveling
or even a beggar in the market, rough and only avoiding giving in to
the despair of hard times because all times were hard.

The bag she carried contained a few bits of silver and plate, or
some others of Roffe's goods, and she sought out the parts of town
where the merchants of more dubious integrity might make their
homes — the sort of shops that might buy a thing of more value than
the person selling it should logically possess. All towns of any size had
such a place.

She haggled just enough to not be too egregiously cheated. Not
enough to be remembered for driving a hard bargain, nor little
enough to be thought a fool or an easy mark.

At the third such shop, something seemed off.

The shopkeeper nodded and agreed to the price, then stepped to his back room to get the coin, while Cat exchanged a brief, level stare with the bully-buck who wasn't, quite, a guard. The man perched on his stool off to the side — unobtrusive, but obviously watching Cat to see that she touched nothing while his master was away. The stare went on too long, was too direct, and the shopkeeper took more time than should be needed. Cat's back muscles tensed as though there were someone behind her, though she knew there was not — her neck itched and her mouth went dry at the certainty that something was wrong.

The shopkeeper returned with a pouch. Cat weighed it in her palm, looked inside to see the coin, then took one out to check it. She should check them all, but there was that itch, and the expectant stare of the shopkeeper, so instead she nodded, smiled, and eased out of the shop.

The street outside was busy, wagons and carriages vying for space with those walking, but Cat picked them out of the crowd in an instant.

To her left, at an alley's entrance — two men, lean and sharp with rougher clothing than the street was used to, but finer than Cat's *Flowergirl* garb. She turned the other way and walked, not looking behind because she knew they followed.

She walked casually, the pouch of coin slipped into a pocket at the front of her skirt so that it came to rest securely between her legs.

A draywagon passed her, and a carriage was coming the other way, so she darted into the street behind the dray, rushed along its far side, having to turn sideways so as not to be crushed between the two, then behind the carriage quickly before the next came, and into an alley.

She heard curses and shouts behind her as the two men tried to cross.

The trouble was that Cat didn't know the town and hadn't scouted an escape route — she was in a hurry to return to Emma and not after robbing the merchant, after all, so what need of that was there? The alleys were as twisty and unpredictable as anywhere and a wrong-turn sent her to a dead end with no likely route to the rooftops.

She skidded to a halt, feet sliding in something dumped from above overnight, and rushed back the way she came.

More turns, more scrambling around the refuse and debris, then another dead end, and this time when she turned she heard the heavy tread of running men.

She tried a doorway — locked and no time to pick it.

A glance up showed laundry hung on a line between the two buildings — the line too high to reach, but someone's trousers hung draped over it and not from pegs. She dragged a decaying, wobbly crate to the center of the alleyway and clambered atop it.

The sound of steps grew louder, then a shout.

Cat looked back and saw one of the men rushing toward her, calling out to his partner where she was.

She crouched, leapt, and caught the pants with both hands, bunching them together in her grip so they stayed hung over the line, and started to scramble up, hand over hand.

Something struck her head as she reached the rope and grasped it, then her back and her leg. She glanced down and saw the two men scooping up whatever debris was to hand and hurling it at her. A rock struck her forehead and she blinked away the pain, feeling a trickle of blood run down between her eyes and along her nose.

Cat started along the rope toward the nearest window, but one of the men threw a large board that struck her head and hand both. The wood *cracked* against her skull and her fingers flew open. Her other hand slipped, the rough line burning her palm, and she fell.

The top of the crate, still under her, gave way at the impact and her attempt to tuck and roll away along the ground merely immersed her in the debris.

Hands reached in, groping for her, and Cat drew her belt knife to slash at them. The men retreated with curses and that gave Cat time to gather her feet under her and leap from the pile of splintered wood. She rolled and regained her feet, but going the wrong way — toward the alley's dead end — and had to turn.

The two men blocked her way, arms wide, knives in their own hands, and grinning.

"All right, girl, enough," one said. He was taller than the other, with dark, greasy hair that shined in the sunlight. "Hand over the coin."

The other had a bleeding forearm from Cat's slash at him and his grin was less pleasant. The blood soaked his sleeve and dripped from his hand, which was more than she'd expect from such a simple pinking as she'd given him.

"An' take us to yer stash." Bleeder glanced at Greasy. "Don't think she sold all o' what she has."

Old instincts and Clanton's training taking hold, Cat slid her hands into her skirt pockets. In her left she palmed her purse-knife, sliding fingers and thumb into the loops that held it steady, in her right a thin cord with knotted ends.

"Hand it over," Greasy said.

Cat shrugged. "As you wish."

She rushed them. That wasn't what they were expecting and there was a moment's hesitation from Bleeder, but Greasy came to meet her.

Cat lunged at Greasy then dodged aside as he grasped for her. She moved to his left, away from both men, but unable to pass them completely due to the debris in the alley.

She reversed course suddenly, catching Greasy as he turned, and rushed past him on his right. The knotted cord whipped out with a flick of her wrist, looping around Greasy's neck. The knot at the far end looped around — once, twice, three times and she yanked the end she held, pulling it tight against the man's neck.

Greasy's hands went to his throat, trying to gain some space between the cord and his skin.

Cat moved on to Bleeder, who'd drawn a knife, but the man's eyes widened as he saw his partner stumble away.

"What —"

He moved toward Greasy, who'd turned about to face them and whose face was red, eyes bulging as he scratched desperately at the cord about his throat.

Cat dodged past, the alley and escape open before her, but her steps slowed. She stopped and turned.

Greasy was on his knees now, his face darker. Bleeder was trying to get his knife blade between the cord and Greasy's neck, and Cat wished him luck with that, for she'd felt how deep it had been pulled.

Part of her wished to leave, but another part — the part that had sent her after Roffe with her blade out and ready that last night before he'd taken her, the part that held a certain satisfaction in Brandt's death, hard as it was — made her stop. She had coin in her pouch that she needed — needed for food, for shelter, for safety. Needed to keep Emma safe, so they'd not be parted. Yet these men had tried to take it from her. Would have taken that and more, if she was less capable. They would have made her reveal Emma and their wagon of valuables outside of town, taken those, and done as they liked with Cat and Emma after.

Anger boiled up and she reached her hand into her skirts again, coming out with her own blade.

How many had they done that to before and how many would they after if Cat left them to continue? How many left destitute to make their way on the street or bruised and battered in an alley?

She rushed at Bleeder, taking him from behind. Her knife sank into his lower back, twisting and jerking to the side as Clanton'd taught her. Her other hand, the one with the purse-knife, grasped the side of his neck and pulled back, the tiny, razor-sharp blade just enough to make the blood spurt.

Cat stepped back.

Bleeder, truer to the name she'd given him now, fell to his knees and then toppled to the side, blood from his neck painting the alley in shortening arcs. Greasy's eyes were already wide, but he followed Bleeder's fall with them, then looked back to Cat. His hands at his neck stilled some, barely scrabbling at the cord now, and he, too, slowly toppled to fall beside his partner.

Cat cleaned her blades on their clothes, walling off a bit of herself that was asking what she'd done, then sheathed her knife and returned the purse-knife to its place.

She went and squatted between the two men, watching until both stilled and there was no motion at all. Greasy's face was dark and purple, while Bleeder's was stark white against the pool of blood he lay in.

She stared at them for what seemed a long time, but may have been only seconds. It was the first time she'd killed with intent, and she wondered what she should be feeling. She examined that, but found, really, nothing. A bit of satisfaction that it was done and a bit of pride that she'd taken down two grown men — as Clanton had told her, skill would overcome the brawlers.

The pool of blood was spreading across the cobbles, so Cat unlooped her cord from about Greasy's neck and pocketed it.

Was this what Clanton felt? She wondered. Or Roffe?

She searched for the horror that had been there after she'd stabbed Brandt, but couldn't find it. Perhaps that had been merely the further shock after the surprises and shock of the night before. Perhaps it had been only because of Roffe's interference and insistence that she do it.

Regardless, she knew what she felt now.

She took a deep breath, a last look, then stood and backed away.

Wait —

She thought for a moment, then shrugged and bent again to retrieve the men's purses. They certainly wouldn't be needing the coin anymore.

Pocketing those, Cat turned and walked away, leaving both the bodies and her thoughts behind — white and purple on the cobbles.

CHAPTER 31

Cat almost left the city behind her. She almost went straight back to Emma and the cart and their journey.

Almost.

She was halfway there, in fact, before her feet turned about in the road's dust and began carrying her back. It took a time of walking for her to accept why and more for her to plan it — she turned about again, then, for she'd need some things from their baggage for her plan.

So, back to the village inn and pay for their rooms for one more day.

She tucked most of the coin from the sale of Roffe's goods into their baggage and filled her pockets and a bag with what she'd need.

Emma watched her curiously, but accepted the explanation that there was one more bit of business Cat had in the city.

She was back and walking the city streets by dusk, idling away the time and wondering if this was the right course.

That shopkeeper had set the pair of bullyboys on her, there was no doubt of that. He'd tried to take back what he'd paid Cat — and more, if they'd gotten her to tell of her cache of funds. Certainly, he'd done this before, to who knew how many others.

Yet what should it matter to Cat?

She and Emma could be gone in the morning, well on their way to another place by noon, and need never spare a thought for this city or that shopkeeper again. They might never return here, never see or speak to him, and certainly need not fear him.

Yet it nagged at Cat's middle and set her jaw to clenching.

She'd made a proper bargain with him, worth for worth and neither the poorer for it, and he'd still set about robbing her.

No, she couldn't see him get away with that.

So, nightfall found her on the rooftops, dressed in green and grey.

She crouched, waiting for the streets to quiet. Watched the shop until the downstairs lights went out and the upstairs lit, then longer until the last of them was extinguished.

Then she leapt the narrow alley to his roof, attached her line to the chimney, and lowered herself to the window that had been last lit.

The latch gave way to her implements and she was inside — closed the shutters behind her and crouched in the shadows under the window for her eyes to adjust to the deeper gloom.

The shopkeeper was asleep, snoring lightly.

She approached slowly and gently pulled the bedclothes from his form. The man stirred, frowning in his sleep, and she froze until he settled again.

Her right hand stole to her pocket, her left slid into a glove.

Finally, she moved quickly.

Her gloved hand clamped in place over the man's mouth and her other slapped one of Roffe's brass disks to his stomach just below his rib cage and angled up.

She really hadn't known when she'd taken those from Roffe's workspace why she did so — they were vile, evil things, but they did their work well.

The shopkeeper woke and cried out, but Cat held her hand in place to muffle it. She had to clamber onto the bed and straddle him, nearly thrown off as he bucked, but the disk worked quickly.

The little legs clamped down, piercing flesh and eliciting more muffled cries, then the whirring came and the shopkeeper's eyes grew wide and panicked.

The thin, corkscrew blade dug deep and up under his ribcage until it found his heart and stilled it.

The man slumped, eyes open and staring at Cat's face close to his.

Cat climbed off him and deactivated the disk, then lit the candle the man kept on his bedside table.

Roffe had told the truth about them — there was remarkably little blood. Four small tears in his bedclothes and drops of blood barely half the size of a penny where the legs had pierced him. Smaller and less blood for the main blade, even as it withdrew.

She raised the shopkeeper's nightshirt and wiped away the blood on his skin, examining the holes closely. If one were to know what to look for, then they were obvious — but if not, then they were naught but scratches.

Cat searched the room and shop below, taking some, but not all of the coin and the most portable pieces of value. With luck, all would think the shopkeeper's heart had gone out in the night and never suspect he'd had a visitor.

Pockets and pack full, she slipped out through the window and into the night.

CHAPTER 32

The autumn sunlight was dimming as they entered the outskirts of the village and made their way through it to the inn on the far side.

To Cat, it seemed like every other village they'd passed through in the last —

Lord, it's been nearly a month!

A month of travel, up at dawn to take to the cart, staring at the horses' rumps through the long hours of the day, then every night a different inn, a different taproom, yet somehow all the same.

They'd traveled, doubled-back, and changed their course for all that time and Cat was nearly certain there was no way Roffe, no matter his abilities nor the depths of his purse, could track them through all those twists and turns.

Now they were nearing winter and she'd not want to travel in the cold, so they'd have to find a place to settle soon.

Leeds was near, and she thought that might do. She'd heard the manufactures were doing well, with interesting innovations that might give her something to do in the line of mechanicals. A set of rooms — not too fine, but not shabby — in some anonymous part of the city would see them through the winter.

For now, though, it was one more night in one more village inn.

The village itself, Cat thought, could have been taken up and plopped down anywhere along the road they'd traveled.

A blacksmith, a shop or two, the inn itself — a small church and grave-yard down the lane they were passing now. Two dozen cottages, no better than those on the farms surrounding the village, only on smaller plots.

Emma seemed to like it, though. She'd perked up as they drew near, stirring herself from the torpor of long hours on the road.

Cat counted the hoofbeats and cart rattles, waiting for her to speak, as she was sure she would.

"It's lovely," Emma said.

Cat grinned, but looked away so the other girl wouldn't think she was laughing at her. There'd been some tension between them since she'd gone back after the merchant — Emma didn't know what she'd done, couldn't, but she seemed to sense something.

"It's much the same as every other we've come to," Cat said, resuming the village-entry ritual they'd fallen into.

"It's like where I grew up," Emma said. "Look! That could be my church, there!"

Cat chuckled quietly. There was always something — the church, the blacksmith, even one of the cottages, that was just like a one from Emma's home, and the girl delighted in seeing them.

They were nearing the inn.

It was a large one, bigger than most they'd encountered. Two stories, both large, with a long line of stables leading from one side. The chimneys were topped with plumes of smoke, promising some warmth against the day's chill — and the coming night.

Beside it was a cottage — different than the others. This one was ill-maintained, with a grown-over garden and one of its shutters hanging at a slant from the bottom hinge. No smoke came from its chimney and the thatching of its roof was rough and patchy.

"How sad," Emma said.

"What?" Cat asked.

"That cottage."

Cat looked at it.

"I wonder why it's not kept up," Emma said.

Cat shrugged and steered the cart into the inn's courtyard. A stableboy came out to take their horses, summoning another to help with their bags. Cat kept a careful eye on him, as their bags held all she and Emma had in the world, their stash of coin secreted amongst them.

Inside, the innkeeper greeted them, alerted by their dress that the new visitors were two ladies and not farmgirls.

They got a room for themselves, though no bath — the inn didn't have a proper bathhouse, only a tub which could be brought to the room and filled with buckets from the kitchen. The price for that was dearer than Cat thought they should pay, no matter how she longed for a bath after hours on the dusty road.

"Will you wish supper sent up?" the innkeeper asked as the last of their bags set down and Cat slipped the stableboy a penny for his efforts.

"No, thank you," Cat said. "We'll dine below."

She wanted to hear the news and the common room, rowdy as it might get, would be the best place. There might be word of happenings in Leeds, being this close, and she'd like to know as much as she might before deciding if they'd winter there.

THE COMMON ROOM was as crowded as Cat expected, but not so rowdy — the villagers and travelers were all worn from their day's labor and wanting only a peaceful meal or mug of beer before taking to their beds.

The conversations were low, but Cat gathered enough — that Leeds was prospering as she'd already heard and growing daily. There'd be room for two anonymous girls to hide away there and not be noticed.

Dinner was a rich stew, fresh bread, with only a bit of wine, and a berry crumble with fresh cream for dessert. Cat sopped up every bit of it, while Emma picked at hers.

"Do you wish aught else?" the innkeeper asked at the end.

Cat shook her head. "No, thank you. That was marvelous."

He smiled. "I'll tell the missus — she's always glad to hear that. Where're you bound for?"

It was a question everyone asked. Cat and Emma, traveling alone, were unique enough to make even an innkeeper curious.

"Leeds," Emma said, easy now with their story, "to stay with family."

Cat fought back a groan, as she'd wanted to lay another false trail off in some other direction, not leave word of where they'd really stay so close.

The innkeeper nodded. "You've an easy road tomorrow, then, only be sure t'see the crossroads — the sign falls down a'times."

"Thank you," Cat said.

The man pursed his lips. "Travelin' alone? Is it safe fer ya?"

Cat lowered her eyes and set her mouth in a somber frown. "We've little choice, I'm afraid. Our father … passed recently."

"I'm sorry t'hear that."

Cat gave him a small smile of thanks, blinking to show how hard she was holding back tears.

"Our uncle is in Leeds and he's agreed to take us in, but …" She shrugged, both for the story's sake and being unable to lay a false trail here, now that Emma had let it out. "He's not a wealthy man himself and we have little to our own, so we must make our own way there."

The innkeeper nodded and patted Cat's shoulder. "Well, yer almost there, girls. Almost there."

"Thank you."

"Sir," Emma said, surprising Cat, for she usually remained silent during their story. "Do you mind a question?"

"No, miss, ask away."

Emma spoke slowly, obviously concentrating on her accent. "The cottage next door — what is its story?"

The innkeeper frowned. "The cottage?" He shrugged, his large shoulders heaving. "No story t'speak of. It's ourn — me and the missus. Widow Tibbet had the rent of it, but she went to live with her daughter — couldn't move so good no more. Let it go, a might, she did. That all, miss?"

Emma nodded. "Thank you."

"Why did you ask that?" Cat asked after the innkeeper was gone.

Emma shrugged. "It just seemed sad."

CHAPTER 33

The next morning dawned clear and crisp. Not too cold yet, but the air held a sharpness that told of real cold not too many days away.

Cat slipped a penny into the stableboy's hand before circling around and climbing up into the cart's seat beside Emma. The boy grinned at her and stepped back from the horse, fist clutched tightly around the coin. She shook the reins and the horses leaned into the harness, pulling the cart into motion, out of the inn's yard and onto the road.

Emma had helped load their bags into the back of the cart. She'd been silent most of the morning, merely accepting Cat's suggestions that she dress, get some bread and cheese from the inn's cook, and take her seat in the cart.

"You're quiet this morning," Cat said, once they were clear of the inn and any others who might overhear.

Emma nodded. She looked back at the village as they left it.

Cat looked back too. It didn't take long, it was a small village as she'd noted on their arrival. An inn, a store, a blacksmith for the surrounding farms. One or two other shops she hadn't seen the details of and a handful of homes for those who didn't live over their shops.

212

It was the sort of place that catered to the surrounding farmers, the occasional traveler, and where no one would stop at by choice nor look twice at as they didn't.

There was no bustle in the market square, and only a market at all but once a week. No fishmongers calling their wares nor carters with heavy loads. Even the inn brewed its own beer, so there were no draymen plying the single road and rutted lanes.

It was as boring a place as Cat had ever seen, really.

Emma sighed.

"What is it?" Cat asked.

Emma shrugged.

"'Twas a peaceful place," Emma said, finally, as they passed the first real farm outside the village.

Cat frowned and glanced at the girl. Emma looked as pensive as Cat had ever seen. Melancholy, even.

"We'll be in Leeds soon," Cat said. "I've heard it's growing — factories and engines abound. It might be the perfect place for us to settle. With so many newcomers, two more girls will hardly be noticed."

Emma looked to the roadside and the passing pastures. She nodded.

Cat stared forward, silent. The horses' haunches moved steadily as they pulled the wagon, like a metronome, ticking away the steps from the village to the city.

Emma had never lived in a city, and hadn't liked the ones they'd traveled through. Too crowded, too dirty, too fast — she preferred a quieter place, with fewer people.

Cat looked at Emma for a moment, trying to imagine the girl in Leeds. They'd live in rented rooms, with others above and below them and on all sides. The day would start with a fishmonger's call outside their window, not birdsong. A step outside their door would put them into the bustle of the street, dodging carts and wagons, instead of the peace of a well-tended garden. Their funds didn't extend to luxury, so there'd be no private kitchen for Emma to prepare their meals, only a small hearth, and that fired by coal instead of wood, so the soot would get into the food.

"Did you note the little cottage as we arrived yesterday, Emma?" Cat asked quietly. "The one with the overgrown yard?"

"Y'know I did," Emma murmured.

"Quite in disrepair," Cat said.

"Needs a loving hand, sure. Someone t'care fer it and keep it straight."

Cat looked away, her eyes and heart filling. It was one of the things she loved most about Emma, this way she saw the world. Most would look at the cottage and see all that was wrong with it. The overgrown garden, the brambles in the ditch that would have to be cleared, the fencing in disrepair, the roof thatch all in need of replacing ... Emma thought of what the cottage needed for itself, as though it were a living thing.

And what it might give in return, if it received that love.

For some reason, she thought of the merchant who'd tried to have her robbed, left dead in his bedclothes, his bullyboys, left white and purple in the alley, and of Brandt's blood covering her hand.

Souls can fill with brambles, too.

What could she repair of herself, with Emma's loving hand? And what could she give in return?

The wagon jerked as one wheel fell into a rut.

Cat stopped her reverie and turned to look back at the village.

They were perhaps a mile down the road now. She'd set the stage well enough last night in the inn's common room. Their story had been accepted. Orphaned sisters traveling to family who were none too thrilled at the prospect of their arrival. How could that be changed?

She reined in the horse and stopped the cart. There was no one about on the road yet and no farmhouse in sight.

"Why're we stopping?" Emma asked.

Cat secured the reins and hopped down. She dug through the packs to find some tools and took a rough file to the cart's front corner.

"Cat?" Emma said.

The file wasn't a saw — it was meant for metal, but it would do.

The wheel's spokes yielded to it quickly, bits of wood flying as she carved the first spoke nearly all the way through.

"Cat! What're y'doing? The cart!"

"Ssshhh!" Cat hissed. She started on the next spoke. "And keep an eye out so no one sees. We need an excuse to return."

"What d'ye mean?"

Cat moved on to the next spoke. Just enough so that they'd break easily, but not so much that the tooling would be clear.

"We need an excuse to return to the inn," Cat said, "and to stay a few days."

"Why?"

"Time enough for a letter to our 'relatives,' informing them of the delay. And a letter in return rescinding our invitation — I haven't figured the why of it yet, but I will."

Emma frowned. "Why'd y'want to do that? I thought we was to tell all the story of why we're passing through?"

She nearly had the spokes done. The wheel was wobbling a bit, but held in place — it would never make much way down the road, but it didn't have to.

"To explain why we're not passing through," Cat said, "as we'll have nowhere else to go."

Emma's eyes widened as realized what Cat was saying.

"We'll stay?"

Cat set the file to the last spoke.

"We'll stay."

Emma was off the cart in an instant, bowling Cat over into the dirt of the road and raining kisses on her face and neck.

"You mean it?" Emma asked.

Cat laughed. The warm weight of the girl on top of her took away the morning chill and more.

"I do," she said.

More kisses and Emma's arms wrapped her so tight it forced a bit of breath from her.

Emma pulled her face back and stared into Cat's eyes.

"I love you."

~

THE CART WRECKED MUCH as Cat planned it.

She left Emma standing in the road, got the horses up to a decent pace, then tossed a hefty branch into the wheel spokes.

The spokes shattered as the wheel spun and the cart lurched to a stop.

Cat climbed down and inspected her work.

A suspicious man might find the tool marks, she thought, but not a casual one. And why would anyone in the village be suspicious?

She took another branch to bash at some of the more obvious marks, though, dulling them, and collected some of the spoke bits from the roadway. Those she thought might be too obvious she packed away in their things for disposal in the inn's fireplace.

The cart was obviously going nowhere far for some time. They could likely get it back to the village with the help of some others, but their journey was done until they could have a new wheel fitted. There'd be an expense to that. The expense and the delay being the cause to write to their "family" while staying at the inn for a response.

It lacked but one more thing.

"Cor!" Emma exclaimed rushing up to the cart. "Y'did a proper job on that!"

Cat had to admit she had. The wheel itself, now spokeless, had rolled some way down the road and the cart tipped precariously anytime weight was put to the wheelless corner.

"We'll unhitch the horses and walk them back," Cat said. "But first —"

She drew her belt knife and checked its edge, then lifted her hair away from her forehead. She rapped herself sharply there with the knife's hilt, then again.

"Cat!"

"I need to look injured," Cat said. She tapped her brow again, blinking away the tears the sharp pain brought. "Will it bruise, do you think?"

Emma examined her brow.

"There's a bit already."

"Good."

Cat rapped herself twice more, to be sure, then drew the blade swiftly across the same area.

"Cat!"

"I'm fine, it's only for show," Cat said, holding her head back to let the blood run down her face. She'd have to sacrifice some of the *Parson's Niece* garb for this, but could always purchase more.

The head wound bled freely and she let it flow down her face and onto her clothes for a few moments.

"How do I look?"

"A fright," Emma said. "I'd think you near dead, if I'd not seen you do it!"

"Good."

Cat clambered into the cart and let a good bit of blood flow and spatter about the bench area, leaving it in such a state that anyone coming along before the cart was retrieved would likely think its occupants had been murdered by highwaymen and the bodies devoured by wild beasts.

She and Emma hung all their baggage on the horses, then turned them back down the road toward the village and began the walk, Cat now holding a bit of cloth to her head to staunch the blood.

CHAPTER 34

*O*ur *Dear Uncle,*

It is with much Sorrow and Trepidation that we write to you in order to inform you of Our further Travails.

In as much as we thought to see you in only Three Days' Time, and have Longed for the Embrace of Family after our so recent Bereavement, we find that Fortune has turned Her Frown upon our family once more.

No sooner had we left our Inn this morning, but we did meet with Foul Providence upon the road, causing untold Damage to our Transport, which has lost a Wheel, all entirely!

I, Catherine, was injured most Grievously in the Event and may not be able to travel for some days. Take no Fear from this, as the injury will heal with time, but I require Rest and Solitude to become once more Myself.

Emma is unhurt in body, but the Fright and Effort of the Crash and bringing me to Safety has quite Overwhelmed her.

I fear that neither of us may be fit for Travel, even by such means as the Postal Coach, for some time.

Please do not seek to Trouble yourself on our account. We are Safe and Snug and remarkably well cared for by the fine people of this village, and shall continue our Journey to your Loving Bosom when we are Able.

We shall remain here, at this lovely Inn which has become our Haven in the face of such Adversity, until such time as our transport is repaired and both Emma and I have recovered Ourselves.

Your Loving Nieces,

Catherine and Emma

Cat eased herself back in the bed. Their room at the inn was more comfortable than the first. The innkeeper and his wife nearly going into fits when Emma staggered into the courtyard under the weight of Cat's half-dragged and fully-bloodied form.

Once the story was out and Cat examined to determine that she wouldn't die of the "Grievous Injury," the two girls were ensconced in the inn's best — Cat neatly tucked into a feather bed, rather than the straw tick of a common travelers' room, and the fire built up so she wouldn't take a chill.

Emma curled up beside her and listened as Cat read the letter to their "uncle" aloud.

"What do you think?" Cat asked.

Emma pursed her lips. "Seems all flowered an' such."

"Speech, Emma, if we're to be safe here, you must play your part."

"It seems quite flowery," Emma said distinctly.

"Yes, well, the *Orphaned Daughters* would be a bit flowery, wouldn't they? Raised to be able to take the next step up in society if they found a decent match, I think."

"If you say so." Emma frowned. "Still, why must you write it if there's no one to receive it?"

"Verisimilitude, Emma," Cat said. "No matter that it will never be delivered, if someone here were to see it before the Post comes, it must be believable. It also helps me to compose the reply."

"An' how'll the reply come?" Emma asked.

Cat pinched the girl in the side, eliciting a giggle and then a heavy sigh.

"And how will the reply come?"

"That," Cat said, "is for tonight and why you must let no one in these rooms while I'm gone — I'll be two days, perhaps more. Tell them the excitement of the crash and my injury have me unable to see anyone and that I must rest."

Emma nodded.

"If they begin making noise about payment, there's money in our bags. Hand over half a crown and don't dicker, then say you must rush back to my side — let them feel guilty about the asking and they'll leave you be. And be sure you eat some from both meals they bring up — lightly from mine and say my appetite has not yet returned."

"Should I stir the chamber pots, as well?" Emma asked with a chuckle. "So, it'll seem there's two of us?"

"Yes," Cat said, her face serious. "In fact, use the pots exclusively, but walk out to the privy from time to time, as well. That way there'll be no questions in that regard."

"Cat —"

"It's the little things, Emma, that draw suspicion. Some little thing, not quite right, and it's remarked on — we're remarkable enough here as it is, there's no need to make it more so."

CAT SLIPPED out the inn's window as soon as the night was far enough along that those still in the pub weren't making regular trips to the privy.

She hung from the window's sill and arched her back enough to swing a bit away from the building, then dropped to the ground with a muffled *thump*.

Their room's window was on the back side of the inn, with nothing but the privy between Cat and a copse of trees that extended away and eventually met the curving road out of town.

She paused, hunched in the shadows, and waited for any sign of movement or that her drop had been heard, then moved swiftly for the trees. She was dressed as the *Serving Girl* — hardworking, honest, something that would pass here in the country or in the larger city where she was bound. Not so poor as to make people wary, nor so grand as to cause them to take notice. Just a serving girl, moving from one place to another. She did have the *Merchant's Daughter* in the sack slung over her shoulder, though, along with some of their coin and a bit of bread and cheese.

Through the woods, swiftly and silently, to the road far enough from town that she'd not be seen by any up and about early.

She wasn't worried about farm folk seeing her. Few of them had been into town to have made note of her and Emma at the inn, and, besides, *Serving Girl* looked nothing at all like *Orphaned Daughter* — they were entirely different people.

Once at the road, she settled into an easy run, which warmed her against the cold night air. The rutted lane was no poorer footing than the ill-kept tiles and slate of a late-night roof run, so she was able to keep the pace for some time.

She made the crossroads she sought before dawn, though it was a bit of a squint in the darkness to be sure of the sign, and made the turn. It was near enough to the sun's rise then that she simply walked.

The sun was barely a hint on the horizon, not yet warming things even a bit, when farm carts began to pass her. Cat waved and smiled as they went by, for *Serving Girl* was a friendly lass, quick with a grin and good-humored — though she waved off the offers of a ride toward the city until one was made from a cart with the farmer's wife along, for *Serving Girl* was not naive.

They rolled into the outskirts of Leeds and Cat hopped down with a thank you, another smile, and her wish the farmer do well in his bargaining.

The city was already bustling, with its many factories and work-shops starting work early in the morning or even running all night. Cat merely wandered for a time, familiarizing herself with the place and gaining a feel for the neighborhoods she walked. She was looking for a particular place — a particular sort of man, in truth.

It was nearly noon before she found some answer to her veiled queries and a name.

Chadbyrne Jessel - Solicitor

The sign on the door was worn and shabby, much like the man who answered the door, looked Cat over with an appraising eye, and ushered her inside.

The office was likewise, adding cluttered and dusty to the mix, and the furnishings contributed battered.

Altogether, Cat was certain it was the right sort of place.

Jessel hurriedly pulled a chair away from his desk, swiped a hand over the seat, and gestured grandly for Cat to make herself at home.

"What can I do for you today, Miss —?" Jessel asked, making his way to his own chair.

"Moseley," Cat said, giving the name she and Emma were using. "Catherine Moseley, sir. I have some business with which I require assistance. *Discreet* assistance."

"Of course," Jessel said. "Discretion is, after all, the very bedrock of a solicitor's practice, is it not?"

"One would hope so."

"Indeed," Jessel said, "and the nature of this assistance?"

"To begin, I wish a letter sent." Cat handed over a letter she'd prepared earlier. "Copied in a good hand, and posted, in four days' time, if you please."

Jessel took it, weighed it in his hand, and examined the outside. He grinned and held it up so she could see its front.

"It would appear that you have misaddressed this," he said, "the recipient noted here would seem to be yourself, though not here in Leeds."

Catherine met his gaze and said nothing.

"I see," Jessel said, his smile widening. "Well, I can certainly drop this in the post whenever you like, for a small fee. You said, 'to begin?'"

"I should also like to leave a sum of money in your care," Cat said.

Jessel's smile widened more. "And you wish me to do what with this sum?"

"From time to time, perhaps monthly or of a fortnight, you will send a bit of it to me at the place on the letter you hold."

"Ah," Jessel said. "And the source of these remittances? For me to reference in the monthly packets?"

"An inheritance," Cat said, "kept in trust for my sister and I."

"A relative?"

"Our mother, some time ago."

"I see," Jessel said. "And your father?"

"Also passed. More recently, but without estate."

"Very sad," Jessel said, his smile never faltering. "My condolences."

"Thank you."

"So," Jessel said, "two girls, alone in the world, and settled ..." He looked at Cat's letter again. "Ah, somewhere small enough that the neighbors take note of such things as where a body's income might be from." He spread his hands. "So, give them something to see, yes?"

"You have the right of it, sir."

"Very good, very good," Jessel said. He took a deep breath and his expression sobered. "I must, I fear, ask a question of you — in the discreetest terms, of course — but it will be central to my fee, you understand?"

"Of course, sir."

Jessel clasped his hands and leaned forward.

"Are there any bodies involved at all?"

Cat met his gaze evenly. Jessel was a man who would prefer the truth and hold it close, she thought, so long as he was paid. And there were other duties he might perform for her, so better he not be surprised if such a time ever came.

"Not as should impact our arrangement, Mister Jessel."

"Excellent!" Jessel said. "Let's settle the details then!"

CHAPTER 35

My Dear Nieces,

It was with a heavy heart that I received your letter and learned of your more recent travails. Glad I am that you are not so injured as to threaten your life or longer health.

Now it is with a heavier heart, and great regret, that I must add to your woes.

As disaster has so recently struck your father, my dear brother, I fear the same, though not so dire, has occurred in my own home.

Recent reversals of fortune, which I hope to soon put right but which require all of my attention and resources, have greatly degraded the aid I and my family may offer to you.

It is with the very heaviest of hearts that I must inform you there may be no place for you in my greatly reduced household at this time.

Perhaps your recent travails have not been the misfortune you originally thought, for had you continued in your journey you would have found your hoped-for new home shuttered and empty, my family moved to more parsimonious rooms and our own circumstances so greatly reduced that you would not recognize us. Perhaps, in what you describe as a fine village of kindly people, you may find a place more suited than what you would find here with me.

I may soon find it necessary to leave this place myself and seek shelter from certain obligations in foreign climes. Were you to be part of my household, the holders of those obligations might, though without true legal recourse, seek to take hold of that which is yours by right.

To that end, I have informed a local solicitor of your current location and circumstances, and of your dear mother's estate, small though it be. He shall see it remitted to you there until such time as you may inform him of some other arrangement.

I trust you will think kindly of me and continue to hold me in your hearts as I do you, praying nightly for some improval of your fortunes and some small relenting of the hardships cruel fortune has rained upon our family.

With familial love and great hopes for all our futures,

Your dear uncle,

Frederick

"*Dear Uncle's* a bit of a cobber, ain't he?" Emma asked.

Cat giggled. "He is, indeed. Though not completely, as he's made arrangements for our portions to get to us, rather than keeping them for himself. Yes, the fortunes of the *Orphaned Daughters* are taking a bit of sadder turn now, thanks to him, but we'll have an explainable source for our receiving funds — not so much as to raise comment, but enough to get by."

Emma sighed and snuggled closer to her.

"Don't get too comfortable, love," Cat said, "it's nearly time for you to react to this. You know what to do?"

Emma nodded. "Rush out in a state. You've fainted from the shock o'this topping all else — cry and wave the letter about until someone takes it to find out what I'm on about."

Cat hugged her. "Good. Then just sit and cry until they've 'revived' me, and I'll handle the rest. And watch your accent."

IT WENT MUCH as Cat expected, with a very few weeping *whatever-shall-we-dos* on her part before the innkeeper's wife, rather tentatively, suggested that, if it weren't too rough for such as these fine sisters, and if they truly had nowhere else to go, then would their portion, perhaps, be sufficient to cover the rent of a small cottage — if such were available for a certain very reasonable sum?

Then there was more weeping necessary, of course, but this of joy, as Cat asked, "Really? That very cottage? And we could make a home here with you, who've treated us so very kindly already?"

She even came to regret the necessary subterfuge, for the villagers as a whole were truly, so very kind about the thing. Nearly the whole place turned out after the next church service, shucking their best togs and rolling up their sleeves to make the cottage livable for their new neighbors. New thatch for the roof, the brambles cleared away, the damaged shutter rehinged, and the whole place made clean and ready before Cat, still "recovering" from the blow to her head, and Emma, were led over and proudly shown their new home.

There was more weeping then, at least amongst the women — the men celebrated their work on the place with a newly broached barrel of ale in the inn's common room.

Cat and Emma bid the last of their benefactors goodbye as darkness fell and they settled into their new home.

The night outside was cold, with a hint of frost for the morning, but a cheery fire warmed the place and their pantry was filled to bursting with gifts. It seemed the women of the village had made up a list of everything a proper household needs and seen to checking off every one. Wheels of cheese, a ham, crocks of jam and pickled vegetables, as well as stocks of potatoes, onions, and turnips, two fresh loaves of bread and a sack of flour that would see them through the first weeks of the coming winter.

Outside in the coop there were four chickens and a rooster, though Cat had paid for those, they being so dear.

Their horses had space in the inn's stable and there was interest from more than one local farmer to buy or let them for plowing and harvest come the time for that. The cottage had no fields in need of tending, so the horses and cart were more than Cat and Emma needed for daily chores.

The cottage itself was small, with but one real room and the bed in a loft with a ladder to reach it — but it was clean, it was safe, and it was theirs together.

CHAPTER 36

"'T ain't natural."

Brimhall, the innkeeper, was dressed roughly for his afternoon chores, but not as roughly as Cat who'd been working in the trench dug between the inn and her cottage. Spring was well along into summer, but there was still enough rain to make the ground muddy.

"You just never mind, Scottas," his wife told him. She was taking a break from her kitchen to see the last of the connections made on what Cat had convinced her would be a help to her and her work, as well as the inn's guests — and by no small means to Cat and Emma in their cottage.

Cat took hold of the last of the pipe joins she'd made and found it solid.

She smiled at the two innkeepers, one smiling expectantly and the other scowling.

"Girl!" Sarah Brimhall yelled out to her scullery maid. "Work the pump!"

With that, she turned and hurried back to the inn's kitchen.

Cat followed along. "You won't need to work the pump each time you use it, Mistress Brimhall," she said. "Only to keep the water high enough — so gauge its use."

"Aye, dear, y'said, but if there's t'be hot water for the turning of a crank, then I know a tub what'll be filling in a moment, as I'll be the first to try mine." She eyed Cat's mud-covered dress. "And I'd not be mistaken to say *two* tubs."

Cat's laugh followed her. "No, you wouldn't, Sarah, not at all." She waved at her mud-covered skirts. "Emma'd have words for me if I didn't take myself straight to a bath after this, and they wouldn't be kind."

The device was simple — no different than what Cat had observed at Roffe's manor and townhouse. A copper vessel in the kitchen's oven — which the inn's ran nearly twenty-four hours a day, from bread-baking in the wee hours until supper was served to the guests. Pipe ran from that to an upstairs closet and another tank, so that the heated water could flow up and the cooled water down. Then pipes from that to the stable which shared a wall with the inn — the Brimhall's had sacrificed the stall nearest to the inn's wall, enclosed it, and the inn now had a bathhouse available, and without the need of carrying pails of hot water up to a guest's room.

"'Tain't natural a'tall," Brimhall said again. "A christenin' splash, a dip before yer vows, an' a wipe-down fer yer box — all the bathin' a man needs."

His wife fixed him with a hard look. "Not if yer expecting a bit of what y'say a man needs more regular than that, Scottas Brimhall."

Brimhall flushed and stalked off, muttering about unnatural women and their devices.

"He's just gruff," Sarah said to Cat once he was gone. "Don't mean a thing by it."

"I know," Cat said with a smile.

"An' we're appreciative, we are, of yer doing this — much as the mister may grumble."

"It's really nothing."

Sarah gave her a speculative look. "More'n nothing, I think. All that copper an' piping an' special made knobs an' such."

"It benefits Emma and me, as well, Sarah — you've the kitchen, after all, and space for our horses."

Sarah and Cat entered the stable and then the set aside stall. With a quick look at Cat for approval, she turned the tap and water began to stream into the linen-lined wooden tub. It took but a moment for the cooler water to run out and soon the flow was hot.

Sarah Brimhall's grin was wide and Cat couldn't help but match her.

"And the same in the kitchen?" Sarah asked.

Cat nodded. "Hotter, as it's closer to the tanks, so be mindful."

"We will, and both I and the girl thank you for it, Miss Catherine."

Cat left the woman to her new bath and sought out her own.

The trench from inn to cottage was still open, and she'd have to see that filled, but the piping was laid. Wrapped in several layers of tarred burlap to keep it sealed and hold in the heat, it ran from the inn, across the cottage's side yard, and into the building itself.

She and Emma would have hot water for their own cooking and bath now, which was a boon to both.

No steam, though, the inn's ovens weren't kept hot enough to really get a good head on and Cat wasn't yet confident enough in her knowledge of how to tame that beast.

Soon, though, she thought, glancing toward the blacksmith's across the road and not too far away. If she could harness *that* heat, what could she accomplish with it?

Emma looked up from the cottage's table when Cat entered. She was arms deep in some sort of pastry dough and a bowl of fruit mixture stood by, making Cat's stomach rumble after her exertions. The cottage had no proper kitchen, only a hearth, the main table, and a bit of a pantry for storage, but Emma liked to try and make things herself rather than relying on the nearby inn.

The one main room of the cottage was crowded, especially with the workbench and crates of mechanical bits Cat had taking up one of its walls, but they made do. Emma called it cozy, even with Cat's clutter.

Cat stripped at the doorway, keeping the muddied clothes in as neat a pile as she could. Their own tub was smaller, more of a half-barrel, really, sealed with tar to keep it from leaking and several layers of linen for comfort, but it was theirs and it was private. Something proper would be next on the list, though, as this would not fit two at all.

She grinned as the barrel started to fill and she saw the water was very nearly as hot as it had been in the inn's bathhouse. Her work on insulating the pipe seemed to have done well, but they'd have to see how well it did next winter.

Cat bound her hair up — it was longer than she'd ever had it, ten or more inches now, and she thought to let it grow longer still. It was curling, also, and the color was more defined, so that it very much resembled her mother's portrait. That was something she wished now that she'd taken with in her flight — the portrait was bulky, but it would be nice to have it here, even with Roffe in it.

She stepped into the tub, relishing the burn of the hot water on her cold skin, and lay back.

Perhaps I could steal it, she thought.

It would serve Roffe right to have his home burgled by his own daughter and that portrait, which she was certain he looked on to remind himself of his revenge, taken away.

And I could have Roffe painted out — perhaps turned into some sort of jester or fanged monster.

Emma set her pastry in the oven-box built into the hearth and knelt beside the tub, giving Cat a peck on the cheek.

"All done?" she asked.

"Nearly — there's still the trench to fill, but Sarah's already trying her own out." Cat stretched. The water was cooling and draining theirs was still enough of a chore that it offset the pleasure of refilling it for a longer soak. A proper bung and drain to the gardens was on her list.

She stood and took the drying sheet Emma offered. Once she stepped out of the tub, though, there was a longer kiss and a bit more than strictly drying going on. Her rumbling stomach and the scent of baking pastry interrupted them, though.

"That smells good," Cat said.

"I've made you a tart."

Cat nuzzled at her neck. "Oh, aye, you've made me *your* tart, but what's baking?"

Emma laughed, pulled back, and stared into Cat's eyes.

"I have to go away again," Cat said before she realized the words were coming.

The hurt in Emma's eyes was immediate and Cat couldn't understand why she'd said it just now. She'd simply spoken, unbidden and without thought.

Oh, she'd known for some time she had to tell the other girl, but she'd been putting it off, so why had she now?

"I see," Emma said. She dropped her arms from around Cat and stepped back, turning to the hearth. "An' what's it for this time, then?"

Cat cursed herself for speaking and ruining the moment they'd had. She resumed drying herself and forced her voice to be casual.

"The copper vessels were costlier than I thought."

Emma stirred the fire a bit more vigorously than Cat thought strictly necessary, then reseated the poker with a heavy *crack* against the hearthstone. Cat winced at the sound.

"So, more thievin'?" Emma asked.

"We need the money," Cat said, "and I don't take from any that can't spare it and don't deserve the taking."

"So you say," Emma said, "but how're you to explain it? Us havin' so much of a sudden?"

Cat could tell how upset the other girl was because she'd reverted to her old accent, but didn't correct her. She had a right to be upset, Cat supposed — Cat had left their little home five times now since they'd settled here last fall. First to get "just a few things to tinker with" and come back with the start of her workspace. Then for a bit more. Then to speak with Jessel about how to seed their visible nest-egg with enough more to justify the packages Cat had arriving for her work.

All that had depleted their funds.

Oh, they still had a tidy sum tucked away. Six months or so of their "remittances" still in the care of Jessel. Cat wouldn't trust him with more than that, and the rest was split into caches around the cottage — under the loose hearthstone, at the bottom of one of Cat's crates, even a bit, just enough to satisfy a more traditional robber and send him on his way, underneath their mattress.

It was going faster than she'd anticipated, though, so needed replenishing for Cat to feel comfortable.

So the last two trips had been for thieving, and Cat hadn't lied to Emma about what she did. She'd not killed anyone, nor lied to Emma — not since the two thugs and the merchant. That lie weighed on her and Cat vowed she'd not break the girl's trust again.

"The villagers have no real idea what the parts for my mechanicals cost," Cat said, "and rarely see them anyway."

"They know the cost of copper well enough," Emma said. "An' saw it by the wagonload for next door."

"An investment of our principal," Cat said. "They know, or Sarah and Scottas will say soon enough, how we're to receive some meals and have our horses housed in return. Those, in addition to my reputation as a tinkerer, should justify the expense to any curious minds."

Emma took the tart from the oven-box and set it on the table to cool.

"So you say," Emma said. She shook her head and went to the cottage door. "I'll see to the chickens before dark."

Cat watched the door close behind her and sighed. It wasn't the first such disagreement they'd had, nor would it be the last. Emma didn't like the thieving at all, but Cat felt the need to add to their finances.

She looked around the cottage. Small though it was, it was comfortable and theirs.

But she feared — no, *knew* — knew in her bones that it could disappear in an instant. Without the rents, without money for food, it was only the matter of a few coins between the comfortable life she and Emma knew and a return to the streets Cat grew up on.

They had years to prepare for — *years* to ensure they had enough coin to keep themselves from want. She'd done the math enough in her head to know that what they'd taken from Roffe might keep them in some sort of state for the rest of their lives, but it wouldn't be the state Cat preferred.

She didn't need luxury, she thought, though her time at Roffe's manor had been luxurious enough and she would admit she liked it fine, but she did need the certainty she and Emma would be free from want.

And what of my mechanicals?

Cat made her way to the workbench that took up one full wall of the cottage.

It would look cluttered to any observer, but the sort of clutter that had an odd organization to it. One could certainly imagine that the owner of such a bench could reach out without looking and put hand to any particular part in any particular pile at their whim.

Cat sat down and took up her latest project. She'd begun working on clocks, as they were easy to come by and she wished to learn the gearing better. Few clockmakers would talk to her — they had their secrets and they'd share only with their apprentices, not random girls — and there were fewer texts on the subject. What few texts on mechanicals she'd been able to find lined the shelf above the work-bench and they were well-thumbed even beyond the worn condition she'd got them in.

She was reduced, it seemed, to working most of the bits out for herself.

Two clocks lay before her on the bench, faces down and mechanisms exposed. One was a purchase and the other a device of her own design — as were the two other pairs on the workbench. Her design wasn't a copy, not exactly, there was no learning in that. No, she found that if she studied a working example, then ideas would come to mind — for improvement or simply a different way to do things.

She hadn't perfected her own design yet — each of the three she'd made tended to run much faster or slower off-time than those she purchased — but she felt she was close.

Her eyes followed the mechanisms of the two clocks, side-by-side, and she fell into a peaceful sort of trance as the springs unwound and the little gears moved in perfect regularity.

Emma had no idea of the cost of these — either the clocks themselves or the parts Cat used for her own. Each of those parts was her own design, scribbled on paper with its shape and notes for the sizes and spacing of the gear teeth. Then she'd send the paper off to a craftsman who could work the brass or copper or steel as she required.

Her hands reached to the side as she watched the mechanism, as though independently seeking some activity of their own. She took up a lock at random from a box of them and picks from their place nearby.

For hours her fingers danced, setting and unsetting a lock, then taking up another, only setting the picks down to scribble some idea her eyes had found to improve her mechanism.

She was oblivious, almost, to Emma's return, to the girl's bustling about the cottage and putting it to rights, to half a cooled tart placed beside her with a glass of milk, and even to the kiss Emma left on her cheek before climbing to the loft and their bed.

Hours later, she came aware, eyes burning, fingers needing a stretch to work out the cramp, and stomach rumbling even louder than it had hours before when she'd lost herself in her work. She ate the tart, drank the milk set beside it, and made her own way up to the loft in darkness after quenching the workbench lamps — which she didn't remember lighting.

Emma was asleep, back to Cat's empty side of the bed, so Cat kept as silent as she could as she stripped off her clothes and slid her nightgown over her head. She raised the blankets slowly and eased her way inside.

The bed was small for the two of them, but so was the loft. They made a show of mentioning it from time to time at the inn and talking of having a larger made, or even two smaller, but never did. There were plenty enough families in the village who all shared a single bed, so none would truly remark on the two "sisters" doing so.

She barely had time to close her eyes before Emma moved, rolling over and pressing herself against Cat.

Cat smiled — that meant they were all right. Emma'd not have waited up for her if she were truly angry.

"Satisfied yer baser urges, have you?" Emma whispered, her breath warm on Cat's neck.

Cat couldn't help but grin. Emma always thought the mechanicals were like another lover for Cat, and she was not quite wrong, but she did understand — the urge to know, to *understand*, how the things worked, and to put something together that was both different and *better*, gnawed at her like an unsatisfied hunger.

The things she'd seen in Roffe's attic workspace, the mechanicals coming to market even now, the *steam*, if they could ever stop the bloody engines blowing up — all of it was like a vast new world opening before her, and Cat wanted part of it. She could see a picture in her head of a time when pipes like those to their cottage from the inn ran to every home, carrying both hot water and steam — for bathing and cleaning, sure, but what about for heat in the winter? What if one fire could send its heat to a dozen homes? Why, that would mean the work of a dozen men chopping wood or shoveling coal could be used elsewhere.

And the mechanicals were just as important. Why, the little cleaning device from Roffe's workspace, the one he'd destroyed when Cat got it working — what if there were one of those in every home, not just those rich enough to have it made by the single craftsman who kept the secret close? What if every woman in the village suddenly had the time she spent sweeping floors to herself, for … whatever she liked?

Her mind began whirring again, like the clocks she'd been watching, but sped up a thousand times. There were a thousand, a million, tasks that could be eased … not only in the factories, but in homes as well …

The tart!

The tart Emma'd made — and the dozens like it made by Sarah at the inn for dinner — well, wasn't slicing the apples for it just one of those tasks? Only a knife blade going up and down, wasn't it? And a bit of a slide to push the apple into place after each stroke?

She could almost see it — the gear would have to be *thus* for each slice to be the proper thickness, and the blade must move *like this* to move out of the way as the apple came back into place.

Some sort of hopper to catch the slices — and another to hold several apples waiting for their turn. Could it peel them, as well? That would be a delicate bit, wouldn't it? Perhaps a razor's blade, but how to keep it from taking too much — a spring! Yes, a spring with just the right tension to pierce the skin, but not enough to cut off too much flesh ... if I were to —

Emma's hand on her brow stilled the thoughts.

"Sshhh," the girl whispered. "I see yer mind spinnin' like them gears."

She stroked softly and Cat's thoughts stilled, then Emma squirmed in that particular way that seemed to erase Cat's thoughts all entire.

"Time enough fer them things tomorrow, yes, love?" Emma whispered, then pressed her lips to Cat's.

"*Mmmm-hhmmm*," Cat agreed through the kiss.

Afterward, Cat's mind began to spin again, she couldn't help it, but Emma pulled her close, stroked her forehead, and sang her whispered song.

"Rhown ein golau gwan i'n gilydd, fy nghariad — Ar hyd y nos."

We'll put our weak light together, my love — All through the night.

Cat fell asleep to the thought that together, their light was very bright indeed.

CHAPTER 37

*C*at went off a week later.

The horses were harnessed in the early morning as other travelers also took their leave of the inn to continue their journeys. Emma walked her to the cart and handed her up a bag of bread, cheese, and fruit.

"Five days, you said?" Emma asked, careful again with her accent, as Brimhall was about in the courtyard to see that no traveler left without a hearty goodbye — or with any owing on his account.

Cat hid a smile as a gentleman handed his lady into their coach, then turned to Brimhall and pressed a coin into his hand.

"A fine place, you have here, innkeep," the man said. "My wife insists we break our journey here from now on, with the ease of bathing."

Brimhall cut his eyes to Cat, but smiled widely and accepted the coin while tugging his forelock with his other hand.

"Thank you, sir, and thank yer lady, if it's no impropriety," he said.

Cat stored the bag under the cart's bench and took up the reins.

"Or more," she said in answer to Emma's question. "I'll need time to … look about. And there's a craftsman I wish to speak to about a trick he has with —"

Emma nodded, but smiled. "Some piece of work I'm not like to understand," she said. "Well, send word if you're to be more than the five days, will you?"

Cat nodded. She longed to wrap her arms around the girl and give her another proper goodbye, but they'd had to settle for accomplishing that in the cottage. It wouldn't do for Brimhall or the travelers to see the "sisters" too affectionate with one another.

Brimhall walked by and Cat caught his eye with a nod to the departing coach and a wink.

The innkeep pocketed the coin and scowled. "Unnatural," he muttered.

CAT WAS NEARLY seven days in the city. She posted a note to Emma on the fourth day, when it was clear she wouldn't be starting back soon, but received no reply. That wasn't unusual — Emma could read Cat's missive well enough, but she wasn't practiced enough at writing to be comfortable doing so. The untidy scrawl was a bit out of character for the *Orphaned Daughters*, so she wrote rarely.

The delay in Cat's journey was twofold.

First, there was the need to find a suitable target for her nighttime excursions. She'd promised Emma that she wouldn't steal from the innocent, so not just any merchant would do.

Second, the craftsman she wished to speak to was proving a bit canny. He answered some questions and not others — but seemed willing enough to do so later, so Cat kept returning to his shop, and then, later, to a nearby pub where she plied him with beer.

"It's not that the boy's an idiot," the man said over his cups on the last night Cat felt she could spend with him. She'd strike her target later and wished to be out of the city thereafter, "it's only that *why* would anyone want to be a bloody priest?"

Cat nodded in sympathy.

Fairleigh Bryant's son had no wish to follow his father into the trade and the sudden announcement, when Bryant had no other apprentice to take over his shop and work when he was gone, had shocked the man and made him worry about the future.

"It's enough t'make me wish I were Church instead o' Catholic," Bryant muttered. "I mean, there'll be no …" He glanced at Cat. "Well, you know …"

Cat nodded again. "It is a quandary you have, Master Bryant."

"Yer an understanding lass," Bryant said. He sighed. "I could wish the boy'd meet a girl who'd *make* him understand what he's givin' up, if y'see?"

"I'm afraid I can't help you with that," Cat said.

Bryant had the good grace to flush red.

"Apologies — not what I meant at all," he said. He sighed again. "But it is a letdown, you know? No grandbabies to spoil? No one to take over the shop when I'm gone — I'm too old to take on a newcome apprentice."

"It is a shame," Cat agreed.

Bryant signaled for another mug and waited, silent, for the serving girl to bring it.

"Those were some fine drawings you brung me," he said.

"Thank you, Master Bryant."

"A bit rough in the detail, but the descriptions were clear."

"I'm getting myself some finer paper," Cat allowed. "I understand there's a fellow in France who's invented a sort of steel quill."

Bryant grunted and Cat could see his mind turning over the thought. "Like to see one of those."

"I plan to order one, perhaps I could show it to you when next we meet?"

"You're a clever girl," Bryant said. "Cleverer than my Rob, for sure. Fine hand, even with the poor paper, and I'm curious to learn what you plan to do with the parts you've ordered."

"As I am curious to know your process for getting the parts so refined in so short a time," Cat said.

Bryant nodded. "No such thing as a girl apprentice."

"Nor have I the time for such a commitment, but it *would* be a shame for your processes to be lost with you."

"No plans to get myself lost too very soon."

They sparred some more, but in the end Cat thought they had an agreement of sorts. Bryant would begin sharing his secret processes with her and she would begin sharing what she made with him. She couldn't, after all, produce and sell her own devices — word of *that* would certainly get back to Roffe. Bryant could manufacture and sell them as his own, something that did gall Cat a bit, but it would keep her and Emma safe — Bryant would no more tell his customers they'd been invented elsewhere than he would take on a girl for an apprentice.

In return, Cat would get his secrets and satisfy, for a time, the never-ending itch she had to see her devices out in the world.

She left Bryant to his drink, settling enough on the pubtender to cover anything else the craftsman might wish for himself that evening and stepped out into the night.

SHE MADE a brief stop at her own inn to change her clothing, donning the shadowy gear of her rooftop running along with enough bits of the *Flowergirl* to give that impression, and slipped out the window.

The run worked off some of her nervous energy and excitement at the thought of Bryant sharing his secrets. He'd promised her a sheaf of designs she could take with her, to be picked up in the morning on her way from town. If she could improve upon them, as they'd discussed, then there'd be more for her to examine in addition to her own work.

She took a more roundabout route to her destination than was necessary, letting the effort and pleasure of dashing across the slate and tile work that excitement out of her so that she could concentrate on the very different task ahead.

That task, the robbing, went almost easier than convincing Bryant to begin sharing his secrets with her.

Cat prowled the seedier areas of the city for a time, identified a few likely bullyboys, then followed them as the *Flowergirl* while they went from stall to stall in the market, always coming away with a little bundle of coin — their take went to a particular tavern and a man at a back table, who never seemed to leave.

She watched him for a time, nursing a cup of beer, until the place grew so rowdy that she knew the *Flowergirl* shouldn't be there alone, then left to set up a watch post on the roof across the street.

She never saw the man leave, so that meant he had rooms there.

Not the big boss, then, but he'd have the market take for several days before that was sent for by his employer, and that would be enough to keep her and Emma for a time.

Now she only had to determine which were his rooms, and where he kept the chest she knew must be there.

It was late for most, but still early enough that the tavern's custom was strong, so she looked for upstairs lights in a room, figuring the man would leave a guard, and that guard would need a light, and any other residents would not seek their beds while the common room below was in full bellow.

Window marked, she reached the tavern's roof and set a light rope about the chimney, easing it down just to the level she needed so that it wouldn't be visible to any in the alley below.

She slid down headfirst, rope threaded through a hooped belt Clanton had given her, until she could peek in through the closed shutters. It was a warm night, so those closed shutters were another sign this would be the right room, for any resident abed this early would prefer to have what breeze there was.

Right the first time, she noted, seeing the back of an obvious bullyboy in a chair facing the room's door. The man sat slouched over, tossing a knife to stick into the floor then picking it up again, with a repetitive *thunk-siss,* of strike and removal from the wood flooring.

She quickly greased the shutter hinges with pork fat, working it between the metal with a thin, dull blade. The guard's knife-game covered the sound of that same thin blade slipping between the shutters and lifting the latch, the *clack* of the latch's metal on wood being less than the next *thunk* of the thrown knife.

Cat eyed the distance between window and chair, then eased

herself back up out of sight. She turned right-side up and walked down the wall to the side of the window, flexed her knees in concert with the *thunk-siss* from inside the room, then pushed herself off the wall and to the side.

She crossed the window's sill just before the next *thunk*, her feet hit the floor with it, and she rolled toward the chair, coming up just as the guard, his knife embedded in the floor, turned in startlement at the sound of her arrival behind him.

She came up from her roll driving hard, her gloved hand holding a roll of heavy lead, and caught the man just under the jaw and at an angle from right to left.

"*Wha —*"

The man staggered back a step and Cat brought her weighted hand back around to clip him below the right ear. She then caught him, as much as she was able as he was a large specimen, and eased him to the floor.

She pocketed the lead and shook out her hand, staring with a bit of surprise that it had worked so handily.

Just as Clanton said it would. She shook her head in wonderment — the myriad ways to strike a man, and to what effect, playing over in her head.

The chest she was searching for was in plain sight — why should it be hidden when there was a guard sitting right beside it and, if the scuffle of a shoe she heard from the hallway told her true, one in the hallway as well.

The lock yielded easily and the spring-loaded trap was one Clanton would box her ears for if she couldn't disarm it in a trice.

Cat's eyebrows rose at the contents — she must have hit the group near the point where they'd transfer this chest to someone higher up in the gang, as it was full of bags of coin. She cleared those out quickly into her own bag, tied that to the end of the rope, and then slipped back out the window, easing the shutters closed behind her and taking the time to set the latch again. When the man in the tavern came up for bed, he'd be in a state to explain the missing gains — or the guard she'd left behind would be when he woke. She spared not a moment's care for how those two might be treated by their employer, for they were at the business end of taking the day's profit from honest merchants.

She got to the rooftop and pulled up the rope with money-laden bag, grunting at the effort.

There may be something in this take-from-the-thieves-and-scoundrels that satisfies Emma — lord knows few honest merchants would have this much for so easy a taking.

Rope and pack in hand, she skittered across a couple rooftops, then down to an alleyway where she arranged her skirts and clothes to hide anything out of the ordinary. That done, and looking like nothing other than a girl making her way home from a hard day's labor, she made her way back to her inn and up to her room.

By morning, she was in the cart and on her way home feeling quite satisfied with her trip.

CHAPTER 38

The cart clattered into the inn's courtyard at midafternoon and Cat tossed the reins to the stableboy. He gave her an odd sort of look, but she ignored it, already on her way to the cottage.

With the amount of coin she'd taken, they would have enough ready money that Cat wouldn't need to gain more until the following spring — and with Master Bryant agreeing to send some few designs by post, she'd have little other reason to leave. Both of which would please Emma.

She nearly skipped with happiness as she neared the cottage door and called out.

"Emma!"

She entered, the cottage door squealing on its hinges, which was unlike it and sent a chill down Cat's spine that had little to do with the sound.

The cottage was empty and dark — no fire burned in the hearth and no lanterns were lit. The curtains were all pulled tight against the afternoon sun, which was also unlike Emma — she'd normally have them full open until after nightfall when she'd pull them closed against the dark outside, as though fearful someone would peep in unseen.

"Emma?"

Cat's eyes adjusted quickly to the gloom and the condition of the cottage told her all was not right.

Chairs were overturned, drawers pulled out and emptied, the contents of the pantry strewn about and all opened, so that flour and eggs and honey coated the floor nearby.

Cat froze for only a moment, then dashed inside and up the ladder to the loft.

"Emma?"

The loft was in a similar state — the mattress sliced and its stuffing flung about.

Cat slid down the ladder in a panic. This could not be, she wouldn't accept it — what could have happened?

Robbers, she decided, come one night, but Emma wouldn't have stayed. Who would with such a mess and fearful of robbers? She'd be at the inn, with the Brimhalls, safe as any and only waiting for Cat's return to —

The light in the doorway darkened even as Cat turned from the ladder. Sarah and Scottas Brimhall stood there, alerted by the stableboy who ducked around them to peer into the cottage.

Brimhall's head was bandaged, his right arm in a sling and bound as well.

Cat stared at Sarah's face for a moment, hoping beyond hope that she misread the look of sorrow and sympathy there, then Sarah moved to the side and the light fell on the table — the table Emma used for her cooking, to make her tarts, and where she and Cat had their meals.

The light highlighted the table's surface, now marred and gouged with rough-hacked lines

R

∾

"IT WAS three days after you left," Sarah said, but the words seemed to buzz in Cat's ears and made no sense.

They'd got her to the inn, sat her at a table, and shooed away the other guests, something that Cat would never imagine Scottas Brimhall doing. Yet here he sat in his empty taproom, pouring her a mug of his best brandy, kept under lock and key for those few visitors who'd not accept a local beer or what poor wines he stocked.

"Wait 'til she's drunk a bit, Sarah," he said. "She's not hearing you."

He wrapped Cat's hands around the mug and helped her raise it to her lips.

"Drink," he ordered. "Two good gulps, then let it sit a moment."

Cat did, coughing and nearly choking at the first, but Brimhall tipped the mug again and she drank.

The liquor burned her throat but settled in her stomach and sent out tendrils that barely warmed the chill that filled her.

Brimhall waved a hand in front of her face.

"You there, girl? You with us now?"

Cat nodded. She was, surprisingly. The buzzing in her head had stopped and she could focus on what Sarah was saying, though her head still felt like it was wrapped in cotton.

Brimhall nodded and Sarah began again.

"Three days after you left," she repeated. "Scottas heard a scream, he thought, and went to check on Miss Emma to see she was all right — then when he didn't return straightaway, I went and found him laid out on the cottage floor."

"It was one man," Brimhall said, his eyes narrow. "I'll swear to that, but how one man took me down I'll never recollect. All the lamps was out and only the coals in the hearth, so it was dark, but I've fought in the dark before — know how the shadows work. I had my cudgel and swung, but —" He held up his arm. "— sliced clean. Then a blow to my head and I was down."

"I found him like that," Sarah said, "arm and head bleeding —"

"Like to take half my ear off," Brimhall added.

"Miss Emma was gone," Sarah said. "No one saw a coach nor heard a horse a'tall."

offe — for that was certainly who had taken Emma, Cat didn't think he would send Clanton for such a thing, he'd come himself — had done a thorough job of searching the cottage. All Cat's carefully secreted caches of coin were emptied, and all of her devices deliberately taken up and smashed to bits. She found the charred remains of her drawings and designs in the cold hearth.

Her father had been nothing if not thorough in the cottage's destruction, she thought the only reason he hadn't set the place afire was that a charred shell would be less distressing to come home to than the destruction he'd wrought.

Cat picked idly through the debris for only a few minutes before concluding there was nothing left of any real value. She had the coin in the cart and whatever she might recover from the solicitor, Jessel, and that was all she had to mount her rescue of Emma. That Roffe had taken Emma to lure Cat back, as well as punish her, she had no doubt.

She left the cart and horses with the Brimhalls and took the coin they offered. She had a moment's thought to refuse, but with all her caches looted by Roffe, she'd need the few shillings.

"And they're yours again, should you come back," Sarah said, her eyes questioning.

Cat only nodded, she didn't want to make promises she couldn't keep, nor think about the future until after she found where Roffe had taken Emma. That would be her focus and her only goal now.

She took the post coach to meet with Jessel and retrieve what funds he still held. He asked no questions at all, merely thanked her for her business and wished her well, assuring her his services were available to her should she ever need them again.

Then a series of post coaches to London, in a more roundabout way.

She had the *Orphaned Daughter* and the *Flowergirl*, still, along with what of her roof-running gear had been in her bags instead of the cottage. After visiting Jessel she picked up a new friend, whom she dubbed the *Weary Traveler* — a deep-hooded cloak that hid her face in shadows.

She pulled that close about her and bowed her head so that few of the others in the coaches dared disturb her — those who did seemed discomfited when she turned the cowl's shadowy front to regard them and said simply, "Thank you, but I fear I must rest."

The cowl would also give her what shelter she might have from any of Roffe's men watching for her to alight there.

She gave some thought, upon seeing a group of them working their fields beside the post road, of going in the guise of a nun, but dismissed it — best not to steal from God when just starting out on this particular journey. Though she did make a note that such could prove useful — after she'd got Emma back and dealt with Roffe.

Once back in London she let a poor set of rooms, after assuring herself she wasn't being followed from the coach, and took a moment to relax. Her thoughts had been a whirl of planning for the whole trip and she wanted to give them time to settle.

She'd have to move fast, though, for her stash of coin was much diminished. Oh, there was an impressive row of guineas in her travel bags, along with bags of other coins, but she'd learned this last year on the run that none of it ever lasted as long as one thought it would.

The memory of her first encounter with Roffe came to her, and how she'd perched on that rooftop weighing his purse and dreaming

— thinking that the coin it carried would keep her nearly her whole life.

She'd learned since then — there was never enough coin. They ran through one's fingers like water and she might as well cup her hands and try to carry moonbeams from one window to the next as think she could hold onto wealth.

A good deal of what she had now would have to go to hiring help and gathering information — where Roffe was and where he was keeping Emma, as well as how many men he had guarding them both.

The trouble was, she knew no one in London but Roffe and Clanton and those they'd introduced her to — who would surely be Roffe's men. and report to him as soon as she contacted them.

Well … nearly no one else.

CAT HUDDLED next to the chimney, her roof-running clothes blending into the shadows, and watched the building across the narrow alley.

The gang was nearly all inside and if whoever'd taken over after Brandt kept them to the same sort of schedule — which he would, she thought, because the boys did like to know what was expected of them — then they'd be doing the shareout soon. Everyone would put their day's takings into the pile and the new leader'd decide what would go to the gang as a whole and what would go to each member — after kicking up to Marven, the next higher-up, of course.

Their lookout on the other roof was watching the alley and the market street, not the other rooftops, so Cat's hiding place was in no danger of discovery.

Given the boy's attention, she thought she might be able to turn cartwheels without him noticing, which was all to her good.

She ran and leaped over the alley below, landing on the gang's roof with a muffled *thump* that finally drew the lookout's attention, but it was too late for him.

Cat grasped his arm as she came up from her roll, spun him around, and pressed him firmly to the brick of the building's chimney.

She put the dull side of her knife blade to the back of his neck. She didn't know him — he was young, maybe six or seven years old, and must have come on after she left.

"Still and quiet, yes? And you'll be all right."

The boy nodded carefully.

"Good," Cat said. "Now you stay right there and I'll whistle for you when it's time to come down. I'm only going to have a talk — who's leader now?"

"Os — Osraed," the boy stammered.

That was surprising. Cat would have thought Dome, for Osraed was none too bright. He'd done well enough as Brandt's second, but that only entailed taking orders.

She made her way down the stairs, avoiding the ones she knew creaked, until she saw light ahead, then slowed and eased her way to look. The gang was all gathered around a couple of lanterns and the sight of it brought back a lot of memories for Cat — some good, most bad, and all more than she needed to deal with just now. The only memories of this gang she had need of were the ones that would help her get them working for her.

She threw her hood back and stepped into the light.

The gang numbered about two dozen now, she thought, ranging from the littlest of perhaps five — still small enough to fit through near anything but old enough to follow instructions — to Osraed and Dome, who were not much younger than Cat. She'd have been second under Brandt if she hadn't seemed so scrawny — and hadn't avoided the attention — both those boys were still bigger than she was now.

Osraed had pride of place nearest the lamps, a pile of coin in front of him and he was adding to it what another boy'd just handed him when Cat stepped out.

They all looked up, some startled, some merely suspicious. A few hands went to belt knives, but Osraed held his hands up to still them. He rose and turned to face her.

"For someone who run off, you sure come back a lot, Runt."

"It's Cat —" No, that wouldn't do at all. She needed to establish their roles immediately and it wasn't as equals. "It's Miss Catherine now, Osraed, and you'll remember it."

"Will I?"

"If you don't wish to wind up like Brandt," Cat said.

Osraed's eyes narrowed. "Last I saw Brandt, he was about to have a taste o'your poke-hole."

Cat smiled thinly. "And note that was the last you saw of him."

"You had help," Osraed said. "Someone knocked us all about and run off with you — weren't you alone, for sure."

"I was a bit distraught that night, Osraed. I won't be caught unawares again."

Osraed matched her smile. "Won't you?"

The faintest scuff of boot upon wood warned Cat that Dome, who she'd noted making his way behind her in the shadows, was lunging for her.

She side-stepped his rush, caught his arm, rapped it sharply as Clanton taught her to send the knife clattering to the floor, and sent him staggering into Osraed.

She stooped to pick up his knife and tossed it hilt-first back to him as soon as he recovered.

"You always did shuffle your feet too low, Dome," she said.

Osraed drew breath, perhaps to order the whole gang to go for her, but she pulled her hand from her pouch and the glint of coins stopped him. His mouth stayed half-open as she approached and let a rain of pennies fall to his pile of coin with a rapid *clinking*. She let fall enough that every boy there could see himself with a full belly the next two days or more, even with Marven's share sent up.

"There's more," Cat said to Osraed. "Not with me, so shall we talk about how you get it?"

THE GANG WAS CELEBRATING their good fortune by sending a runner out to bring back sausage and bread, but Osraed pulled her aside as soon as the boy was off.

They stepped out onto the rooftop, where they could have a private talk, and Cat caught sight of a figure nestled against the chimney.

"Oh, dear."

"Garwin!" Osraed bellowed. "You worthless dung-head! What're you doing?"

The boys head barely moved, but he nodded slightly at Cat.

"I told him not to move," Cat explained. "Go downstairs, boy!"

Osraed sniffed as the boy went past. "An' clean your pants!" He turned to Cat. "Well, you've impressed the young ones, at least."

"But not you?" Cat asked.

Osraed settled himself on the roof's edge and looked out over the dark and vacant market. Cat sat beside him.

"You lied to us, Runt," Osraed said. "Why should I trust you?"

Cat frowned and watched him out of the corner of her eye for a moment. Osraed had always been a believer in the truth, but there was more to him now. She was surprised he was the gang's leader, after Brandt, and he seemed less ... dunderheaded than ever she knew him.

"When last we met," Cat said, "you were holding me down while Brandt tore at my skirts, Osraed. Trust isn't in it."

"You're jumping to the last of what's between us, Runt, when we've still to deal with the first. You lied to us for years."

"I should have told?" She grasped her chest and shook them at Osraed. "What would have happened to me if you'd all known about these? Bent over for Brandt and any others who wanted a taste, then sold off to the buttock-brokers, that's what!"

Osraed grunted. He reached into his pants and drew out a flask, opened it, and took a drink, then passed it to Cat.

She took it and drank, surprised at the taste — apple brandy, and not a harsh one. She looked at the flask for a moment, frowning, and passed it back.

Osraed drank. "You stole that purse from us," he said. "That was a big score — we were counting on it for the week. Marven was none too pleased we came up short."

"There was nothing in it — naught but some rusty, iron disks." She shook her head and snorted with laughter. "Believe me or not, but it's the truth. That man — the one we took it from — he was … planning something."

Osraed grunted. "Something for you?" he asked.

Cat nodded.

"He have anything to do with this work you want of us?"

Cat nodded again.

Osraed grunted again, drank and passed the flask to her. Waited for her to pass it back, then, "Sounds a dangerous man."

"He is."

"He who came that night? He who killed Brandt? You've not said a'certain, but he's dead, ain't he?"

Cat considered what to say. Osraed had never shown much of whether he liked Brandt or not, so did he want revenge? Would he agree to help her if he thought Roffe had done the killing?

Finally, her mind settled on the thing Osraed said to her at the start, how she'd lied to him.

"I killed Brandt," she said.

Osraed pursed his lips and drank again. "Hard or easy?"

Cat thought about all the screams and whimpers in the dark. She turned her head, met Osraed's gaze, and stared at him for a moment.

"Hard."

Osraed's eyes widened a bit.

"You're not Runt no more," he said.

"No, I'm not." Cat accepted the flask and sipped again, the scent of apples in her nose. "You're not the same Osraed I knew."

Osraed nodded to her chest. "Some things needed hiding under Brandt, I'll admit." He sighed. "I always thought, another year an' that bastard'll move up, you know? Marven tap him for some job — maybe he goes for the high jump and half the little 'uns rejoice, but Brandt, damned if he didn't like being the big fish in the little pond, see what I mean?"

Cat nodded.

"So, I did as I'm told," Osraed said, "no matter what, and I wait. Now Brandt's gone and Dome backs me, so I'm in charge."

"So, *you* lied to us all those years, Osraed? Playing the boy with rocks for brains?"

The boy shook his head. "*I* never said I was stupid, Run —" He frowned. "What was it, Miss Catherine?"

"It'll do."

"All right, then, Miss Catherine. Like I was saying, *I* never said I was stupid — so no lie, see?"

"If you say so."

Osraed drained the flask. "I do."

Cat nodded to it. "That's not rough drink," she said. "It must be nice at the top."

Osraed shot her a sideways look. "Brandt was a fool," he said. "We've twice as much in the pile as when he was in charge. Brandt, he took near all of it as didn't go to Marven, so the boys had to hold back some to eat — you remember?"

Cat nodded.

"But we were all afraid to hold back too much and if the rest just goes in the pile, then why bother bring in more than your share for Marven, eh?" Osraed chuckled. "Now I see they all see the split and its fair — so they work harder. More for them, more for Marven —" He tucked the flask back into his belt and smiled. "— more for me."

Cat thought she could almost like this new Osraed.

"So we can work together?" she asked.

"Aye, Miss Catherine, we're yours — long as you have the coin."

CHAPTER 40

*O*sraed was true to his word and the gang soon set about earning more of Cat's coin.

She dipped into her dwindling cache again and again over the next fortnight to keep them at it, but their reports soon gave her a decent idea of Roffe's comings and goings from the club where he kept rooms. Perhaps he cared more for the company there than at the townhouse, but he spent no more nights in his own home now than he had while Cat was there with Clanton — visiting only seldomly, Cat assumed to work on some device.

There was, though, no sign of Emma anywhere. Neither Roffe nor Clanton, who was also shadowed by the gang, went anywhere near a sniff of the girl.

It was morning when Cat decided to confront Roffe and the street outside his club was bustling with activity already. Cat rode in a hired carriage, followed at a distance by another containing Osraed, who was decked out in new clothes Cat had dubbed the *Poor Lord's Son*. Shabby and several seasons out of fashion, but good enough to be hiring carriages without the driver worrying about the fare.

She alighted quickly, not waiting for either the driver or the club's doorman to open the carriage door and put down the steps — instead she flung it open herself and hopped down.

She wore the *Parson's Niece*, no longer the *Orphaned Daughter*, though she was herself for the most part — the conservative cut and dark color lent her the necessary gravity, she thought.

The doorman, caught with his hand extended and smacked with the flung open carriage door, took several steps back in surprise, which allowed Cat the opportunity to walk swiftly — not running or dashing, but purposefully and brooking no interruption, as the *Parson's Niece* would in searching out some parishioner in need of a lecture.

She was into the club before the doorman could recover and the door swung shut behind her.

Inside, the club was all dim lights and dark woods, just as she'd suspected from glimpses of the male-dominated studies she'd had at the parties Roffe took her to.

The entry hall had a marbled floor and the heels of her shoes set off a sharp echo, the pace of which never altered or slowed as she strode forward.

A suited majordomo or other servant of some kind widened his eyes and rushed toward her.

"Miss? *Miss!* May I help you?"

"I seek my uncle, Mister Edward Roffe, is he in?"

Cat saw the man's eyes cut toward a particular door and she started that way before he could begin to answer.

"Mister Roffe is in the Reading Room," he said, "but —" He struggled to keep up with her, his feet on the marble adding a shuffling, desperate counter-beat to her own. "*Miss!* Ladies are not allowed in the —"

He broke off as Cat made the Reading Room door and strode through with no hesitation. His voice lowered to a hissing whisper as he followed along.

"Ladies are *not* permitted in the club, Miss Roffe!"

The Reading Room was perhaps half full of men in heavy, leather, wingback chairs, all set about in groups of two or four around low tables, with carefully shaded lamps casting pools of light for each reader. Coffee cups clacked against saucers, newspapers crinkled and *snapped* as they were read and folded, the low murmur of some few conversations filled the room for an instant as Cat entered, then silenced as heads turned to observe her, eyes widened, and all action stilled.

Cat ignored them. She caught sight of Roffe, made her way to him — also ignoring the increasingly urgent pleas of the majordomo — and sat herself in the chair opposite him.

"Mister Roffe, *please*," the majordomo whispered. "Inform your *niece* that she is *not* permitted *in* the club."

"Please excuse us this one time, Franklin," Roffe said, voice calm. "I'm sure my niece would not disturb us so if it were not an urgent matter."

The majordomo's throat worked as though there were a great many words caught there and in need of swallowing.

"A few minutes, only, I assure you," Roffe said.

The servant clenched his jaw, nodded once, then backed away.

Around them, the sounds of the Reading Room began to resume, though fewer and more muted.

Roffe smiled thinly. "Catherine."

"Father."

"Good of you to come, it's been too long without word. Are you well?"

"Where is she?" Cat demanded.

"Who?"

"You know who, damn you!"

"The maid do you mean? Have you lost her?" Roffe shrugged. "Perhaps she's run off with someone — the lower classes, you know. Can't trust them."

They sat in silence for a moment, Roffe smiling his infuriating smile and Cat's mind working on how to get any information from him at all. She'd hoped to throw him off by confronting him here, but he was unshaken.

"What do you want of me?" she tried instead.

"You know what I want of you, Catherine."

Cat shook her head. "I won't return to you."

"That's what your mother said, and look what happened to her. I will not allow you to defy me, Catherine. You are mine, as she was, and nothing, *no one*, will deprive me of what is mine."

She stayed silent then lowered her eyes to her lap and let her shoulders slump. Perhaps if she appeared to give in —

"And if I do? Return, I mean."

Roffe shrugged. "I suppose that all will return to as it was."

"So, she's alive?" Cat asked. "Emma?"

"Alive?" Roffe snorted. "Of course — so long as she's of value to me, of course. I'm surprised it's taken you so long to come for her — perhaps she is surprised, as well."

Cat ignored his dig. "And she's well, you've not harmed her?"

"Harmed? Far from it, she's getting the best of care for her affliction."

"Affliction?" Cat asked, her blood running cold. What had Roffe done?

"That ... aberration of hers." Roffe's eyes narrowed. "There's a physician I know who has the most ingenious theories for the cure of that."

Cat's blood chilled, but she kept enough of her senses to wonder why Roffe would tell her that. The information had been got too easily — she could find the doctor, find where Emma was kept.

"Because it won't matter," Roffe said, answering her unspoken question. "You'll find her and run again, yes?" He shrugged. "Very well. *I* will find *you* again. You're not your mother, Catherine — not a bit. Too much of me in you. The taste of the mechanicals will call you — and I'll find you. You'll have need of money, for you've far finer tastes, now you've had a bit of finery to yourself, than you can bear to part with, so you'll pull a job for more coin — and I'll find you." His smile widened. "You'll feel the *urge*, girl, to set yourself and take from others, even if you don't need the coin just then. You'll make an excuse for it, any excuse to feel that rush — *and I'll find you.*"

He wasn't wrong, she knew. They'd had enough for a year or more

— far more if she'd stopped buying in parts for her mechanicals — before she'd made that last trip. They hadn't *really* needed the coin, but she'd wanted the freedom and feeling of setting herself to beat some closely guarded thing and take it.

"I'll find you," Roffe repeated, "and do worse to teach you not to run. And again, and again, and again — for however long it's needed, until you realize that you cannot escape. You are *mine*, and I will not let you go, girl."

CHAPTER 41

"Poking stick? Poking stick, miss, just a tuppence!"

Cat brushed the boy aside and moved forward with the others, about three dozen, who wished to tour the facility this afternoon. Most were men, but there were several other women, so Cat didn't feel too out of place. She ignored another youth selling bottles of water with which to spray the inhabitants.

The building before her, Bethlem Royal Hospital, was imposing, and disturbing to look at, with walls that seemed to tilt slightly off true.

There was talk of a new site and a new building, but for now, the building itself reflected those within.

Up ahead there was an uproar in the line.

"What do you mean I can't enter?" a man was saying. "I tell you I had a ticket just here! Signed by Governor Rhodes of your board!"

The line shuffled to a halt. Little Garwin, the boy she'd terrorized on the gang's rooftop, hurried by, a pack of sticks in one arm and the other hand just brushing Cat's to pass off a folded bit of paper.

The first stick seller put a hand out to stop him, but Garwin merely handed the other boy his bundle and ran off.

"No! I tell you I had it just here in my pocket this morning. It must have —"

Cat could see a pair of attendants in white uniforms. One shook his head, but she couldn't make out his words.

"We will see about this! You'll hear from Governor Rhodes, my good man, I assure you!"

The line resumed moving forward as the angry man made his way past them back the other way, face red and muttering he gave the stick-seller a shove that put the boy on his backside and continued on without a backward glance.

Cat reached the front and handed the paper over to the attendant.

"Right this way, miss," he said after reading it. "And please let me know if there's anything else I can do for you. Would you like a stick? I'll get you one complimentary, if you like."

"No, thank you," Cat said.

"Well, anything a'tall you'd like, you just let us know, yes?"

Cat smiled. "I will."

He ushered her in, and she heard him mutter to his partner behind her. "Have'ta be especial nice to them signed by Governor Rhodes today — just in case."

THE STATE of the building grew worse as they entered, with uneven floors and drips from the ceiling, though it hadn't rained in days — as though the building itself were sagging in on itself and weeping at the use it was put to. The white-tiled floor and walls were thick with grime, so that the color of the tiles was only visible where the black and grey had been scraped away.

The din nearly drove Cat to cover her ears, and some of those around her did so — screams and wails echoed through the corridors, as though the hosts of hell itself awaited them ahead.

"This way! This way!" an attendant called. His white uniform was soiled as well, but had seen a wash nearer than the floors and walls had.

They followed him down corridors and through another locked gate to a long hall with windows on one side and barred cages on the other.

The attendant rattled a heavy stick along the bars and the wails redoubled.

"Poke 'em up, gents, poke 'em up!" he called. "Make 'em spin an' dash about! Good fer the blood, the doctors say!"

Cat's stomach rebelled at the sight of the poor creatures within those cages. Men and women, some alone in their cages, others crammed in tight, naked as the day they were born, with long, greasy hair, and as filth-covered as the institution's floors.

She clenched her jaw and forced herself to look, both longing to see Emma and afraid she'd find her here.

It had not taken long or too much coin for her to find the "physician" Roffe had spoken of, with his way of treating Emma's "affliction". The man had patients at Bethlem and it was here he carried out his work.

"Ladies use yer bottles," the attendant called out. "Hose 'em down good!"

He approached the bars where a naked man stood on the other side. The man's face was split in a rictus grin and he fondled himself almost absently. The attendant took up a bucket, setting the mop aside, and flung the contents into the man's face, soaking him and splashing those behind him with the filthy water.

The patients behind shrieked and rushed about madly, knocking some to the floor to be trampled by the others. The man at the bars stared back dumbly until the attendant threw his own head back and laughed, mouth wide, then the madman behind the bars did the same.

He laughed, again, and again, until Cat longed to slit the attendant's throat and flee this place.

"See? They likes it!" the attendant called out, and the women of the group stepped forward to spray water from their bottles on those behind the bars.

"Takes yer time, have yer fun," the attendant called out.

Cat scanned those in the cages, but caught no sight of Emma. She thought she might have — the hair and figure were close — but the woman was older.

One of the gentlemen stepped away from the crowd and approached the attendant. Cat watched carefully while he passed on a few coins, then the attendant nodded and motioned for the man to follow.

Cat marked the doorway they entered and watched the other attendants for a moment, seeing they were all occupied with those at the cage bars, that none got too close to be grabbed by the inhabitants and encouraging them to "Stir 'em up! Stir 'em up!"

With a purposeful stride, she made her way to the marked door and slipped inside.

Behind was a narrow corridor that met another, wider one ahead.

She crept forward, noting voices echoing.

"No," a gentleman's voice said. "Not to my liking."

The sound of metal sliding on metal, then a pause, and the sound again.

"Hhmm ... perhaps. Are there any younger?"

The metal again and the attendant's voice, "This way, sir," then footsteps receding.

Cat edged to the corner and peeked around, seeing the two men walking away down a long hallway lined on both sides with solid doors. Metal slides covered a window in each of the doors. The men turned a corner farther down the hall and Cat stepped from around her own.

Carefully, slowly, so as not to make the grating metal sound she'd heard before, she slid open the window on the first door.

Inside, a woman sat on the floor, naked but her long, lank hair covering her form. She hugged her knees to her chest and rocked back and forth slowly. A single blanket, crumpled in the corner, was the room's only furnishing.

She closed that window and moved to the next, seeing much the same, save this woman paced — one hand across her midsection, the other gesturing wildly about her head. Her mouth moved, but no sound emerged.

"Hst!" Cat called, whispering close to the opening so that her voice wouldn't carry down the hall, but there was no reaction. She called again, *"You there!"*

Still nothing, so Cat frowned, slid the window shut, and moved on.

The next two rooms were much the same, and Cat realized what went on here.

A bit of coin to the attendant and take your pick. Do as you like, they'll not resist — I'm certain some physician somewhere has said it's good for them.

She swallowed bile, suddenly certain that Emma was in one of these rooms. What else might any "physician" chosen by Roffe "prescribe" for Emma's ailment?

She checked door after door, time after time, slowing and opening the windows more carefully as she neared the next corner where the two men had turned. She was uncertain how it would work, whether the man would be left alone to his pleasures or whether the attendant would remain until he finished. All of the women in these rooms seemed docile, none responded to Cat's calls, so perhaps there was no fear of them harming their visitors.

She was nearly to the corner when she found her. Emma sat against one wall, immobile, not rocking as so many did, gaze fixed on the far wall — or something only she could see.

"Emma! *Emma!*" Cat whispered frantically. "I've come to get you out!"

Her hands went automatically to her stays, through the clever slits and pockets that allowed her access through the other layers of clothes. In a moment, her picks were in her hands and she had them nearly to the lock before she heard the footsteps.

That sobered her — even if she were to get the door open and Emma out, how would the two of them, with Emma unclothed, make their way from the hospital? What would they do once they were on the streets?

No, she'd come only to find where Emma was, then make a plan according to those circumstances. Though it broke her heart, she couldn't get the girl out now.

"I'll return for you, Emma," she whispered urgently. "I'll be back soon — hang on." The footsteps drew closer. "I love you."

Cat drew the window closed with a grating that cut to her soul. Her last glimpse of Emma was the same as the first — the girl had neither moved nor acknowledged her at all.

CHAPTER 42

The line to enter Bethlem was again rife with boy's selling sticks and water, but this time Cat was not alone.

She wore the *Parson's Niece*, with some few additions and renamed the *Haughty Tutor*, in honor of Mistress Hinds, who Cat now modeled her own behavior and bearing after.

Beside her ranged no fewer than five boys from the gang, stretching in age — or what an observer might believe to be their ages, since none of them knew for certain how old they were — from five to Dome's possible fourteen. All of them in fine, fresh, starched clothes, the purchase of which, along with payment to the gang and these boys in particular, had stretched Cat's purse to the very limit. She had, if she were careful, perhaps enough for a fortnight's lodgings and food — and that at the poorest of places, not much better, and some ways worse, than the gang's abandoned building.

Garwin, the youngest of those she had along, tugged at his collar and Cat forcefully took his fingers from it and replaced them at his side.

"It *itches*," Garwin whined.

"Leave it," Cat whispered. "And stand as I showed you."

Garwin sighed, but put his hands at his side and straightened his back, throwing his shoulders back as a proper boy of quality should.

"Feels like a lamp post up my arse," he muttered.

Cat bent close to whisper in his ear. "Do as you're told and no more muttering, or I'll see to it you're able to make a proper comparison."

The boy's eyes widened and he looked askance at Cat, then straightened further.

The group awaiting entry began to shuffle forward as the attendants arrived and opened the gates. Cat was relieved to see that there were none among them who'd handled the visitors on her first tour.

Though the *Haughty Tutor* looked nothing like the *Orphaned Daughter* who'd visited before — Cat even going so far as to add a bit of paints to her face in order to look several years older — she *had* spent some minutes speaking with the attendant who'd caught her in the hall outside Emma's room.

That one might recognize her, no matter the disguise, despite her distracting him with talk of the noise and stench quite overcoming her and where, good man, might a young lady find a bit of water — *clean* water, mind you — to refresh herself with?

She'd taken his escort to the gate, careful to avoid his getting *too* good a look at her, and left — just another flighty girl, overcome by the experience of Bethlem Hospital.

Cat stepped forward with the rest and handed over her ticket, this one lifted from someone farther back in the line, so there'd be no outrage before she was inside. The attendants might remark on so many lost tickets this week, but no more.

The attendant scanned the boys she had in tow and frowned. "We don't get many so young," he said.

Cat drew the deep, affronted breath she'd learned from Hinds, so that her chest expanded as her shoulders rose.

"I have a pass, good man," she said, her tone and inflection brooking no objection and making it clear that volume was a single questioning word away — as well as the switch or paddle, come to that.

"Well, yes you do," the man said, "but it's —"

Cat snatched the paper from him and held it before his face, snapping her finger against its bottom. "Signed," she said, "by one of the hospital's governors. Do you, sir, know better than Lord Tummons who should enter?"

"Well, no, mum, but it's not a place for children, this. Very —"

Cat lowered her free hand and flicked her fingers in signal.

Albern, the ostensible eight-year old, shoved Jeremie, who might have been nine. The latter shoved the former back, and a tussle ensued until Cat, not taking her eyes from the attendant, handed back the pass and caught both boys by an ear, nearly lifting them off the ground.

Cat inhaled again, this time to give vent to the sigh of the long-suffering.

"There are reasons, sir," she said, "for these boys to see what ends await those who do not properly follow the ways of good, Christian folk. We shall tour Newgate, as well, I think, before returning to the country."

The attendant looked from Cat to the two boys, still nearly elevated off the ground by Cat's grip on their ears, then to the other boys who were standing ramrod straight, their eyes fixed ahead and not looking at their "brothers'" condition.

"O'course, mum," the man said, taking her pass from her. "Step on through."

ONCE INSIDE, things went much as before. Cat settled the boys in a place where her own absence would not be noted and waited for a chance to slip away.

"Start the count when I leave," she told Dome and the oldest of the boys nodded.

Her chance came soon as a gentleman approached an attendant as she'd seen before. In a moment, the two were off, leaving fewer attendants to watch the "guests" and Cat was able to slip away after them.

She began counting in her head as Dome, behind her, would be doing.

She entered the hallway not far behind the pair she followed, taking less time about it than before, and walked on, paying no heed to the sound of her heels on the tile and the backs of the two men ahead of her.

The attendant turned at the sound, frowned, and slowed his pace, the gentleman beside him did likewise.

"Miss," the attendant said, "the exhibit's back that way, please."

He held out a hand to block her way as she approached. The gentleman turned away, as though not wanting to be seen here.

"Miss, you've got to go back, this way's not for —"

Cat's blade, hidden behind her forearm as she approached, took the attendant across the throat. Her free hand grasped his arm and spun him against the blade and away from Cat so that his blood spurted against the grime-covered wall.

The gentleman turned, eyes wide at the sight of the great gout of blood on the wall, still being added to by spurts from the attendenant's throat.

Cat was on him before he could exclaim in shock, driving a knee into his groin, then a shove to put his head into the tiled wall, and finally to grasp his hair, pull his head back, and draw the blade across his throat as well.

She let his body fall across that of the attendant and left them there.

Not a shred of pity or remorse crossed her mind, which was filled only with the thought of getting Emma out. The bodies behind her were those who'd sell the helpless to those who'd buy them, and there was the one truth she felt she'd ever hear from her father — there were some men who needed to be dead.

There was no time wasted hiding the bodies, either. So long as they weren't discovered before she had Emma in hand, then the finding would only add to their chances of escape. This was no sneak job in the night they were about.

She turned the corner, made her way to Emma's cell, and in a moment had the lock picked — the locks here were no challenge, which she'd seen on her last visit. They were blocky, crude things, meant only to hold in those incapable of any real effort at escape. They yielded easily to her manipulation, as they would to Dome's, who would already be at the first bit of his work behind her with the main group.

"Emma!"

Cat rushed through the door and dropped to her knees before the girl, pulling her close, then cupping her face to pull her gaze from the far wall.

"Emma?"

There was no response — no movement save what Cat's grasp imparted, not even a glint of recognition in the girl's eyes.

For the first time since she met with Roffe, Cat felt real fear. When her father'd said Emma was alive, Cat felt there was hope. She'd find her, get away, and find some way for them to be safe. She hadn't considered —

Cat pushed all thoughts of what might be wrong with Emma aside. Perhaps they drugged the girls in these rooms to keep them from harming the "visitors."

She pulled packets of cloth from beneath her skirts and began dressing Emma. All the while she counted in her head and cursed — this was taking more time than she'd thought. She'd planned for Emma to be awake, aware enough to help.

"Emma, you must help me, please!" She pulled the girl up to stand, grateful that she did so, and thrust bits of clothing into her hands. "Dress! Please, help!"

Dully, slowly, Emma did so.

Cat felt some hope at that — the girl was hearing and could do as she was told. She remembered how to dress, so that meant she was in there, somewhere, behind that vacant mask, didn't it?

She'd brought only the barest clothing needed, only what someone would see, not the complicated underthings and stays that made up the base. They only needed to look … normal, for a time.

Cat caught Emma's hair in her hands as the girl finished buttoning her jacket. She pulled it back and bound it. There was nothing she could do about it being greasy and wildly tangled, but in what was about to come, a bit of disarray would only be expected.

She grasped Emma's arm and pulled her along, out of the cell and into the corridor.

"Oy! What're you about?"

CHAPTER 43

Cat shoved Emma ahead of her, sparing but a glance for the Bethlem attendant who was now walking quickly toward them from the other way.

"Stop there! *You!* Stop, I said!"

She prodded Emma again and the girl moved faster, then a shove and she began to run. It wasn't enough to outpace the attendant, but it was enough to make the turn before him. Cat grasped Emma's arm and swung her into the hallway toward the exit, then shoved her hard.

"*Run!*"

Cat stopped. The attendant's footsteps were sounding the pattern of a run themselves, and approaching quickly. She tucked herself against the corner and as the man rounded it, she dropped to the floor and tangled his legs. He went flying, arms outstretched to land on the hard tiles with a muffled *oomph* of escaping breath.

She was on him in a second.

Her knees in his back drove him down to the tiles as he tried to rise. The blade, drawn while she leapt at him, sank deep into his lower back. Cat jerked and twisted, savaging the man's insides, then rocked forward and slammed her forearm against his head to bash his face into the tiles.

He had time for one, brief scream before that blade made it to his throat.

Cat rose, wiped blade and hands on the man's garb, leaving bloody streaks behind, and tucked the blade away again.

Emma had stopped ahead, no longer prodded, so no longer running, she stood still and stared down at the other bodies, the attendant and gentleman Cat had done for on her way in.

There was noise coming from the gallery ahead. Shouts, screams, and wails, along with the shrill call of the attendants' whistles shrieking for aid. They weren't too late, but nearly so.

Cat took Emma's arm, easing her around the bodies. The girl's face fixed on them, expression still blank, but staring at the carnage, taking it all in.

The sounds from the gallery were stronger now.

Cat pulled Emma's arm and the girl came along obediently.

They passed through the gallery door into chaos.

DOME and the boys had done their jobs well.

First Dome, to edge to the front of the crowd, poking and jeering along with the rest, while he worked the locks. Then the boys to grip the bars or sit and place their feet against the cage doors and keep them closed.

Then five cages sprung open at once, the crowd of onlookers drawing back and blocking the way for the attendants to get through, even as the cage's occupants found a new route for their agitated movements. Mad they might be, but they knew their tormentors — recognized the white clothes of the attendants and the sticks and water sprayers of the Quality come to jeer at them in their misery.

Some left the cages with intent, others with mindless motion, but all contributed to the shouts and chaos that followed.

Dome met Cat and Emma at the doorway.

"The lads are run already like you said!" he shouted over the din. "Come on!"

He grasped Emma's other arm and the two of them pulled the girl along between them into the panicking crowd.

Cat and Dome added their own shouts to the cacophony.

"*Help!* They're loose!"

"*Murder!*" Cat yelled, shoving bodies from her way. "Bloody murder! Help!"

Cat hooked a foot between an attendant's legs and gave his shoulders a shove as he raised a baton to strike at two naked men. The man went down and was soon covered in naked, grimy bodies that swung their arms and came up with bloody bits.

They shoved their way through the crowd to the exit, Cat and Dome using fists, knees, elbows, and blades as necessary to clear their path.

Outside, people crowded about, wondering at the louder shrieks and whistles — they might be used to some noise from the hospital, but this was new. The crowd reversed itself and rushed away as naked men and women came pouring out, along with no few visitors and attendants, all of them screaming murder along with Cat and Dome.

The two of them hurried Emma along, away from the worst of the crowds and dispersing madmen, to the open space of Moorfields Park which fronted the hospital. Before they reached the first pathway, a coach clattered to a stop before them and Osraed flung the door open.

Osraed reached out to take Emma's arms and pull her inside, then Cat shoved Dome in and climbed up herself.

She pulled the door shut after her and pounded on the ceiling.

"Away! Away, driver, away — as though the hounds of hell are after you!"

CAT PAID OSRAED FOR THE BOYS' help, adding a promise of more coin and more work. She wasn't sure if she'd have either for them, but the promise would keep them silent for a time, and that was time she needed.

Emma said nothing through the whole carriage ride to her rented rooms. Her gaze remained vacant and distant, even when Cat knelt before her in the carriage and whispered urgently for her to speak, blink, do something — *anything* — to let Cat know she was aware. That she knew she was safe and out of that horrible place.

Nothing came and Cat finally bowed her head to rest it in the girl's lap and give vent to the tears she'd had to hold in for the rescue.

Osraed and Dome hopped from the carriage and scurried off without a word. Cat pulled Emma out to the street, handed payment up to the driver, and led Emma to their rooms, poor as they were.

The building was shabby and not much more stable than Bethlem itself had appeared.

She settled Emma in a chair and knelt before her again, searching for some sign of life, some spark in the girl's eyes, then buried her face in Emma's lap and let her tears overcome her again.

Silently, beneath her sobs, she cursed herself — for taking so long to get to the city, for leaving Emma in Bethlem for so many days, finally, with more guilt than she thought she'd ever be able to bear, for making the trips away from their cottage that she was sure had led Roffe to their sanctuary.

"I'm sorry, Emma, I'm so sorry." She gripped the girl's waist tightly, fingers clenching into claws. "Please come back to me — you're safe now. *Please!*"

She looked up but Emma's face was blank and still as any stone.

Cat stood and paced the room, always turning back, searching for some sign of awareness. She begged, she pleaded, she screamed — until there came a pounding on the wall with the muffled demand she shut up — all for naught.

Finally, exhausted, she stood and took Emma's arm to at least put her to bed for the night. The girl stood at the pressure and Cat had a moment's hope, but her face remained still, her eyes unseeing.

She responded to other commands — to lift her arms, to step out of her skirts, as Cat helped her to undress. That gave Cat some hope — with time, with rest ... perhaps there was a physician who could understand and help her —

That thought nearly sent Cat into a rage again, for physicians would cost and she had barely enough for a few more nights in these dingy rooms after paying the boys. She had nothing to pay a physician with, much less to keep Emma safe and warm and fed for however long it took her to recover.

Rage filled her, and she wanted to lash out, to break everything in the room that came to hand. Roffe had done this. Roffe and his obsessions — Roffe and his demands.

God damn him for the evil he is! I'll see him hang — no, I'll see him dead and gutted by my own hand!

"Some men deserve their name in your ear, indeed, Father, but yours is in mine now, have no doubt."

She eased Emma into the bed, naked for she had no night shift, and saw so many bruises and marks on the girl's fair skin that Cat's heart broke again.

The sheets were rough as Cat joined her — rough and stuck through with the straw that filled the mattress. The sharp jabs must be painful, but Emma made no sound or movement and Cat accepted them as the smallest of penance for her role in bringing them to this.

She pulled Emma close and nearly cried out when Emma's arms went around her, then clenched her eyes shut as the girl's face betrayed nothing more. She pulled Emma's head to her breast and stroked her hair, murmuring.

"I love you, Emma. You're safe — come back to me, my girl, my love."

Cat's fingers traced Emma's cheek and she sought the words, the language strange on her tongue.

"I oleuo'i chwaer ddaearen

Ar hyd y nos.

Nos yw henaint pan ddaw cystudd

Ond i harddu dyn a'i hwyrddydd

Rhown ein golau gwan i'n gilydd, fy nghariad,

Ar hyd y nos."

We'll put our weak light together, my love, all through the night.

CHAPTER 44

*C*lanton's back was scarcely out of sight before Cat was at the townhouse door. He'd be at the pub for hours, unless Roffe told him to return, so she had time.

The lock there on the door was an old friend, familiar to her picks from long practice, and she had it open in almost the time as if she'd used a key.

Cat wasted no time looking about, but went immediately to the kitchen and seated herself at the table, her back to the pantry where she could see both the stairs from the first floor and the steps up to the delivery door. She'd wait for Roffe there.

It was a struggle not to worry, to think about what might happen if Roffe didn't come alone as she requested. What would she do if he came with Clanton or some others of his bullyboys?

She forced that thought aside and smoothed her skirts, resting her kid-gloved hands on her knees for a moment and taking a deep breath to calm herself.

She'd done all she could, thought all she could, and she saw no other choice.

That was fitting, as she had nothing else at all, so why not be out of choices, as well?

Emma was in their rented rooms — rooms she owed on for the last three nights, as she'd sought to conserve what little coin was left. The only thing keeping the girl from being thrown out on the streets this moment was Osraed's bulk and cold stare cowing the landlord for a time, but that wouldn't last.

He was with her now, following, if he could be trusted, Cat's last instructions.

"Keep Emma safe today," she'd said as she readied herself. She handed Osraed a purse with all their remaining coin. "If I don't return by morning, get Emma to Lower Feltstone and give this to Sarah Brimhall, the innkeeper's wife there."

Cat could only hope that the Brimhalls would continue to be as kind as they had been already and give Emma some kind of place to live out her days if things went wrong here with Roffe.

Well, if things go the worst here with Roffe, for there's nothing but wrong about it now.

Her note to Roffe had said to come alone. She had to rely on the man's arrogance that he would.

On an impulse she rose and retrieved a bottle of wine from the cellar and two cups from the cabinet. She set those on the table and resumed her seat.

The waiting was interminable, almost unbearable.

Finally, she heard footsteps outside and the grating of a key in the lock. More footsteps on the floor above her, then the creaking of the stairs.

She waited. From the sound, Roffe, or whoever entered, had gone up first.

Soon enough the footsteps returned and grew closer.

Roffe came down the stairs into the kitchen and paused as he caught sight of her.

"I'd thought to find you in my rooms, mooning over your mother's image," he said. "Or at least in the Mechanicals Room." He gestured about. "The kitchen? Really? Why?"

Cat shrugged.

Roffe came closer, his eyes narrow and taking in everything about her, the room, the table.

"Will you sit, father?"

Roffe smiled. "Of course."

He paused at the chair opposite her as though thinking, his eyes darted from the chair to her, then he sat.

"Where is it?" he asked.

Cat frowned.

"'It?'"

"The trap you think so clever," Roffe said. "The one you think will get you free of me."

Cat shook her head.

"I've set no trap here, father."

Roffe studied her for a moment.

"Wine, father?" Cat asked.

Roffe raised an eyebrow.

Cat sighed and reached forward. She took up the bottle and poured into both cups, then drank from each of them and the bottle. Roffe took one of the cups and pushed the other toward her — she drank from it again and set it aside.

"'Come alone,'" Roffe quoted from her note to him. "How dramatic."

"I wished a private talk, father."

"And you have it."

Cat swallowed, her lips thinning. She closed her eyes and took a deep breath.

"I'll not come back to you," she said.

Roffe stared at her waiting.

"Is that it?" he asked finally.

Cat nodded.

"You brought me out from my club for that?" He chuckled. "We'll see, then. How is your little friend, by the way? Did she respond well to her treatments?"

Cat's jaw clenched and her hands made fists, straining the thin leather of her gloves.

"You can kill me if you wish, father, but I won't return."

"I'll do more than that," Roffe said. "Do you think Bedlam's the worst of what can happen to your precious Emma?"

"Then I'll kill myself — you can't stop that."

Roffe laughed. "Your mother threatened that, as well, until I told her what I'd do to you. Will you take your girl with you to keep her safe?" He paused. "I thought not."

He leaned forward, arms on the table.

Cat unclenched her fists and slid her hand through the slit in her skirts.

"Give it up, Catherine, and come home. Take your playmate back out to the manor — the fresh air and sun will do her good. It's nothing to me if you wish to spend your nights there tipping the velvet, and none will say a word about it. You have no other choi —"

She took the chance. Now, when he was just the slightest bit off balance, his weight on those arms.

Her hand closed about the hilt of the knife strapped to her thigh — cold through the thin glove.

She lunged for him.

Roffe stood as she came, chair skidding back, its wood legs clattering against the cobbles of the kitchen floor.

The knife blade reached for him, then Cat's arm went numb as he struck her. Her wrist was pinned to the table by his and his elbow *cracked* against the side of her head.

The knife fell to the table with a heavy *thunk*.

Roffe grasped her other wrist, pulled them together, then shoved her away.

Cat staggered back until she struck the cabinets heavily.

By that time, her knife was in Roffe's hand and he was shaking his head at her in disappointment.

He gestured at her chair with the knife blade.

"Sit *down*, Catherine."

CHAPTER 45

"Stupid, clumsy girl," Roffe said.

He picked up his chair from where it had toppled over and returned to sit at the table. He pointed the knife at her, blade bobbing up and down.

"I should speak to Clanton about your training," he said. "I might as well have received a note informing me of your attack. Slow, girl, it will never do. *Sit, I said!*"

Cat did so. Her arm was numb where he'd struck her, but she fancied the palm felt cold and wet through the glove. She clenched her right hand into a fist and cradled it with her left, setting her teeth as well to give Roffe no sign that she was worried. If her trap took her down too, then so be it.

Roffe sighed. He set the knife on the table, blade pointing at Cat, and drank some wine.

"Catherine, Catherine, Catherine," he muttered. "Whatever will I do with you? Running is one thing, but attacking me? Had you been faster, I might have hurt you with my reaction — we cannot have that."

"I will not return to you," Cat said, her voice soft and shaking a bit.

Roffe slammed his fist on the table, half rising.

"You are mine!"

"Is that what you told my mother?" Cat asked. "Before you threw her off that ship?"

Cat knew as she spoke that she had the right of it. Roffe's face stilled, the anger melting away.

"In bloody pieces," he said.

Cat clenched her eyes shut against sudden tears. She'd thought, but not been certain, that Roffe would not set a hireling to that task.

Soft lips against her forehead, the scent of safety — "I love you, Kathleen, never forget."

"Why?" Her voice was raw.

Roffe stared at her for a moment, looking bewildered.

"Because she took what was mine," Roffe said, "and had to be punished. *Why* is this so difficult for you to understand, Catherine? This, all of this, has always been about that. She was mine — *you* were mine. She left and took you, so she must suffer — and suffer still, as you will even if you take your own life, for I shall mete out your punishment on that girl for as long as I allow her to live!"

"So this —" Cat swallowed to keep her voice in check. "All of this? Finding me, bringing me to your home — it's all some way of punishing my dead mother?"

Roffe smiled and scratched at his palm. "Of course, Catherine. What better? She hated what I did, when she found out — it drove her to run. What better punishment than to turn the precious daughter she tried to protect … into me?"

"I will never be you."

"You already are, Catherine." He rubbed his palms against his thighs as though to dry them, then took up his cup and drank. "That boy in this very house? Good Lord, girl, the bodies you left behind at Bedlam! Tell me there were no others while you sought to escape me?"

Cat couldn't deny it entirely. There had been the merchant and his two bullyboys on their way to Leeds, and she couldn't be so certain that some of those she'd robbed might not have found the experience more final than she intended. She felt nothing for them — every one of them had deserved it, she was certain, but that didn't make her like Roffe, did it?

Roffe put his elbows on the table and tented his fingers, scratching idly at his palm before stilling.

"Will you honestly say you felt one moment's remorse for a single one of them?"

Cat opened her mouth to speak, but it was too honest a moment for her to lie. She hadn't — not after those hours in the cellar with Brandt, at least. Once the boy was dead, her mind had eased quickly enough. And why should she feel remorse, in any case?

Brandt was a bully and worse. The men in Leeds had tried to rob her. The men she'd killed in Bethlem Hospital had been selling and buying the helpless into the worst kinds of abuse.

They'd deserved no better, not any of them.

She closed her mouth, thinking and watching Roffe. The man sat back and rubbed his palms against his thighs again.

"I am not you," Cat said firmly.

Roffe smiled.

"I'm *not! You* forced Brandt on me! I didn't kill those other men for money, I did it to protect myself! To save Emma from where you put her!"

"You will, though," Roffe said, "now you've a taste for it."

Cat shook her head.

Roffe's smile widened. He rubbed at his chest.

"Oh, you'll rationalize it for a time as I did. How they deserved it and how your own lack of regret merely means you were in the right. But then it will come one night — the urge to feel your blade open a man's flesh. It'll come and you'll respond, Catherine, but —" He cleared his throat and worked his mouth, frowning. "The money I take for the job is merely a happy coincidence when we get right down to it. As it will be for you. What is money for, but to save —" He cleared his throat again and frowned. "To save yourself."

He made to take another drink, then his frown deepened and he lowered the cup. His eyes darted about the table, from his cup to the bottle to her cup, and finally came to rest on her face, though his head was beginning to bow as though too heavy for him to keep up.

"What have you done, Catherine?" he asked. "You drank too." He coughed. "Pray, tell me you've not … gone noble on me."

Cat took a deep breath and sat back in her chair. She relaxed her hands, carefully flexing her fingers within the kid-skin gloves.

"It wasn't the wine, father."

Roffe's eyes narrowed. He started to rise, but his legs refused to obey. He braced his hands on the table's edge and let his head fall back so that he could look at her.

"Then, how —" He rubbed his palms against the table's edge.

Carefully and gingerly, Cat peeled the glove off her right hand. Her hand was covered in grease and the grease then wrapped in parchment. She set the glove on the table, well away from her. The palm was dark where liquid had soaked it.

Roffe stared at it for a moment, then looked to the knife on the table before him.

"Slow and clumsy," he whispered.

Cat stripped her other glove off and set it with the first.

"I could never best you in a fight, father. I know that."

Roffe took a deep breath and let it out slowly, as though testing his ability to do so. He closed his eyes and chuckled. When he opened them again, the lids remained half-hooded.

"Such a wonderful girl," he murmured. "Your mother … would be … horrified."

CHAPTER 46

Cat rose once Roffe was still, his eyes vacant and unseeing.

She took a cloth from the cabinet and scrubbed at her hands, removing all of the grease and parchment, careful not to let any of the outermost touch her skin.

She could fancy her right palm was growing cold, but a quick pinch once the grease was gone made her sigh with relief.

Then she shucked out of her skirts, holding them carefully by the waist and pooling them next to the gloves.

The knife sheath along her thigh was next, and even her drawers, under it, until nothing the knife hilt had or might have touched remained on her person.

She sat again, nearly naked from the waist down, and filled her cup — keeping well away from Roffe, the knife, and pile of clothing. Her shoulders slumped as she sipped her wine.

Some time later, there came the sound of a key in the kitchen door, but Cat somehow couldn't summon the urgency to move. She wasn't certain what she'd tell Clanton, when he found her here in the kitchen with her father's body. *Roffe.* Not her father. She'd never name him that again.

The door swung open and Clanton entered the kitchen with a keg balanced on one shoulder and a bag in his free hand.

He stopped at the foot of the steps, staring at Cat. His eyebrows rose, possibly the most expressive bit of surprise she'd ever seen in the man.

Clanton took two steps more into the kitchen, which brought Roffe's body into view. The valet's eyebrows rose higher.

He slowly bent to lower the keg to the floor then straightened. He glanced from Roffe's body to Cat again.

"That how it is, then?"

Cat nodded.

Clanton grunted and pulled a chair from the table to sit between Cat and where Roffe sat slumped back, head bowed.

He took a deep breath and shook his head, then reached for the wine bottle, his hand stopping just short. Clanton pointed to the bottle, then to Roffe's body.

"This have anything to do with that?"

Cat shook her head. "No, it's safe."

Clanton grunted and raised the bottle to drink. "Never hurts to ask in this house, it don't."

Cat almost smiled.

Clanton tilted his head to one side, examining the body.

"No blood, eh? Will it hurt the pigs? He's not one should turn up on a riverbank, I think."

Cat's shoulders slumped with relief and she almost cried out.

If Clanton was willing to help dispose of the body, then he might be willing to help with other things as well. She'd been despairing of where she'd go from here, with no funds and no home. She might have succeeded in killing Roffe, but she was no closer to helping Emma. Nor herself, come to that.

"I wouldn't risk it," she said. She nodded at the knife. "I'd wrap the hands, both of them, and knife and burn them —" She paused, running through the things Roffe had touched. "No, wrap the whole body before its moved. The chair, table — everything on it. All wrapped in heavy oilskin, then burned … careful of what's downwind."

"Good to know."

They sat in silence for a time, sipping at the wine.

"If he's disappeared," Cat said tentatively, "Some papers would be helpful, perhaps."

Clanton glanced at her, face impassive.

"Some bit of a note … that my … my uncle has felt a sudden need to return to the Orient?"

Clanton nodded and pursed his lips. "Monthly allowance to you, for the household, until your majority? Amounts to draw on for special things?"

Cat's chest was tight as she nodded. She very much wanted to throw her arms around Clanton and kiss the man.

"Perhaps some letters over time. Describing his travels?"

Clanton nodded again.

"I'll see to it," he said. "Then word of some … accident, when you've reached your majority?"

Relief washed over her in waves. With Clanton's help and those documents, she'd be able to keep the townhouse and manor, keep them paid for from Roffe's accounts, and provide for Emma. That Clanton would retain his place and pay would not be far from the man's mind, she was sure.

How long would that money last, though? How full were Roffe's accounts and how much might be owed to others?

The tale of Roffe visiting the Orient would be only a stopgap — she'd almost certainly have to find some source of funds.

Clanton sighed and raised the bottle to drink again. "Put the word out on the other, as well. That there'll be no more of the … special work done."

Cat started to nod, then stopped. That *special work* had been Roffe's main source of income. How much did he have on account? Enough to keep the households, even small as they were, going for … how long? He'd been a profligate spender, always at his club.

She frowned.

Moreover, there was Emma to consider. She'd need a quiet, warm place. And doctors … they would not be cheap.

Cat swallowed. "No."

Clanton's eyebrows rose to hitherto unknown heights. "You're certain."

"Not certain, no. But … best to leave the option, yes?"

"Best?"

Cat took a deep breath. The money would be needed — she couldn't hope to support the two houses and the servants through thieving alone. Attempting that would mean taking things of such value that they couldn't be easily sold — and that way led to capture.

She supposed she could consolidate — sell one or both of the properties — but how would that work until she reached her majority and Roffe was *officially* dead? Until then, any significant change would be looked at more closely.

No, she needed the funds.

And she owed it to Clanton for his help, didn't she, to provide him with the same place and comforts he'd grown used to? What of Singley and Skiff back at the manor? Where would they go if she closed that place? Skiff, for certain, could not come to the city — he'd have to stay forever in the townhouse for fear of being recognized and taken up on the years-old warrant.

She toyed with her cup, running a finger around its rim.

It wasn't just for her and not only that she *liked* the manor and townhouse both. Not for her ease alone, either, to lack for nothing. She could be said to owe it to those who'd helped her. And to Emma, for certain, who would do far better in her recovery to be housed at the manor with its fresh air and gardens.

Cat took a long drink of wine, stared at Roffe's body for a moment, then met Clanton's eye.

"If a man's name finds its way to my ear, Clanton, there must be a reason, don't you think?"

AUTHOR'S NOTE

Thank you for reading *Of Dubious Intent*, I hope you enjoyed it and it will come along on more of Cat's story in the *Dark Artifice* novels to come.

If you did and would like to help support the series, the best thing you can do is leave a review at Amazon, Goodreads, or even your personal blog — reviews help other readers determine if a series is to their liking and authors, especially indie authors, rely on such word of mouth to get our books in front of new readers.

You can also join my email mailing list at:

http://eepurl.com/dm6fYv

The list receives no more than one or two emails a month, with updates on my next books, as well as recommendations of other authors you might like.

The lullaby Emma sings to ease Cat's mind, and which Cat sings to her later in the story, is *Ar Hyd y Nos* (https://en.wikipedia.org/wiki/Ar_Hyd_y_Nos), a Welsh tune first recorded in 1784.

The lyrics do not include the words *fy nghariad* (my love) in the final couplet, as Emma sings them, but it is not, certainly, unthinkable that first Emma, and then Cat, would add such a thing to those words.

In starting a slightly more traditional Steampunk series, I struggled with the question of *why*. Why would, in my new world, steam become the predominant power source, rather than electricity?

And so, we have the notion of an alternate history, where Halley's Comet arrived early for some unobserved reason and part of it, or part of what caused it to arrive early, even, collided with our Moon to create Halley's Crevasse — a large deposit of something on the Moon's surface, likely magnetic, given its interaction with pigeons, compasses, and "electricals." With those "electricals" behaving so erratically for the days around the Moon's perigee, it is entirely probable that steam would become and remain the dominant power — who wants to trust something that will spark and spit at you for a week every month?

Of Dubious Intent takes place earlier than most Steampunk, with the series beginning in the early 1800s, still in the Georgian era and only a few years before the Regency.

Bethlem Royal Hospital, Bedlam, is still at its Moorsfield location, in the old building built over the rubbish dump of the "Town Ditch" and buckling under the strain of that foundation being unable to support a building whose span measured nearly 500 feet. It will not be moved to its Southwork location until 1810, or perhaps later in the *Dark Artifice* timeline.

Access to the wards was generally open to the public until 1770, when it was changed to require a ticket signed by one of the hospital's board of governors. It was actually during this period, with far less in the way of public scrutiny, that the very worst of the patient abuses occurred. While in the "real" Bedlam men and women were housed in separate wings, I've mixed them at least in the "viewing" areas.

Homosexuality was illegal in Britain well into the 20th century — and the beginning of the 19th century saw a wave of prosecutions against homosexual men, including a raid on The White Swan, a pub on Drury lane with an exclusively gay clientle (https://en.wikipedia.org/wiki/Vere_Street_Coterie). Most of those caught up in the raid were sentenced to pillory, but two, John Hepburn and Thomas White, were sentenced to hang at Newgate

Prison on March 7, 1811. This is later than the hanging Roffe uses to threaten Cat, but *Dark Artifice* does have its own timeline, so perhaps the raid happened earlier in this world.

Cat's character and upbringing is quite different than most, with only the barest memory of her mother, her first years spent with an aged servant more intent on teaching her how to stay alive than the niceties of affection, having to hide her true self from a gang who'd sell her off into virtual slavery if they found out she was a girl, and then to find her "father" in the form of the despicable Edward Roffe.

Her entire drive, everything she threw her most capable self into, has to do with protecting herself from being left in that state ever again — achieving the security of never being hungry again and never being vulnerable to others. Save Emma, the one person she loves and who loves her in return.

Should you ever find yourself between Catherine Roffe and her Emma, dear Reader, I suggest you run far and fast — and even then, sleep with one ear open to the *snicker-snack* of your window's latch being thrown.

Richard Grantham
    October 22, 2017
    Burnsville, NC